Return on or before the
last date stamped below.

Learning Resources
Centre

D0335567

Kingston College
Kingston Hall Road
Kingston upon Thames
KT1 2AQ

ALSO BY JONATHAN TULLOCH

The Bonny Lad

Jonathan Tulloch

THE SEASON TICKET

V

VINTAGE

Published by Vintage 2001

3 5 7 9 10 8 6 4 2

Copyright © Jonathan Tulloch 2000

First published in Great Britain by
Jonathan Cape 2000

Vintage
Random House, 20 Vauxhall Bridge Road,
London SW1V 2SA

Random House Australia (Pty) Limited
20 Alfred Street, Milsons Point, Sydney,
New South Wales 2061, Australia

Random House New Zealand Limited
18 Poland Road, Glenfield,
Auckland 10, New Zealand

Random House (Pty) Limited
Endulini, 5a Jubilee Road, Parktown 2193, South Africa

The Random House Group Limited Reg. No. 954009
www.randomhouse.co.uk

A CIP catalogue record for this book
is available from the British Library

ISBN 0 09 928466 9

Papers used by Random House are natural, recyclable
products made from wood grown in sustainable forests.
The manufacturing processes conform to the environmental
regulations of the country of origin.

Printed and bound in Great Britain by
Cox & Wyman Ltd, Reading, Berkshire

For Shirley

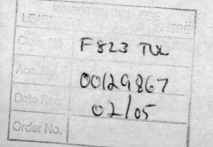

THE SEASON TICKET

On the southern bank of the River Tyne, where the water widens over tidal mud, stands the Metropolitan Borough of Gateshead.

Two figures, one tall, one small, were walking alongside the river. They were both teenagers. Perhaps the large one was two or three years older, but it was the smaller who led. His was a busy walk, swaying him nimbly from side to side, elbows out, setting his head in a constant swivelling, a continual searching, like a lean, trotting, urban fox. The taller one, always following at a distance of half a pace, walked slanting forward with hunched shoulders and wrinkled brow as though being led unwillingly by the forehead. His step, nearly twice the size of his companion's, appeared slow and vague. The pair of them were deep in discussion. 'We'll nivver see them again, man. Nivver,' sighed the taller one.

'We will,' replied the smaller.

Despite their difference in size, one wide and well over six feet tall and the other no more than five, they were identically dressed in black tracksuit bottoms, sweatshirts and white training shoes. Their hair was short and greased down in little points that fell an inch over their foreheads like the teeth in a comb. The large lad also wore a heavy jacket, the type that football managers and their players wear whilst sitting on the bench. Zipped right up to the throat, he stooped into the bench coat so that his mouth and nose were entirely covered. His hands were thrust deep into two of the many pockets. Only the top of his head was on permanent show. If his friend had the look of a famished fox, then his was the slow appearance of an overgrown tortoise.

As they talked their voices rose and fell on the tender summer evening air. Voices which followed the trend of their bodies. One spoke slowly, ponderously, the other's words were more marked, clipped. 'Ha'way man, admit it,' the tall, slower one repeated. 'We'll nivver see the lads again.'

'Aye, we will,' urged the other tersely.

Falling silent, they walked on and, turning up from the river, ascended a steep bank of newly planted trees and scattered rubbish. With each step the tall one's face grew redder. 'Pack it in, man Sewell,' said the small one abruptly without looking back at his friend. Sewell made an inarticulate but questioning noise. 'Ye're holding yer breath,' the small one told him. 'Pack it in.'

Sewell deflated like a balloon, the expelled air throwing him back a few paces. 'Oh, Gerry man,' he said, plodding up behind his friend again. 'Ah was trying to beat me record. One hundred steps withoot a breath. Ah nearly had it an' all.'

Gerry looked at Sewell quizzically. They reached the top of the bank. Crossing a busy road they walked on to the streets. 'Ha'way, how we gonnae gan and see them?' Sewell began again. 'Ye just cannet . . .'

'It's easy.'

'But how like?'

Gerry stopped for a moment, then, speaking the words slowly as though relishing appetising food, 'Season Ticket,' he explained.

'Eh?'

'We'll get Season Tickets.'

Sewell stood rooted to the spot, his mouth opening and closing as though he were chewing. Gerry carried on walking. Sewell looked about him and slowly shook his head.

The streets and roofs of Gateshead are grey. Fog often rises from the river, taking the lampposts by surprise, becalming the tower blocks into melancholy islands. The concrete is the colour of river mud exposed at high tide.

Sewell tried to catch up with Gerry. His walk became

lumbering as he speeded up, and his bulk bent so far forward that he looked in danger of toppling over and falling slap on his forehead.

'Well aye!' said Sewell, settling into his place of half a step behind. 'Talk sense, Gerry man. How can we get them?' They walked on for a few more yards. 'Ye cannet just walk in and ask for them, y'kna.' They turned a corner and walked over the remains of a smashed car windscreen, the pile of glass crunching under their feet. 'They divven't hand them oot on the social like,' Sewell started again after a silence. Gathering his thoughts, he pushed his head forward and down so that it was level with Gerry's. 'Put it this way, man,' he said with slow deliberation. 'If ye spent all your benefits on a Season Ticket, all of it, mind, nowt on tabs or tac or owt else, it would take six months. That's half a year, man. And ye're not even on benefits. Ye're still at school. Or supposed to be. Talk sense to us, man Gerry. We'll nivver be able to afford a one.'

In Gateshead, people walk slowly through the rain on waste ground, picking over the broken bricks and rubble. Grown men walk alone with plastic bags tugging on their wrists like a dog. Women and girls chatter in twos or threes, one of them pushing the baby. And the young men roam in ever-watchful pairs.

'Na, man Sewell. We've gorra have a one. A one each.'

'Nee chance, Gerry. Purely nee chance.'

'Listen to us, man Sewell man. Divven't ye see? There's nee question. We've just got to get a Season Ticket.'

Rubbish rots in alleyways. Shoes. Kiddies' clothes. Broken pushchairs. Mattresses. In Gateshead everything rots in the rain. And the bus shelters are always full of people nattering like starlings.

'Ah've been working it oot,' said Gerry, pausing for a second on a raised paving stone and then springing lightly off it like a fox pouncing on a small prey in long grass. 'All the money we get, your benefits, everything we twoc, we'll save

3

it. We'll collect it together and put it in a tin in wor lass's cupboard.'

'Your lass?' asked Sewell, side-stepping Gerry to avoid the collision.

Gerry moved off again. 'Aye. It'll be areet there. Wor Bridget's never stolen a thing in her life.'

'Canny weird, eh?' replied Sewell, catching his balance and then stumbling after Gerry.

'Canny weird.'

In Gateshead people cough loud, hacking, lung-stripping coughs. Even in the summer the air is damp. But their doors are always open. And they talk to strangers in the street, sharing the time of day with them, or the smoking of a tab. 'It's June now,' said Gerry. 'By the start of the season we'll have enough.'

In Gateshead the people dream dreams, and their dreams collect like litter in the long grass, then the winds come and blow them away, spiralling them high over houses and roads.

For a while Gerry and Sewell continued in silence. They walked behind the Spartan Redheugh factory, past the Superpitz five-a-side soccer courts, picked over the waste ground where the travellers camp from time to time, forded the River Team, small tributary of the Tyne, and crossed the motorway into Dunston. Then they began to climb Dunston Bank up to the affluent summit of Whickham. Below them the Tyne glimmered red in the sunset. The higher they got the more they could see. They saw the Dunston Tower, tallest tower block in Gateshead, standing like a rocket waiting to be launched. They saw the Metro Centre, the largest indoor shopping and leisure complex in Europe. They saw the mile upon mile of roofs and windows. And across the water, raised reverently above the town like a monstrance, they saw St James' Park, home to Newcastle United. 'Field o' dreams,' breathed Gerry. They stopped to look before carrying on.

'Starting from toneet?' asked Sewell, sweating with exertion.

'What we get the neet, gans straight in wor tin,' replied Gerry.

Behind Whickham is a chain of fields cordoning a wooded gorge called Washingwell Woods. Gerry and Sewell waited there, walking about, sitting on logs, smoking cigarettes. Washingwell Woods is part of the Great North Forest, a large area which the local councils have tried to plant with trees and interconnecting meadows on the sites of former collieries and railway lines. In the midst of this area of regeneration, standing on a hump of land so that it towers above the whole area like a watchful giant, is The Angel of the North. This immense statue, its rusty body the colour of sunsets, is visible for miles. It spreads its arms over the Great North Forest, over Gateshead, as though in protection. Gerry stared at it fondly. 'We'll be areet,' he told Sewell. 'The Angel's lookin' after us.'

'Eh?' said Sewell.

'Didn't y'kna? It's the guardian angel of twocers. It's like wor logo, y'kna.'

'Twocers,' repeated Sewell. 'That's us. We take withoot the owner's consent.'

Slowly it began to grow dark, and when the street lights came on they cast a jaundiced halo over Gateshead. 'One last tab,' decided Gerry.

'Ah've got a canister,' said Sewell, digging into his pockets.

'Gis a look,' said Gerry.

Sewell brought out a gas canister and placed it in Gerry's outstretched hand. Flexing his arm, Gerry threw the canister with all his might. It bounced out of sight.

'What ye deein', man?' moaned Sewell, standing up.

Gerry pulled him down with a gesture. 'None o' that,' he said. 'Nee sniffing, nee smoking tac, nee nowt. From noo on we're giving it all up. Nowt until we've got wor Season Tickets.'

The blue smoke from the cigarette drifted away on the soft night air. 'It'll be mint,' said Gerry as he exhaled.

'We could have finished that gas first,' said Sewell, looking fondly in the direction where the canister had been thrown.

Gerry began blowing smoke rings which Sewell watched float higher and higher until they disappeared into the gathering gloaming. 'Just think aboot it,' Gerry said dreamily. 'Every fortnight we can gan and watch the toon. I can see it noo. Where ye gannin' the day? a gadgie might say to us on a Saturday morning. To the match, we'll tell him. Ye'll nivver get in, he'll say. Why not? we'll ask. Neeone gets in nowadays, man, he'll say back with a dead told ye so smile. Really? we'll say, but we've got Season Tickets ye see. How aboot that, eh Sewell? Summink to look forward to. All winter, man. And just think when we're in the ground. Neeone'll be able to chase us or tell us to gan, because they'll be wor seats. Neeone else's. Just wor seats.'

'It'll be great.'

'I cannot wait, man. This is what it'll be like. We'll buy a big cup o' tea each and take them back to wor seats. Two sugars. Milk if ye want. Then we'll just sit there in comfort, sipping wor tea and watching the match.'

'Tea?'

'With milk and sugar. Luxury, eh?'

'Will we have a tab?' asked Sewell, taking the cigarette from Gerry and trying to blow smoke rings too. 'To gan with the tea?'

'Aye, mebbes we'll light up at half-time and stretch wor legs. Or mebbes we won't smoke at all. But then again mebbes we'll light one tab up after another. And y'kna what?'

'What?'

'Neeone can say a word aboot it because they'll be wor seats and not theirs.'

'Ah cannet wait, man Gerry.'

'Sounds belter like.'

'Purely belter.'

Sewell took one last drag on the cigarette and offered it to

Gerry. 'Na,' said Gerry. 'Put it oot and put yer hat on. It's time to make a start.'

Pulling the black Newcastle United football hats so low over their foreheads that their features were barely recognisable, the two set off into Whickham. The streets were wide and tree-lined. The kerbs high. A well-tended strip of grass ran parallel to the pavement. A dog barked somewhere in the distance. The pubs they walked past seemed quiet and forlorn. A lone police siren wailed its way down Dunston Bank. 'That's one of them pollises oot the way anyway,' said Gerry.

On they went. The streets were darker now, the lampposts fewer and further between. They neared the cul-de-sac. Sewell started humming in time with their accelerating steps. 'Whisht, man,' said Gerry. 'Ah've told ye before aboot that humming. Why d'ye dee it?'

'Cannet help it,' admitted Sewell with a shrug. 'Whenever ah'm buzzin' ah start humming.'

'But it's always the same tune. It's always The Blaydon Races, man.'

'Ah kna. Ah love that tune.'

'Well love it later. Ha'way, we're here.'

The cul-de-sac was five or six houses all facing each other. Big houses with gardens at the front and the back. There were none like these in Dunston or the Teams. They were the kind of houses teachers lived in. They walked round the cul-de-sac a few times. 'Doesn't Mr Caird live roond here?' whispered Sewell.

'Mebbes,' replied Gerry. 'Ah divven't kna for certain.'

'Is he still teaching at St Jude's?'

'Aye. Last time ah was there he was.'

'Always shoutin', deeing yer heed in?'

'Still the same.'

'Ah got expelled,' mused Sewell.

'Ah kna.'

'For shoutin' back at 'im.'

'And the rest, man,' laughed Gerry. 'Shit!' he hissed

suddenly. 'Divven't look noo, but there's an auld biddy watchin' wor from that hoose.'

'Oh aye. Ah see her.'

'Ah telt yus not to look. Ha'way let's gan roond once more and then pretend to leave. Look geet casual, as though we're oot walking the dog.' They circled the cul-de-sac and then carried on as though they were leaving it. As soon as they were out of sight of the watching face, Gerry darted into a thicket of shrubs. Sewell followed, crashing through the branches. 'Sewell!'

'Sorry, man Gerry.'

'And ah said walk roond casually. Ye looked as though yus were auditioning for *Crimewatch UK*,' said Gerry. 'What the frigg did yus hold yer hand oot like that for?'

'Ye said pretend to be walkin' a dog. Ah mean how can yus dee that withoot a dog? People'd think ye were a radgie.' At that moment voices could be heard. One of the doors to the houses slammed. 'Ah've always wanted a dog, me,' mused Sewell.

'Get doon,' ordered Gerry, pulling Sewell to the ground with him. The voices on the street grew quieter; another door was opened and then closed. A black cat appeared from behind one of the bushes. It rubbed its head against Sewell's cheek. Chuckling, he stroked it. The cat jumped up and, leaning against him, purred. 'Just like a dog, eh,' smiled Sewell. 'This cat'll dee for yer dog, man Gerry.'

'Eh?'

'That dog yus wanted to walk.'

Gerry shook his head pityingly. 'Ha'way.'

Emerging from the shrubs, they circled the cul-de-sac again. 'That's the one,' whispered Gerry, stopping at a house without lights on. 'They've left a window open. Ha'way, let's ring the doorbell.'

'What are we this time?'

Gerry frowned. 'Sewell man, this time leave it to me. Ah'll dee the talking if anyone answers the door.'

'But what are we gonnae dee? Are we collecting for the blind again?'

'And divven't ye stand behind us and laugh.' The doorbell sounded. No one answered.

'Mebbes they've just popped oot for a minute,' said Sewell. 'We'll wait and see then.'

They circled the cul-de-sac again. 'Roond and friggin' roond. This is deein' me heed in,' said Gerry. 'Ha'way. There's neeone in, let's get busy.' The black cat reappeared and Sewell picked it up before gently pushing it on its way. 'Ye and that cat,' said Gerry. 'Anyway ah've got it all worked oot. Listen. We gan in and take what we can. When we leave we'll come back through the garden and climb the fence. Awer the fence is the burn. That leads to Washingwell Woods. Even if we're chased we'll lose them in the woods. Areet? If we get split up we'll meet where we lit that fire last year. Y'kna the spot.'

'Areet,' replied Sewell, staring past the houses down to the burn where the last light of the long day lingered in streaks in the sky. It was midsummer. It would never be truly dark tonight.

'Listen, Sewell man!' said Gerry, pausing solemnly and facing Sewell with narrowed eyes. 'We're deeing it for wor Season Ticket.'

'Wor Season Ticket.'

Stealthily, they moved to the open downstairs toilet window. Sewell lifted Gerry on to the sill. Although the gap left by the window was tiny, Gerry slipped through easily. 'Remember, if there's an alarm then awer the fence and doon the burn,' whispered Gerry.

There was no alarm. Sewell waited an anxious few minutes then a face appeared through the glass of the back door. He turned to run. 'Where ye gannin'?' hissed Gerry as he opened the door. 'Welcome home, bonny lad.'

Stifling their laughter they crept into the house. It was dark and quiet. 'Give us the torch,' said Gerry as they tiptoed through the hall.

'Eh?'

'The torch, man Sewell man. Give us the torch.'

'Ah haven't got it.'

'Ye haven't got the torch?'

Sewell blushed defensively. 'Na.'

'Ye're joking.'

'Ah'm not joking.'

'Ye haven't got the torch that we always take on a job?'

'Ah haven't.'

'Ha'way, hand it awer. We need it.'

'Ah haven't got it.'

'Ye really haven't got it? Tell us honestly. Divven't piss aboot.'

'Ah thought ye had it, Gerry.'

'Na ye didn't, did ye? Ye always bring the torch. It's your responsibility.'

'Look, man. Ah just forgot it. Ah'm sorry.'

'What are we supposed to dee without a friggin' torch? Ah worry aboot ye sometimes, man Sewell.'

'Ah said ah'm sorry, man, but ye . . .' said Sewell, trailing off below the level of audibility. 'Ah told ye . . . ye . . .'

'Ye're seventeen year old and ye cannet even remember to bring a torch on a job,' said Gerry. Sewell continued to speak rapidly under his breath. 'Eh?' demanded Gerry. 'What did ye say? What ye mumbling aboot?'

'Ah said mebbe ah shouldn't gan on jobs with school kids,' said Sewell, slower again now that his voice had resurfaced.

'Is that what ye think?'

'Mebbes.'

'Listen, man Sewell,' began Gerry heavily. 'We're mates and always will be. But we'll get neewhere until we both admit that my brain is twice the size of yours. I'm the brains here reet. Reet?'

'Ah kna y'are, man Gerry . . .'

'Not that ah'm saying that brains are any better than owt else. Ye're strong. Hard. That's yer talent. Canny strong an' all. That's why we work so well together. We're a partnership, man. Say if we had to force a window then ah'd be nee good. Ah admit it. Ah'd step back. Ah'd say, ha'way Sewell, ye take command. But if we need to be crafty or clever aboot owt then ah step forward.'

'We're mates, eh?' said Sewell. 'Always. That's why we want these Season Tickets. So we can watch the lads together.'

'Together,' agreed Gerry.

'We'll sit there together in wor own seats?' Sewell said.

'And have two big cups o' tea.'

'And mebbes smoke and mebbes not smoke?'

'Aye, all of that,' agreed Gerry. 'All of that will come later. But listen, man. Ha'way and let's get this place done. We haven't got all night. We'll just have to see what we can dee withoot the torch.'

The carpets were thick and soft. 'Ye could sleep on this, eh?' whispered Sewell bending down and sinking a podgy fore-finger deep into the carpet as Gerry led the way through the hall and up the stairs. The carpet was so thick that the stairs didn't even creak. 'It's like snow.'

'Ha'way, man Sewell,' whispered Gerry from one of the bedrooms. 'There's a telly and a video in this one, ye can see the video clock.'

'Ah cannet see owt me,' replied Sewell.

They met on the landing, in the darkness almost knocking each other down. 'Cannet see a thing,' said Gerry.

'Look at all this tackle,' said Sewell from the bathroom. Hearing the drawn-out hiss of a spray, Gerry followed. A street lamp shone through the patterned window of the glass, bathing everywhere in a yellow glow. The shelf above the bath, the shelf above the sink, the window-sill, each was full of toiletries.

Gerry stood on the threshold of the bathroom. 'What's that minging?'

'Lily of the valley or summink,' said Sewell, holding out an aerosol.

'Let's have a look.'

Sewell inhaled approvingly. 'The lasses'll be all awer us with this gear.'

Gerry took the aerosol. 'It's air-freshener, man. Ye divven't spray air-freshener on.'

'Ye can.'

'It's for when ye've been, man.'

'Been?' asked Sewell ponderously.

'To clear the air.'

'What are ye gannin' on aboot, man Gerry?'

'What ye've got here, well, it's not a deodorant or aftershave. Ye spray it after ye've had a shit. If ye gan aboot with that gear on, all the lasses'd think ye've just had a shit.'

Sewell's face fell. 'What's this then, man Gerry?' he asked, pointing to a low porcelain bowl.

Gerry came over. 'They've got everything here.' He whistled softly. 'Even drinking water in the bathroom. See ye can sit on it and then lean doon to drink from that spout.'

'Funny-looking drinking spout,' said Sewell. 'Looks like a bairn's potty or summink.' Surreptitiously Sewell felt for the air-freshener can which was still in his pocket.

'Ah told ye to put that back,' said Gerry.

Sewell pulled out the air-freshener and, holding it up in the yellow light, examined it.

'Fill your pockets with valuables, man,' Gerry told him. 'Ye divven't break into a hoose to steal an air-freshener. Ah said put it back.'

'Areet, but . . .'

'What ye mumbling aboot noo?'

'If ye could smell wor bog on a morning after me auld man's been sitting reading the paper for half an hour ye'd reckon this air-freshener was gold dust.'

Gerry sighed. 'Areet then.'

'Ah can take it?'

'Take it, man Sewell. But nee more junk.'

Happily Sewell stuffed the aerosol into the breast pocket of his bench coat. Tapping it tenderly with the palm of his hand he smiled. 'Pure gold dust.'

'Ha'way,' called Gerry from another bedroom.

'How many bedrooms are there?' asked Sewell as he joined Gerry, feeling his way into the room. There was a rough gasp as Sewell lit a match. The flare seemed to fill the air. 'Wow!' he breathed. 'Purely belter.'

It was decorated entirely in Newcastle United colours. The bedding. The wallpaper. Even the alarm clock on the bedside table had a black and white football as the pointer which bounced around the seconds. There were posters and framed pictures of the players on the wall. 'It's a shrine,' said Gerry, scratching his head through the thick hat. He directed Sewell's match into the corner, where there was a television and a video. Three video cassettes were stacked on top. They were all about Newcastle United.

'Bingo!' said Sewell. 'Three early Christmas presents.'

Gerry fingered the cassettes uncertainly. 'Na,' he decided at last.

'What?'

'Na, it'd be wrong . . .' said Gerry, perching lightly on the edge of the bed.

'Wrong?' returned Sewell less ponderously than usual.

'Wrong.'

'What ye gannin' on aboot?'

'Ah divven't kna.'

'Ye divven't kna?'

'That's reet. Ah divven't kna.'

'But ye think it's wrong?'

Gerry nodded. 'It's wrong.'

Sewell gestured incredulously at the videos. 'Wrong to take them three?'

'Wrong.'

Sewell flicked out the match when it reached his fingers.

The light of the video clock shone green in the darkness. 'But we'd get a tenner for them three easy, mebbes more. Not to mention the friggin' recorder.'

'Ha'way. Let's see what there is doonstairs.'

'What d'ye mean, ha'way?' gasped Sewell, gesticulating wildly. 'There's three videos here but.'

Another rasp on the sandpaper was followed by another flare. Padding over to the cassettes Sewell picked them up. 'History of Newcastle United,' he read. 'Mint! The Top One Hundred Black and White Goals. Belter! Geordie Hall of Fame, Famous Local Magpies. Purely mint and belter.' Sewell fingered the third cassette with affection. 'Ye might be the brains, man Gerry, but ah divven't think ye're acting very clever noo. There's three videos here, man, we'd easily get . . .'

'Sewell?' interrupted Gerry. 'Isn't your uncle in that?'

'Eh?'

'Ah thought your uncle played for the lads.'

'Great-uncle. Great-Uncle Arthur. Used to play centre forward for the lads . . . ah divven't kna when exactly. In the days before colour any road. Long shorts and greasy hair and all that. Smoking tabs at half-time.'

'Mebbes there's a picture of him on the box.'

Gerry came over. 'It's hard to see,' he said, twisting the box round at different angles to maximise the light.

'Gis it back, man,' said Sewell. There was a struggle over the cassette. It fell heavily to the ground. The match died.

They both froze. 'Are ye mental, man Sewell, or what?' Gerry snatched the matches and lit one. It cast a shadow over Sewell's whole body, projecting his silhouette massively on to the ceiling. Crouching, Gerry held the light over the video box. It was covered with little head shots of players each highlighted by a halo-like star. 'Pure dodgy-looking crew,' laughed Gerry.

'Ah wonder what life was like in them days?'

'Same as noo,' replied Gerry.

'Nee chance,' disagreed Sewell. 'They divven't smoke tabs

at half-time any more. Alan Shearer's probably never had a tab in his life.'

'Aye but we dee,' explained Gerry, handing the video over to Sewell. 'Things haven't changed for us. Y'kna. The likes of us.'

'We will nivver forget the stars of yesteryear.' Sewell stumbled over the words on the box. 'They live on in wor hearts. Pity me great-uncle's dead, eh, Gerry. Mebbes he would have been able to get us a Season Ticket.'

'They didn't have them in them days, man. Ye just paid at the turnstile. He wouldn't even be able to afford to watch himself now. Ah cannet see him on here, man. Mebbes he wasn't a star, Sewell. Well, not a big one eh. Anyway.'

The match went out. 'Gerry, please let us have them videos,' pleaded Sewell in a small voice.

Gerry shook his head. 'It's wrong . . . well it's not reet. Ha'way. Cannet hang aroond here all night. Leave them. Divven't mumble, just leave them. And the recorder. There'll be a better one downstairs.'

When they were on the stairs, a clock chimed from somewhere. 'Eleven o'clock,' counted Gerry. 'Let's get busy.'

They went into the kitchen. A night light burnt from a socket. 'At least ah can see me hand in front of me face noo,' muttered Gerry. In one corner a fridge hummed like a sleeping dog. The units were at eye-level, assembled from the cold sterility of IKEA. All the pots and pans hung from rings screwed into the walls. Sharp knives were sheathed in a black enamel knife holder. 'Sword in the stone!' laughed Sewell, unsheathing a knife. Its blade glinted dully as he cut and thrust it against the air. 'They divven't even have to wash their own dishes,' he added, opening up the dishwasher. 'They just stick 'em in here.'

'Microwave,' spotted Gerry. 'We'll have that. And sum-mink for wor dinner,' he added, taking a chicken from the fridge and putting it in the microwave oven.

'Divven't pack it too heavily,' grumbled Sewell. 'Ah'll have to carry it. Is there a cake in there mind?'

Sewell was just about to go through the door into the living room when a low growl from Gerry stopped him in his tracks. 'It's time we were missing.'

'What aboot in here?' Sewell said, gesturing to the rich pickings of the house's main room.

'Na. We've got to be gannin'. The kettle's still hot, man. There's someone aboot.'

As they unplugged the mircowave, Sewell began humming. 'Not The Blaydon Races again,' snapped Gerry.

Carrying the microwave, Sewell followed Gerry across the kitchen towards the hall. 'That'll dee for wor tin,' said Gerry, grabbing a glass jar from the surface as he passed it.

'What's in it?' whispered Sewell.

'Divven't kna. Rice or summink. Doesn't matter. We'll hoy that. It'll be wor tin. Ha'way, there's nee time for owt else.'

Suddenly the front door opened. Gerry and Sewell froze, instinctively stooping, making themselves smaller. A peevish voice filled the hall. 'Do we have to go round to her every time her ladyship calls?' demanded a woman.

'She's our next-door neighbour. She was frightened, pet,' a man responded wearily.

'She does it on purpose.'

'She thought she saw two toe rags hanging about. Real scum.'

'There was nobody there. There never is anything there.' The woman's voice reverberated angrily around the house.

'Since the divorce she's been living alone, pet. She gets frightened.' The man spoke with a timorous rationality.

'She gets you round at the slightest excuse.'

'Not this again, pet.'

'Yes this again.'

'It's Cairdy,' whispered Gerry, his mouth dropping wide.

'Mr Caird,' nodded Sewell.

The front door closed with a slam and the door to the living room opened with a jerk. The conversation continued into that room. 'They think they're so posh living here,' the woman said icily. 'I've never been good enough for them. Just because I used to work on the tills.'

'He sounds different here,' breathed Gerry.

'Ah've only ever heard him shouting,' said Sewell.

'Posh? She's about as posh as an arse. God, did yus see what she was wearing? Common as fuckin' clarts. The way her tits were hanging out. She does it on purpose. I swear down. She's after you, man Paul man. Wants to sink her teeth into you.'

'Ha'way, man Denise,' reasoned the man, 'There might have been burglars. I had to go and see if she was all right.'

'Piss off, man. I saw you looking at her tits.'

The man sighed. 'I wasn't, pet, honestly.'

'I wasn't, pet, honestly,' mocked the woman, imitating him perfectly. 'Ye fucking were!'

'Ah bet he was an' all,' whispered Gerry. 'Ha'way, man Sewell, let's get missing.' But Sewell was rocking with laughter. Suddenly Gerry had to stifle a laugh too.

'Ha'way, I divven't look at other women, pet,' begged the man in a whining voice.

'Stop laughing,' hissed Gerry, but his own head was now shaking too.

'Ye're pathetic,' snapped the woman.

'Oh ha'way, pet,' begged the man. 'Ye've got much nicer tits.'

'Ah'm gonnae die here,' stuttered Gerry, fighting for breath through his silent laughter. 'Let's get gannin', man Sewell.'

'Ah wish we had a tape recorder,' Sewell replied, balancing the microwave on a raised knee.

'Ha'way!' said Gerry, turning to the back door. 'Where ye gannin', man Sewell?' he hissed as Sewell lumbered into the hall towards the front door.

'Eh?' said Sewell turning. In the hall there was a low table with ornaments. English country animals overlooked by a shepherdess with a bonnet and floral crook. As Sewell turned, the plug from the microwave trailed over the table, sending one of the animals tumbling to the ground. The shepherdess teetered on the edge of the table for a moment, and then, dutifully following the lost one of her flock, crashed down too. The conversation suddenly stopped. 'What was that?' shrilled the woman's voice.

'Run for it,' urged Gerry, flying through the back door.

Sewell followed him but tripped on the raised threshold and fell headlong. The microwave hit the path, its door opened and out popped the chicken. The chicken bounced for a few feet before coming to a forlorn stop under the roses. Cursing, Sewell picked himself and the microwave up. 'Run, man, she's at the friggin' door!' shouted Gerry, already astride the fence. Sewell looked back to see the squat, thickset figure of Mr Caird standing in the doorway. 'Pull the hat awer yer heed,' urged Gerry. 'Divven't let them recognise ye.'

'Come here, ye bastards!' the woman yelled. 'Ee man Paul, the fuckers have been in here all along.'

Pulling the Newcastle United hat over his face Sewell stood there paralysed. 'Run, man!' he could hear Gerry yelling. 'Get the fat fucker!' he heard Cairdy's wife yelling. 'Hey ye!' he heard Mr Caird shouting now. Dogs barked. Car alarms were activated. Neighbours appeared at windows. Sewell stood in the back garden like a rabbit caught in headlights. He was dazzled. He couldn't see or think a thing. Then Gerry's voice forced a way through the chaos, and reached him like a slap to the face: 'HA'WAY, MAN, RUN FOR IT!'

Tossing up the microwave, Sewell ran for his life. He bundled himself over the fence like a desperate steeplechaser, and rolled down to the burn where Gerry was already waiting. They sprinted along the burn towards the woods, curses and insults ringing out after them like the howling of a pack of wolves. 'If ah'd known they were going to be like that ah would have taken them videos after all,' said Gerry.

When they could no longer hear any shouting, they threw themselves into a thicket of birch trees, and waited to get their breath back. Sure that no one was following, they lit cigarettes, and smoked until they had none left, emerging some time later. Trudging through the woods, they crossed into the fields. They mounted a little rise and standing there for a long time, looked over Gateshead. Eventually they found the Angel, its shape shimmering in the midsummer night as though it were hovering on gently beating wings. Gerry held his arms out wide in imitation. Sewell did the same. Letting themselves fall, they flapped their arms as though to fly. Hitting the soft grass, they laughed. 'Cheer up, man. At least we've got wor tin,' said Gerry, and with a flick of the wrist he sent the contents of the jar flying through the air.

'Ye can write a name on a one of them,' said Sewell, watching the rice. 'Doon the market, they can write your name on a grain of rice.'

With a pitter-patter the rice landed on the ground, gathering there like snow. 'They'll write wor names on the Season Tickets,' said Gerry, collecting a handful of rice and watching it sieve through his fingers. 'Just ye wait and see.'

2

The morning sun shone brightly through the uncurtained window. Gerry turned over on to his other side to face the wall. The mattress creaked as he moved.

From downstairs he could hear his mother coughing. He pulled the pillow over his head, but he could still hear her. He dug his fingers into his ears, but still he could hear the coughing. It was a dry, relentless, desperate hacking. Unable to escape the noise, Gerry listened to it closely. It sounded as though his mother was struggling in deep water; whole minutes of her gargling as she submerged were followed by a few snatched breaths at the surface, and then down she sank again. A baby started crying. Gerry didn't know whether it was in their house or next door. The crying came in waves as though the infant had been tossed into the same sea as his mother. Coughing. Crying. Crying. Coughing. The noises seemed to confront each other and then intermesh until they became the same struggling, feeble, lost thing. Then suddenly they both subsided and fell quiet. It was as though both his mother and the baby had drowned. Gerry leant over to the empty Viborg lager can he had been using as an ash-tray the night before and selected the most promising dow. Lying back in bed he struck a match and inhaled. Seized by a racking cough, he doubled up.

'Areet, Gerry,' said Sewell twenty minutes later, popping his head round the bedroom door.

'What time is it?'

'Divven't kna. Aboot ten o'clock ah reckon. Sleep areet?'

'What ye deein' up so early?'

'Oh, y'kna. After last neet. Thought ah might come and have a look at wor tin.'

'Make us a cup of tea, man Sewell.'

'Is there any tea an' that in?'

Gerry sat up in his bed. 'Na,' he said yawning. 'There's nee tea in the hoose. Nee milk. And nee sugar. Who's in?'

'Yer mam, Clare and the babby.'

'Nee Bridget?'

'Na.'

'Come with me,' said Gerry, jumping out of bed and pulling on the tracksuit bottoms that were lying on the floor. 'Ah put it in here last night,' he told Sewell as they crossed the landing and went into another room. It was a tiny room just long enough to accommodate a bed, and with a width which allowed you to touch two walls when standing in the middle. Gerry opened the cupboard and lifted out a shoe box.

'What's in there?' asked Sewell, bending down to open the box.

'Ha'way, man,' said Gerry, slapping his friend's hand. 'That's wor Bridget's special box. Ye cannet gan in there. Anyway, this is what ah wanted to show ye.' Gerry lifted up a plastic bag and there underneath it, in the corner of the cupboard, lying on a nest of old magazines like a glass egg, was their tin. He brought the glass container out slowly, reverently.

'It's not very big,' said Sewell doubtfully.

'We're not putting shrapnel in it,' Gerry told him. 'We'll put big notes in. Twenties. Fifties. Hundreds.'

'Not much of a tin either,' continued Sewell. 'Couldn't see it clearly last neet. More of a jar really but.'

'It'll dee us,' said Gerry, rolling it appreciatively round in his palms before replacing it in the cupboard.

'And it'll be safe there?' asked Sewell.

'Why aye, man!' Going back to his room Gerry peeled a T-shirt from the ground and put it on. He took the stairs three at a time. Sewell followed him. They went into the sitting room. 'Areet, Mam,' said Gerry.

'Areet, Mrs Macarten,' said Sewell.

'Areet, lads,' said Mrs Macarten. She was a small woman, bearing a clear resemblance to Gerry. Her teeth were yellow and brown. Her hair fell over her shoulders in long, grey horse tails. Her eyes loomed large in her frail body. She was sitting on a threadbare armchair holding a baby. The baby was naked.

'Stinks, man!' exclaimed Gerry.

'So did ye, man Gerry,' said his mother. Sewell laughed. Then Gerry laughed. They sat down on the settee which was equally as threadbare as the chair. It only had enough room for two people.

'Areet lads,' said Clare from the kitchen which adjoined the living room.

'Areet,' said Sewell.

'What ye deein' here?' asked Gerry.

Clare was different from her mother and brother. Taller, but only in comparison with the size of the rest of her family, she was very thin with a face as white as asbestos. She had the sleeves of her sweatshirt rolled up as she washed a nappy in the kitchen sink. Behind her, dirty washing-up was stacked high on the kitchen table 'Ye stink!' said Gerry, pushing his face at his niece.

'Leave her alone, man Gerry. Anyway it's your fault. Ah've been on at ye to gerrus some more Pampas,' Clare told him.

'Ee! Where's the telly, Mam?' Gerry asked, looking for the familiar screen in the corner.

'They came yesterday,' Mrs Macarten said, coughing up a blob of phlegm and spitting it on to a piece of toilet paper. At her elbow, on the chipped wooden window-sill, stood a toilet roll and about twenty rolled-up pieces. 'They just took it. Ah couldn't stop them, pet.'

'Oh, Mam man. I cannet believe ye,' said Gerry. 'Ye nivver open the door and let them in. How many times do ah have to tell ye?'

Clare came over from the sink. 'Shurrup, man Gerry. She thought it was the doctor.'

Mrs Macarten shifted position uncomfortably in the arm-chair and handed the baby over to Clare. 'Ah'm not so well,' she said without looking at him.

There was an awkward silence. 'Ye look canny good to me, Mrs Macarten,' said Sewell at last.

'Aye, well ah'm not, lad.' Mrs Macarten began coughing. Gerry watched her fighting for air. Sewell looked away respectfully. Then the baby began crying. Handing her to Gerry, Clare went back into the kitchen and then came running in carrying a baby's bottle full of orange squash. She thrust it in her daughter's mouth and took the baby back from Gerry. Mrs Macarten was still coughing, but the baby quietened.

A car drove past the house, its radio blaring. Sewell and Gerry sprang up and looked through the window. They watched the car suspiciously as it turned at the dead end, and drove back past the house. They sat down again. 'What are yous two up to the day?' Clare asked.

'We're gonnae –' began Sewell.

'Nowt much,' interrupted Gerry, giving his friend a knowing look. 'What about ye?'

'Ah'm gonnae get this place sorted, do a bit of washing-up for me mam,' said Clare.

'Where's me nana?' Gerry asked.

'She's just gone to the toon, for her deaf club bingo y'kna,' his mother told him.

'Well, ah'll mebbes see ye later,' said Gerry, getting up.

Clare was bouncing the baby up and down on her knee. She stopped and looked up at her brother and his friend. 'Have either of yous two seen wor Bridget?'

'Since yesterday morning?' added Mrs Macarten, fighting back a cough.

'Where's she gone this time like?' asked Gerry.

'Divven't kna,' admitted his sister. 'Thought ye might kna.'

'Na,' said Gerry, getting up and walking over to the front door.

23

'Na,' said Sewell, joining him.

'See ye then,' they said together.

'See yus both then,' said Clare.

'Aye see ye,' they repeated.

'See yus lads,' said Mrs Macarten.

It was almost hot outside. They walked down the street. 'Take yer bench coat off, man,' said Gerry.

'Na,' answered Sewell.

The Macartens' terrace fronted two public football pitches. Green railings separated the houses from the football pitches. The railings were covered in newspapers and plastic bags; pieces of litter were crucified on the railing spikes. On the pitches three little boys were playing football with their T-shirts planted on the ground for goalposts. Their bodies were white and puny in the glare of the sun like those of insects that have lived under a stone. A dog followed their game closely, barking and chasing the ball, examining every kick the boys took like an over-exuberant referee. Pushing through one of the many gaps in the green railings, Gerry and Sewell paused to watch the game as they walked over the fields. They sat down. 'This'll be us, man Sewell,' Gerry said. 'This'll be us next season at St James' Park.' With a wide sweep of his arm he gestured the emptiness of the fields. 'We'll come in early, getting in before anyone else. We'll sit in wor seats and watch the lads practise before the game. For them few precious moments the whole place'll belong to us. We'll sit there looking doon on it all. Picture it. We'll be like two kings, Sewell, sitting there. Neeone else. Just us. With two big cups of tea. Loads of milk. Two, no, three sugars. What time do they start deeing the tea? When do they open the tea hatch?'

Sewell looked at Gerry. 'They divven't have tea hatches any more. It's like at McDonald's. A counter with burgers an' all that.'

'Oh,' said Gerry.

They watched the boys and the dogs playing for a while.

'There wouldn't be a dog there though,' mused Sewell. 'Saw a fox once at a Celtic match on the telly.'

'Sewell,' began Gerry softly. 'When was the last time ye went to a match like?'

Sewell answered without looking at him. 'A while back.'

On the pitch one of the boys scored a goal. He ran up to Sewell and Gerry with his arms in a celebration windmill. 'Canny goal, son,' said Gerry. 'Ye'll play for the toon one day.'

'Gorra tab?' asked the kid.

'Haddaway,' Gerry told him. The dog arrived, nosing and yelping at the kid, marshalling him back to the field of play. The kid ran back to his friends and started playing again. A throw-in was taken, and the dog launched itself after the flying ball. It twisted and turned in the air. 'Some keeper that,' said Gerry.

'Ah wish ah had a dog,' said Sewell admiringly. 'One like that mutt. He's beautiful.'

'They crap all awer the place, man,' said Gerry. A whole minute passed. Then Gerry turned back to Sewell. 'Tell us aboot when ye went again.'

'Eh?'

'Aboot when ye went to the match an' that.'

Sewell's eyes narrowed slightly for a moment. He shrugged. 'Ah used tae gan with me dad when ah was a bairn.'

'And what d'ye remember best aboot it?' Gerry prompted.

Sewell screwed up his face in thought, then spoke easily as though repeating words often spoken. 'What ah remember best is me auld man's coat. He always wore it on the matchday. Ah can see that coat clearly even noo.'

Gerry grinned. 'He used to get ye refreshments an' all, didn't he?'

Sewell nodded. 'We always had tea at half-time. Warm and sweet.'

'How d'yus get it?' asked Gerry, and lying back with his head resting on his hands he closed his eyes dreamily.

'It came in polystyrene cups. There was a hatch where ye

lined up. Loads of people queuing. But neeone pushed in front of me and me dad. The sugar was in a bowl on the counter. The plastic spoons were coated in sugar. It's all changed noo but.'

Gerry remained motionless, as though sleeping; then suddenly he sprang up. 'Ha'way!' he said, 'it's time we were getting some money together.'

'Ah've already been thinking aboot it,' said Sewell as they walked across the fields. 'Ah've had an idea.'

'Bloody hell, take cover everyone,' laughed Gerry.

'Na. A serious idea.'

Gerry sighed heavily. 'Ah've told ye before we cannet sell tac. Them radgies from the West End'd kill us if we tried. Anyway we just smoked it all worsel' last time.'

Sewell cleared his throat as though he had to cough up his idea before remembering it. 'Scrap.'

'Eh?'

'Scrap, man Gerry,' repeated Sewell proudly.

'Scrap?'

'Scrap metal . . . ye kna. Tackle people divven't want.'

Gerry spat long-sufferingly. 'Ye're joking.'

'Ah'm not. Think aboot it.' Sewell's eyes expanded with his idea. 'There's scrap all awer Gatesheed. It's worth money. People are always throwing away the things they divven't want. There's money just to be picked up.'

'Aye, man Sewell,' said Gerry, stopping abruptly for emphasis. 'They divven't want them because they're useless. That's why they hoy oot. If they were worth anything then they'd keep them.'

Sewell shook his head. 'All ah kna is that there's money in scrap.'

Gerry began walking again. 'And how d'ye kna that like?'

'Everyone does. Ginga told us.'

'Ginga?'

'Ginga. One of me dad's auld mates.'

'That's all we need,' Gerry said to himself, rolling his eyes.

Sewell heard him. 'What d'ye mean by that like?' he demanded, his forehead puckering into a frown.

Gerry thought about it. 'Look, nee offence to your auld man or any of his mates, but, well, man Sewell, they're all as skint as we are.'

'And what's your family then?'

'Ah'm not saying that. They're all skint an' all. It's a tradition roond here. Being skint. And whenever ye have money ye've got to spend it as soon as possible. Which makes ye skint again. What ah'm trying to say is that me and you, Sewell, we're trying to break oot of all that. We're trying to have something that, well y'kna, lasts.'

Sewell grabbed hold of Gerry's arm and tugged. Gerry winced. 'Ha'way, give it a gan, man Gerry. One day. Just one day. We'll collect all the scrap we can and then take it to Ginga. He'll give us a fair price. Y'kna Terry? Terry the scrap man. He sends his daughter to a private school. Ah'm telling ye the streets are paved with scrap waiting to be turned into gold.'

Gerry sighed wearily, pulling his arm free. 'Tell us what ye mean by scrap,' he said.

'Ye kna,' answered Sewell, nodding vigorously.

'Ah divven't.'

'Auld bike wheels, spanners, copper wiring. That type of tackle.'

'Metal's heavy ye kna. How d'ye suggest we carry it?'

'There's stacks of Tesco trolleys doon in the river. We'll catch the tide if we hurry.' Sewell immediately took four or five steps in that direction.

'Na,' said Gerry without moving.

'Gan on,' pleaded Sewell, taking one step back.

'Na.'

'Ha'way,' Sewell begged, taking another step and then another. 'It's for wor Season Ticket.' Sewell stepped beside Gerry. Gerry looked stern for a while. Then he lifted his eyebrows as though he were considering the most important of questions. Finally he smiled. 'Great!' shouted Sewell. 'Let's get gannin'.'

The mud of the Tyne exposed by the ebbing of the tide is thick and grey. A watchful little wading bird runs along it, taking noisy flight whenever it hears a human footstep on the raised walkway. The bird is called a redshank because of its red legs. It is also called The Little Sentinel of the Marshes. Once, many years ago, before the coming and then the going of the ships, the flatland on the Gateshead bank of the Tyne was a marsh. A bleak, windswept place, teeming with creatures. Then they built the Metro Centre. A short time ago they allowed an IKEA and an Asda hypermarket to swallow the last of these wetlands. Now all that is left of this lost marsh kingdom is the strip of mud on the edge of the river exposed by the falling of the tide; and the red-legged sentinel, who endlessly patrols this small space as though searching for a panorama only its instincts recall.

Some steps lead down to the river from the raised walkway. Sewell and Gerry descended them. They stopped at the bottom one and looked out. Twenty yards of thick, glutinous, ashen-coloured mud ran down to the water. Among the seaweed-crowned rocks were all manner of artefacts. Bicycle frames, rusted industrial chains, car wheels, an entire car sunk up to its aerial tip, and there, halfway to the water, a Tesco shopping trolley. 'Ha'way,' said Sewell.

'Divven't . . .' began Gerry. But it was too late. Sewell sunk in the mud up to his ankles. Helplessly Sewell stretched his hand out to Gerry. Gerry shook his head. 'There's nee point me gannin' in and all. Just wade oot and bring it back.'

Sewell lifted a foot and pulled it out of the sucking mud. He took a step. This time he sank a little deeper. 'Ha'way, man Gerry,' he begged.

'Na.' Gerry was adamant. 'One of us has got to look respectable if we're gonnae sell anything.'

'Why?'

'It's the rule of sales, man. Ye might be making money oot of shite but ye cannet smell of it.'

'Ginga wouldn't mind.'

'Ye divven't kna.'

'Aye ah dee. He's me auld man's best mate.'

'Forget aboot that for noo. Just get to that trolley.'

Sewell's progress was tortuously slow as he picked his way across the mud. The redshank lit up from behind a rock and, flying past Sewell with a strident alarm call, noisily disappeared round the concrete girders of the railway bridge. 'Who rattled your cage?' Sewell mumbled.

'Divven't take all day,' called Gerry.

The Tesco shopping trolley was wedged deeply in the mud. Sewell tugged and tugged at it but it wouldn't budge. 'Mebbes ye were the one we rode down on last Christmas,' Sewell recalled fondly. 'Rode it all the way doon from Tesco's. Jumped off before it crashed in.'

'Who are ye talking to, ye daft get?' laughed Gerry.

'Ah cannet shift it, man,' said Sewell.

'Ha'way, ye're supposed to be strong.'

Breathing in deeply, Sewell gave it an almighty tug. His hands slipped and he fell back. There was a dull splat as he hit the mud.

'Divven't piss aboot, man,' Gerry told him from the bank. 'It looks like the tide's coming in.'

Wrenching himself up, Sewell now stood up to his knees in mud. 'Tide?' he asked, puzzlement contorting his face. 'What d'ye mean like? It's not due yet.'

'But it's a moon tide the day. Ye kna, man. The moon tide. Biggest of the month. It comes up, covers all this mud. If ye were to stay there it'd droon ye.'

'Droon?'

Gerry climbed up to the top step and looked down at his friend complacently. 'We had this woman into school one day. She was one of them river pollises. Told us all aboot people getting stuck in the mud and drooning.'

'Piss off, man Gerry.'

'Should have heard her gan on aboot when they dredged the river. Found all sorts in the mud. Cats, dogs, whole skeletons of people. Been trapped up to their knees. Struggled but couldn't get free. What a way to gan eh? Cold. Lonely. And all that shitey water in your mouth and ears. Lungs . . .'

'Please help us, Gerry,' said Sewell in a tiny voice.

'Ee, Sewell, are ye blubbing?'

'Just get us oot.'

Gerry seemed to be inspecting a hole in his shoe. 'Calm doon, man,' he advised.

'Ah'm trapped, man.'

'Ye're blubbing.'

'Ah'm not blubbing.'

'Like a babby.'

'Ha'way, man Gerry. The tide's coming in. One o' them moons.'

'Like wor Clare's bairn.'

'Ah can feel the water lapping at me ankles.'

'Divven't worry,' said Gerry wisely, scanning the river downstream. 'Ye've got ages yet.'

'Please . . .' said Sewell, buffeting his legs wildly to get them out of the sucking mud.

'When it comes, it's a tidal wave, mind. Pure evil, them moons.'

Unbalanced, Sewell fell forward, his hands breaking his fall. 'The water's beginning to rise, man!'

There was a plop as a wooden plank hit the mud. Gingerly Gerry tested his weight. Carrying two more planks under his arm he walked to the end of the first one. He dropped another and stepped on to it. And then a third. Having reached the end of his improvised jetty he still couldn't reach Sewell. Retracing his steps he lifted up the second plank and laid it down as the fourth. The plank landed an inch from Sewell. 'There ye gan,' Gerry said. 'And divven't ye mumble,' he added as Sewell wiped the mud from his eyes where the plank had sent it splattering. 'Bloody hell. Ye stink, man. What a minging. D'ye kna forty per cent of this mud is pure sewage?'

'Haddaway, man,' grumbled Sewell.

'Phor! Get doon wind of us, man. Reet, one, two, three.'

'What ye deein'?'

'We'll get the trolley up first. Then rescue ye. One, two, three!' And with an almighty heave they pulled at the sunken Tesco trolley. It gave an inch or two. 'And again, one, two, three.' The trolley gave another inch or two. 'One, two, three.' With a tremendous fart of suction the trolley blew free of the mud. 'Ye could have waited,' said Gerry.

'Funny man Gerry.'

'Heh, heh, heh.'

With its metal ribs covered in dripping mud and its red Tesco handle discoloured to a kind of flaking ochre, the trolley looked like a corpse dredged up on a dig, the archaeological remnants of some long extinct, peculiarly evolved animal, an ancient beast of burden perfectly preserved in the unique chemical composition of Tyne mud. Gerry dragged it over the improvised pier of wooden planks, carefully throwing the fourth one into the empty gap between three and one. 'Reet, see ye later,' he said when he reached the bottom of the steps.

Even from the bank it was clear that Sewell blanched. 'Ah'll give ye owt ye want,' he said, his voice rising an octave. 'Owt. I swear doon. JUST GET US OOT OF THIS FRIGGIN' MUD!'

'Ah was only joking, man Sewell,' said Gerry.

By the time Sewell was clear of the mud, and had hauled the trolley up to the raised walkway, the sun was hot and high. 'Take your bench coat off, man,' coaxed Gerry. 'It's covered in mud and it mings.'

'Na,' said Sewell, although beads of perspiration wreathed his brow.

They decided to begin round the back of the Spartan Redheugh factory. 'People throw all their rubbish oot behind Spartan,' said Gerry, warming to the idea now. The wheels of the Tesco trolley squeaked as they revolved. The front left one was buckled. 'Why won't ye take that coat off?'

'Ah like wearing it. That's why.'

'Well, at least unzip it from yer neck.'

A path runs parallel to the back of the Spartan Redheugh factory. The path is screened from the football pitches by a strip of trees. The factory is behind a very tall, spiked metal fence. Somehow someone has managed to scale this barrier and write on the metal wall of the factory, in very neat letters as tall as Gerry: CRIME. After Spartan Redheugh the path passes the gasworks and after the gasworks it runs by a large piece of land which is cordoned off for development. Eventually the path meets the dead end of a black metal fence, beyond which Alsatians loll like lions.

The path, more of a lane in summer, more of a track in winter, is secluded. A lovers' walk. A place for escape. A rendezvous for illicit goods. Gerry and Sewell walked down it, pushing their trolley. The trees were luxuriant and thick. The grass and leaves were a vibrant, summer green. Wild rose bushes lined the way, their blooms a surprise of pink and white. 'It's like a forest, if ye close your eyes,' remarked Gerry, listening to the high hum of the bees which drowned out the car sounds and human sounds of Gateshead. 'Ye could have a picnic here.'

'Aye, if it weren't for the gas,' said Sewell, sniffing at the ever-present gas which emanates from the huge works. 'Ah'd be frightened of lighting a tab. Ye'd light up and find yourself taking a drag on the roof of the Metro Centre. Never mind the stink of it.'

'Stink? Ye can talk, man Sewell,' said Gerry wrinkling up his nose.

'It's not me. It's the trolley.'

'Ha'way, take that jacket off. You must be roasted.'

'Na.' Sewell cleared his throat and licked his lips with distaste. 'Talkin' aboot tabs, ah'm clamming for a one.'

'What's more important to ye?' demanded Gerry. 'A few creature comforts or a Season Ticket.'

'Season Ticket,' admitted Sewell.

There was every conceivable piece of household flotsam and jetsam on the lane behind Spartan Redheugh, all of it in the various stages of decomposing into the ground. Gerry and Sewell soon began to fill the trolley with whatever they could lay a hand on. The husk of a recently burnt-out car had already been picked clean but there was still a door and the bonnet.

When the trolley was full it was too heavy to push. 'Hoy oot the rubbish then,' said Sewell.

'It's all rubbish, man,' said Gerry.

'Well, hoy oot the rubbish rubbish then.'

When the trolley was three-quarters empty they were able to push it. It was a long way to Ginga's.

'There's not enough here, man,' said Gerry sadly as they rested. 'Nee quality. We'll get nowt for this.'

Negotiating a high kerb, they came to a decision. 'Areet,' agreed Sewell.

'So we'll gan roond the hooses then?'

'Areet.'

'Askin' for scrap?'

'Areet.'

'We'll leave this lot here,' said Gerry pointing at the Tesco trolley. 'And come back to top it up with what we're given roond the hooses. Quality gear mind. None of your car roofs. And, Sewell man, for the last time of fucking asking will ye take off that bench coat?'

It was very hot now. People sat sweating on plastic foldy-out chairs on the pavements. Here and there they were gathered round radios or television sets wired up on rickety extension cables. Children ran between the chairs, dodging the cans of lager. An ice-cream van played the Blaydon Races three or four streets away. 'Cushdy,' said Sewell.

They walked on a little. 'RAG and BOOONE!' Gerry began to shout. 'Any auld RAAG and BOOONE!'

Sewell stopped and slid his head into the depths of his bench coat. 'What ye deein', man?' he hissed.

'What they all dee,' replied Gerry. 'RAAAG and BOOOONE! Any auld RAAAG and . . .'

'Hold on, man,' said Sewell, grabbing Gerry and dragging him down an alleyway. 'Ye cannet shout that. Someone'll see us.'

Gerry pushed Sewell away from him. 'So?' he asked.

'They'll have a laugh.'

Gerry narrowed his eyes. 'They'll have a laugh?'

'Aye.'

'Someone'll see us and have a laugh?' He spoke very slowly, spelling out each word carefully.

'That's what ah'm saying,' replied Sewell simply.

Gerry took a threatening pace towards his friend. 'D'ye want this Season Ticket or not? Divven't mumble. Tell us oot straight. D'ye want this Season Ticket or not?'

Sewell took a flustered step back. 'Ah . . .'

'Well?'

'Course ah do. More than anything.'

Gerry smiled. 'Then ye've got to put up with it. Any auld RAAAG and BOOOOAN! Any auld RAAAAAG and BOOOOOOOOAAAN!'

'You're not the usual,' a woman told them as she stood watching them from her doorway. Her arms were tightly folded and her mouth was clamped vice-like around a cigarette.

'Youth training scheme,' Gerry told her. 'Y'kna, New Deal, get the young back to work, give wor a fair chance.'

The woman had a sharp face that seemed to taper to a point at her short, jagged dyed-blonde hair, like a sharpened pencil. She wore dirty white towelling jogging trousers and sweat top. Her mouth was all gums. 'Where's your van?' she asked suspiciously.

'We divven't . . .' began Sewell.

'It's parked roond the corner,' Gerry interrupted.

'How auld are yus?' the woman asked, twisting her head abruptly to make the ash drop from the end of her cigarette.

'Younger than ye,' Gerry returned, stifling Sewell's snigger with a glance.

'Less of your cheek.'

'Sorry, Madam.'

'And that an' all. Anyway, does Terry kna ye're deein' this?'

'Terry?'

'Y'kna. Terry. The gadgie what normally comes roond.'

'Terry. Why aye. Terry. Terry, eh Sewell?'

There was a pause. 'Why aye. Terry,' added Sewell, catching on eventually.

'Ah went to school with his daughter me,' said Gerry with a smile.

The woman looked at him as though he were very far away and she had to use a telescope. 'Well, if he knas ye. Come in the hoose, ah've got something for you. Keep that friggin' door closed but.'

After the glare of the bright sun the house was dark. They went into the kitchen. Four dogs of different shapes and sizes were foraging in a cupboard. Another two were lying on the kitchen table. 'Get oot, ye bastards!' shouted the woman, spitting out her cigarette at the dogs with an amazing force. The dogs pushed past her and ran up the stairs, one of them howling. Ruefully she picked up her cigarette and stuck it back in her mouth even more tightly. Her words had to force a way past the cigarette. 'It's me bairn Matthew. Mebbe ye kna him?' Sewell and Gerry nodded. 'He keeps on bringing dogs into the hoose. Ah wouldn't mind, but it's a new one every week. There was twenty-eight o' them sleeping here last night. But ah cannet dee owt aboot it. He gans radge if ah mention it. They stink an' all. Get into every inch of the hoose. Crap all awer. Cup of tea before ye go, lads, since yus are Terry's lads? Ah can make yus a one on me gaz stove.'

'Nee thanks, Missus. We're not allowed to drink tea in the hooses.'

'Terry doesn't mind,' she said with an enigmatic smile.

'It's the rule of wor youth scheme y'kna,' Gerry told her.

'Terry wouldn't like that. He likes a cup of tea does Terry.'

'Good auld Terry,' said Gerry. 'What a laugh. Ha. Ha. Ha.'

'Aye well,' said the woman. Going into the kitchen she dropped the cigarette from her mouth into the sink and turned on the tap. The burning tobacco hissed. 'This is what ah want ye to take.' She turned back to Gerry and Sewell who had followed her. 'The cooncil have promised to gerrus a new one. It's knackt.'

As Sewell and Gerry danced the fridge into the middle of the floor, its door fell open and a dog ran out. The woman threw a handful of insults at its tail. Then she looked about worriedly. 'Help wor catch him. Ah've only just managed to get him in the hoose.'

Sewell's eyes were wide. 'Is that the hoond that was playing football before?'

Gerry nodded.

'Ha'way lads,' implored the woman. 'Me lad'll gan mad if this one isn't here when he gets back. It's his favourite.' The woman lunged for the dog, but it sidestepped her easily and padded over to the other side of the kitchen. The woman approached it again. Evading her once more, the dog leapt up on to the sink and, having opened the kitchen window with a swipe of a paw, sailed through the aperture in one bound.

The woman let out a little whimper. 'If ye see Matthew,' she told Gerry and Sewell worriedly, 'divven't tell him aboot it. He loves his dogs ye see. Can't stand to see them homeless. And whativver ye dee, divven't tell him ah kept one trapped in a fridge. Not that it was cold like. Wor electric's been cut off. But it's such a frisky bugger that one. Well ye saw it yersels. Practically opened the window itself to get oot.'

The fridge was heavy, but Sewell and Gerry were happy. They carried it between them with Sewell taking the bulk. 'Ee, are ye not hot in that big coat?' the woman called after

Sewell, taking back her sentry position in the frame of the open door from where she had first spied them.

'She wants ye to take your clothes off, man,' sniggered Gerry.

'Ah'm keeping me bench coat on.'

When they were halfway to Ginga's they put the fridge down and lolled back on the seats in a bus shelter.

'Ah'm gaspin',' moaned Sewell. 'We should have taken that cup o'tea the ould wifie offered us.'

Gerry smiled slyly. 'Ah knew ye fancied her.'

'Well aye,' shrilled Sewell sarcastically.

'Ye cannet deny it. Ah saw the way ye watched her sucking on that tab.'

'Na man. Ah just wanted a smoke. Anyway, it was ye she wanted.'

'She wanted to get ye oot o' that coat. Mebbes she thought ye were like a Scotsman.'

'Eh?'

'Wantin' to see what was beneath your bench coat!'

The two of them dissolved into laughter. When they recovered, it seemed hotter than ever. The temperature was rising with the afternoon.

'Ah'm climbing up the wall for a fag,' said Sewell. 'What wouldn't ah give for a tab, a toastie and a mug o' tea.'

'When we get wor Season Ticket,' Gerry told him. 'When we get wor Season Ticket, that's the time for snacks.'

Smiling, Sewell sighed dreamily. 'Ah wonder where that dog is,' he said. 'It was a belter hoond.'

They got to Ginga's eventually, toiling down Saltwell Road and then up the Whitehall Bank. It was in Bensham. The road had never felt so long. 'This is the one,' decided Sewell, stopping at the end house in a long, crumbling terrace. 'This time ah'm sure.' All the other houses in the terrace, with slates missing from the roofs, and windows and doors boarded with metal shutters, were not occupied. A thin line of smoke issuing from this last chimney advertised human presence. Taking one hand from underneath the fridge Gerry knocked on the door. There was no answer. 'Ye'll have to knock louder,' Sewell told him. 'Ah think he's getting deef.'

'Hold this then,' said Gerry, taking one arm away from the fridge to knock at the door. Sewell buckled under the weight of the fridge as Gerry pounded on the battered front door. There was still no reply. 'Hello?' shouted Gerry. 'Anyone in?' At that moment Sewell's strength gave way and the fridge fell to the ground. It bounced once, twice, then its door fell off. 'What ye deein', Sewell man?' Gerry demanded.

'Ah couldn't hold it,' replied Sewell.

'Hello?' said a face appearing through a gap in the opening door.

'Couldn't hold it?' shot back Gerry.

'Na. Couldn't hold it.'

'Hello?' the face repeated.

'So ye've gone weak?'

'Na, ye let go of your end.'

'Hello?' The face still spoke in a calm, even voice.

'Ah divven't kna what to dee with ye me, Sewell,' said Gerry angrily.

'And ah divven't kna what to dee with ye me, Gerry,' responded Sewell.

'Have ye two come to see Ginga or to have a battle on me doorstep?' remarked the voice mildly, a hand settling itself beside the face.

'Ginga,' said Sewell, seeing the face at the door.

'We've brought ye summink,' said Gerry.

'Ye'd better come in then,' said the face with a smile.

Ginga was an old man, although you couldn't tell it by his face. His hair was thick, long and flamingly ginger. His beard, which seemed to totally fill his face, leaving only the smallest of portholes for his eyes, nose and mouth, was likewise red. His eyebrows were also ginger. And even the hair on his hands, one of which held the door wide now while the other gestured Gerry and Sewell hospitably in, was ginger. It was only when the rest of him was added to the face and hands, that he was seen to be shrunken and stooped with age. 'And divven't think ah henna it,' Ginga said to Gerry with a wink.

'Na,' said Gerry still staring at the ginger hair.

'Bring yer treasure in an' all,' Ginga said, pointing lovingly at where the doorless fridge squatted on the pavement. 'Set it doon here,' he said in the hall. They did. 'Ha'way,' he called, leading them along the pitch-dark passage. They surfaced into a room which was only slightly brighter with one small window high on the far wall. Ginga tugged at a cord and a dim light filled the room. Every single object in it, every single fixture and fitting, every single ornament and utility had been salvaged. The waste of Gateshead was resurrected here. 'Things have never been the same since ye young uns took up joy-riding. It's been a godsend. Ye provide all me upholstery. Sit doon.' Gerry and Sewell sat on the settee which was the back seat of a car, while Ginga eased himself into the passenger's seat. Gerry and Sewell looked about, fascinated. 'Ye wouldn't believe what people hoy oot the hoose,' laughed Ginga, tugging at his beard with both hands. There was a hollowed-out upright Hoover which served as a walking stick and umbrella stand; two tea chests covered by curtains were his table and cloth; washing hung below the ceiling on twine attached to a pulley controlled by a pan handle fixed to a bicycle wheel; yards of old Formica panels ran along the walls, giving shelf space to countless ornaments – standing figures made from wire coathangers, farmyard animals crafted from plastic carrier bags, and the most outstanding fleet of newspaper ships, sepia with age. 'Having a good look roond, lads?' laughed Ginga.

'Aye. It's a treasure trove,' said Gerry, emitting a low whistle of appreciation.

'Ye what?' asked Ginga, cupping his ear with a hand.

'Ah said it's like a treasure trove,' repeated Gerry. 'Aladdin's cave y'kna.'

'Aye, it is everything ah've saved.'

'Na. Ah said yer hoose is like an Aladdin's cave. A magpie's nest.'

'Aye, ah think it's the best.'

'He cannet hear very well,' Sewell reminded Gerry.

'Ah divven't kna ye,' said Ginga, pointing at Gerry with a smile. 'But ye're Billy Sewell's lad, aren't ye?' he said with a nod in Sewell's direction.

'Aye, Ginga,' said Sewell.

'How's he deeing, yer auld man? Haven't seen him for a canny bit.'

Sewell blushed. 'He's areet,' he said.

There was an open fire burning in an elaborate-looking fire place. 'Ah picked this up before they knocked the hooses doon in Dunston,' Ginga said, following Gerry's and Sewell's eyes. 'The Mayor of Gateshead used to warm his backside in front of this y'kna.' He picked up a cube of wood sawn from a fence post and threw it on the fire. 'Ah love Gatesheed me,' he told them. 'Used to be a sailor, seen half the world. Worked as a miner a mile below the groond. But ah'd take Gatesheed every time. Except for one thing. The weather's shocking. Divven't kna aboot ye, Billy Sewell's lad. Ye must be canny hot in that snorkel jacket.'

'It's a bench coat, Ginga,' said Sewell.

'What d'ye mean a French stoat?'

'Snorkel jackets went oot with the ark,' explained Gerry. 'It's a bench coat. Y'kna, a manager's jacket. What Kevin Keegan and Kenny Dalglish and all them footie managers wear. A b-e-n-c-h coat.' Gerry stopped suddenly. 'Ah kna sign language,' he told Sewell. ''cos of me nana.' Frantically he began to sign. Ginga looked at him, reading his hand words carefully.

'Aye, it is hot for the time of year, but ah still feel the damp,' he said at length.

Gerry looked at Sewell and shook his head. 'Ah was trying to tell him aboot yer bench coat.'

'There's neewhere like Gatesheed for the damp,' Ginga

carried on. 'Sometimes ah wake up and think ah'm still at sea, but ah'm really here in Gatesheed of course. It's the river. It's tidal y'kna.' Ginga broke off abruptly, as though waking up from a dream. 'Sorry ah've nee tea to offer ye lads. Nee sarsaparilla either. Ah usually just drink water. Ah've got some fern brew mind, ah grow it on the allotments.'

'Ye're areet, man Ginga,' said Gerry.

There was a pause. 'We've got ye a fridge,' shouted Sewell and Gerry simultaneously.

Ginga's youthful gingery hand shot up and scratched his thick ginger mop. His eyes shone intelligently. 'What kind of fridge?'

'Divven't kna, man Ginga. The type that keeps cans cold.'

Ginga seemed perplexed for a while then he smiled broadly at them. 'Well thanks very much, lads,' he said.

'Aye,' said Gerry.

'Aye,' said Sewell.

'Aye,' said Ginga.

A clock suddenly burst into life. Its mechanics whirred and hummed. A little plastic magpie popped out like a cuckoo. It was three o'clock. They all sat on in silence. After a while Ginga said, 'It's nice of ye lads to bring the fridge roond. What else can ah get for ye?'

'Em,' said Sewell.

'We thought ye might pay us like,' said Gerry.

Ginga shook his head. 'Ah cannet hear ye.'

'Pay us!' roared Gerry. 'We thought ye might pay us. For the materials like, and the labour costs.'

'It took us ages to drag it up here,' explained Sewell, nodding emphatically.

Gerry rubbed his thumb over his forefinger as though feeling banknotes.

Ginga understood. 'Ah would love to. But ah've nee money,' he said with a smile. 'Besides, lads, ah could get hold of any amounts of fridges for meself at a moment's notice.'

'Oh,' said Gerry. 'Oh,' said Sewell.

'Ah'm what's called living beyond the cash economy.'

'Eh?'

'Look, ah'll take the fridge in return for anything ye see in here that ye fancy.'

Sewell and Gerry looked round and examined everything. 'We'll have . . .' began Sewell.

'The magpie cuckoo clock,' said Gerry, getting up and pointing at it.

'A good choice,' approved Ginga. 'D'ye follow the football?'

'Aye,' said Gerry. 'Of course.'

'Ye won't remember Billy Sewell's uncle will ye? A Gateshead lad. Built like a tug boat. Worked doon the pit with us. Made the midfield his own, mind. Used to drink like a fish, always areet on the day of a match but. Didn't need speed y'kna. It was all strength. Bit like wor kiddar here,' he said pointing at Sewell with a smile.

The walk back was long and hot. Sewell and Gerry trailed along the streets disconsolately. There had been an accident on the motorway and the cars were backed up for about a mile. The smog of exhaust fumes rose over the houses. The police helicopter flew overhead and hovered for a while like an angry wasp.

'We're not gonnae have enough, are we?' said Sewell as they stood on the bridge looking at the traffic jammed below.

Gerry's voice was small. 'Na. Ah thought two or three weeks was long enough. Ah was wrong.'

There was a pause. 'Next season,' said Sewell.

'Aye,' said Gerry. 'It'll have to be next season.'

Sewell smiled. 'And we'll enjoy them all the more for the wait. We'll have to get a move on but. We still haven't made a penny.'

In silence they stood on the bridge, the traffic roaring below them like a waterfall. Gerry looked up suddenly. 'Reet,' he said.

Sewell looked up too, staring distractedly at the helicopter which was hovering nearby. 'What?' he said.

Gerry spat. 'We need a bold stroke,' he said. 'A purely bold stroke.'

The helicopter boiled itself away. The two friends stood leaning against the parapet. A bark sounded behind them. Then another one. Sewell looked round. 'Gerry man! It's that dog. The one playing footie. The one in the hoose. It's come looking for wor!' Crouching down, Sewell extended a hand towards the animal, rubbing his fingers together encouragingly. 'Here, boy, come to Sewell.'

'How do ye kna it's a boy?' Gerry asked.

'Look at its balls, man. It must have been following wor.'

Sewell was practically on his knees now. 'Watch oot it doesn't leap up and rip oot yer throat,' warned Gerry.

'Here, dog, here,' Sewell coaxed. The dog took a few steps towards him but then inched back cautiously. 'Ha'way, ah'm not gonnae hurt ye.' The creature whined a little.

'Ye must be giving off a smell,' Gerry announced, sitting on the parapet to watch.

'Eh?'

'Y'kna. A fearful ming, a hostile smell. Dogs can sense these things.'

Sewell unzipped his bench coat and put his face inside it. 'Divven't think so. He's just nervous. He wants to come to me, but he's had his trust broken that many times.'

In Gateshead there are small dogs, vicious dogs, serene dogs. Dogs with patches over the eye, dogs with a tail that curves over the back. Trotting dogs, lowping dogs, sniffing dogs, sitting dogs. Dogs of one colour, dogs of two colours, dogs with many many colours. Sociable dogs, misanthropic dogs. Highly knowledgeable dogs, fearfully giddy dogs. This one was largely white with rusty patches on its face and body. Every so often its ears pricked forward and bristled intelligently. A little larger than a Border collie, it was one of those whose tail curves up over the back. 'Here, hoond. Here,'

Sewell sang with infinite gentleness. The dog took another few steps towards him, its snout surveying Sewell with rapid sniffs. Then suddenly it let out a wild yelp and threw itself at him, bundling him over with his paws.

'Divven't let it get a grip o' yer throat!' urged Gerry from the parapet.

'Calm doon,' laughed Sewell. 'It's just licking us to death. It likes us. That's all. It likes us.' Sewell's face was contorted with joy. 'Ah think ah'll call it Rusty.'

'Rusty?'

'Aye, it's white with rusty patches.'

'Sewell man, ye cannet give it a name. It'll already have a one.'

'It can have two.'

'Two?'

'Just like ye. You're Gerry Macarten reet? Well, he'll be Rusty . . . Rusty . . . Whatever his other name is.'

Gerry shook his head gravely. 'Rusty Matthew. Ha'way, man Sewell. It belongs to Matthew. Ye cannet keep it. He's a radgie mad lad that dog boy. Ye saw, even his mam's terrified of him.'

Sewell stood up, and the dog jumped up at him. Catching hold of the animal's paws, together they danced a few steps on the bridge. 'Look at it. It's geet intelligent, man.'

'Oh aye.'

'Aye, it'll be able to dee all sorts o' tricks and that. Ah'll teach it.'

Gerry jumped down from the parapet and sighed heavily. 'Well, ye can start by asking it how we're gonnae get the dosh for wor Season Tickets then.'

The long, long nights of summer are shortening. Every morning the fog lifts a little later from the Tyne. The leaves on the trees that line the Spartan Redheugh factory are suddenly yellow and red. The grass that has grown strong and wiry in clumps on the wasteland, tires and dies. In the evenings, swallows and house martins gather above the pools of the Watergate Colliery Land Redevelopment Project; one morning they are gone. So autumn arrives in Gateshead.

'How much we got? How much we got?' demanded Sewell one morning, bursting into Gerry's bedroom.

'Eh?' responded Gerry, bleary-eyed. 'What's gannin' on? What d'ye want, man Sewell?' There was a bark, a scuttle of rapid movement up the stairs and then a dog wagged its tail into the room. 'Ah thought ah told ye to get rid of the mutt,' Gerry said sharply.

Sewell's face fell. 'Ah tried. But he keeps on following us. Rusty's grown attached to us, man.'

'Aye, well, he can grow unattached an' all. He's not yours, man Sewell. He belongs to someone else. He belongs to that psycho kid Matthew.'

Sewell stared at the floor.

'Ha'way, divven't blub awer a dumb animal.'

'Ah'm not blubbing, and Rusty's not dumb.'

There was a long pause. Gerry turned over in his bed and pretended to go back to sleep. Sewell watched him patiently. After a lengthy, silent interval, Gerry sat up as though just waking, and said, 'Well areet. Ye can keep him, but just for a while.' At that moment Rusty leapt up on to Gerry's bed and began licking his face wildly. 'On the condition that ye keep him under control, and nee licking wor!'

Leaning over, Sewell picked Rusty up. The animal lay back pliantly in his arms. Gently he set the dog down. Rusty lay at Sewell's feet, his head resting on his left shoe.

'What ye come awer so early for anyway?' Gerry asked.

'Gerry man!' he burst out eagerly. 'How much have we got?' Gerry pulled the sheet over his head, Sewell pulled it off. 'Ha'way, Gerry! Let's count wor money.'

Gerry yawned theatrically. 'Ah thought we agreed. Nee countin' it until we kna we've got enough.'

Sewell nodded his head methodically. 'Aye,' he said. 'That's what we agreed. We haven't counted it yet. But we will the day. Today's the day because it's a special day like. The toon are playing at home.'

'It's first thing in the morning, man Sewell man. Gis a moment.'

Just then the cuckoo clock, fixed to the wall with a nail, began to whirr and chime. The magpie came out on a steady chain. 'It's nine o'clock, ha'way!' Sewell said, ripping off Gerry's bedcovers. 'Jesus man, divenn't ye wear owt in bed?'

Gerry crawled out of bed and pulled on his jogging trousers. 'Gis a tab, Sewell.'

Sewell took out two cigarettes from a packet of twenty. He handed one to Gerry. They lit up. 'Ha'way, man Gerry, let's see how much we've got.'

Gerry inhaled uneasily as he followed his friend across the landing to Bridget's room. 'She aroond?' asked Sewell.

'Haven't seen her for a canny while. Me mam says she was here last week but.'

'Is she areet?'

'Ah divven't kna,' mused Gerry, disappearing into Bridget's cupboard. He came out holding the glass jar. 'Ah've wrapped it up as an extra safety measure,' he told Sewell as he undid the rag of black and white paper and handed it over to him. Sewell took it like a trophy. There was awe on his face. Then he tilted the jar to see its contents better. The coins and notes fell in an avalanche on to the uncarpeted floor, rolling in all directions. 'Well, we can count it easier on the floor,' Sewell reasoned.

For twenty serious, concentrated minutes they moved around the bedroom on their hands and knees, salvaging the money from where it had fallen and counting it carefully. Under the bed, under the floorboards, in corners, in the shadows they rescued it. Rusty watched them contentedly from the doorway, where he lay down. 'Ah thought we were only saving the notes,' said Sewell uncertainly, rolling a twenty-pence piece in his fingers.

'Later on, later. At first we'll have to save it all.'

The first sum total came to eighty-eight pounds. 'Nivver,' said Sewell shaking his head in disbelief. 'Nivver.' The second count yielded only seventy. 'Nivver,' said Gerry. 'Nivver.' The third reckoning mustered eighty-five pounds.

'Eighty-five poond?' stammered Sewell.

'Eighty-five poond,' repeated Gerry.

Sewell was despondent. 'We've done all this for only eighty-five poond?'

'It's a start,' reasoned Gerry.

'It's finished,' decided Sewell.

'Ha'way, man,' cajoled Gerry folding the notes under Sewell's nose. 'We haven't done that much for it.'

'Not much? We washed all them cars in Whickham,' corrected Sewell, his cheeks brightening with disappointment. 'We distributed all them leaflets in toon, four Saturdays in a row mind. Ah was even the Nobles Amusements sandwich-board man. We won all that money on the fruit machine in the Cushie Butterfield. We sold all the Biros we twoced. And all the CDs. We even did Penny for the friggin' Guy even though it's only September. We're off the drink, hardly ever have a tab, ah cannet remember the last tac we smoked and ye're telling me we've got only eighty-five poonds?'

Gerry looked calmly, unblinkingly at his friend. 'Ye sayin' ah took it?'

Sewell dismissed the allegation with a smart wave of his hand.

'Divven't cry then, man Sewell.'

Sewell shook his head dejectedly. 'It's shocking that's what it is. Well, Gerry, what's the point, man? We've done all this and we're neewhere near a Season Ticket not even for next season.'

Gerry looked Sewell in the eye. 'Mebbes it's time to get serious,' he said, walking back into his own room, Rusty trotting after him.

'Time to get serious?' asked Sewell, shambling after both of them.

'Aye, time tae gan into overdrive.'

'Any more overdrive and we'll bloody well explode before we get wor tickets,' Sewell seethed.

'Time for us to make real sacrifices.'

Aggrieved, Sewell punched his own fist. 'What ye talking aboot? We've scrimped and saved for months. We've totally gone withoot the good things in life.'

Gerry looked calmly and levelly at Sewell. Deliberately he blinked. And then he blinked again. 'Na,' he said. 'Ah'm telling ye. We haven't even begun yet.'

'But . . .'

Gerry's voice was low. 'Nivver ever let me catch ye smoking them proper pre-rolled tabs again, Sewell,' he told him, threatening him with the glowing dow of the cigarette Sewell had given him. 'Ah cannet believe it, man. Ah thought we were mates. Then ye gan and waste money on proper tabs. Remember wor rule. Whenever we have any, and that's hardly ever, then we have to roll wor own.'

There was a silence. The pigeons could be heard jockeying for position on the roof, the sound of their toes scraping on the slates seemed separated from the boys by the thinnest of ceilings. From somewhere on the football fields a pony could be heard whinnying happily. 'What we gonnae dee?' asked Sewell miserably, sinking on to the bed.

'Divenn't worry.' Gerry looked out of the window. 'Ah'll work it oot.'

There was a short pause. 'Got any ideas?'

'Na.'

Following Gerry, Sewell climbed on to the bed and stared out of the window. Rusty jumped up too, his front paws resting on the sill. Outside a trotting-pony was circling the football pitches, coaxed on by a driver lying back on the lightweight carriage. 'An idea,' Gerry intoned softly. 'All we need is a good idea. One great idea.'

Downstairs the front door opened and then closed with a bang. 'Anyone aboot?' a voice shouted up the stairs.

'Wor Clare,' said Gerry and, slipping quickly back into Bridget's room, hurriedly collected up the last coins and notes into the jar. Rewrapping it in its rag of black and white paper, he thrust it into the corner of Bridget's cupboard. 'Ah tell ye what Sewell, we won't tell her and me mam until we've got a bit more like. Won't tell neebody. Not until we've got the tickets in wor hands.'

'What's this great idea gonnae be then?' Sewell asked, standing in the doorway.

'Eh?' replied Gerry.

'Gerry? Ah kna ye're there,' Clare shouted again, there was a small henlike cluck from the baby tucked under her arm.

'The idea that's gonnae put everything reet,' Sewell prompted.

'Ah'll tell ye later,' whispered Gerry to Sewell. 'Areet, Clare!' he called down the stairs.

'Ha'way doon here then, man,' she yelled. 'And ye, Sewell.'

'How did she kna ah was here?' Sewell wondered as they walked down the stairs.

'She knas everything,' answered Gerry grimly. 'So remember. Not a word to her aboot the . . . ye kna what.'

Clare was waiting for them in the hall. She was wearing a red miniskirt, a yellow sweatshirt and white stiletto-heeled sandals which were about the same shade of pale as her face.

'Ah cannet stop,' she told them waving the baby at them like a rattle. 'Ye areet, Sewell hinny?'

'Aye. Ye?'

'Ye staying for a bit?' Gerry asked her.

'Na.' As Clare shook her head she elicited another few clucks from the baby. 'Mam was up geet early this morning. She came roond mine. She's canny badly. She's gonnae stay with me a bit. Nana's stopping an' all like.'

'Ah heard her coughing again last night,' Gerry told her.

'Did ye?' Clare's white face was lined with worry.

'All night like.'

'Aye well. Y'kna where everyone is if ye need wor eh. Has wor Bridie been aboot?'

'Na.'

'If ye see her tell her aboot me mam.' Clare marched through to the kitchen but then stopped and turned round to face her brother and his friend. 'Gerry, what ye two deeing the day?'

'We've got wor plans,' Gerry replied guardedly.

'Have ye?'

'Aye. Y'kna, things to dee and sort oot.' Gerry lifted his eyebrows mysteriously.

'Well, ah've got me hands full with mam and nana an' that,' Clare replied.

'Have ye?' Gerry said without enthusiasm.

'Aye, so can ye and Sewell look after the bairn for the day?'

'Em . . .'

Before they could answer, Clare had deposited the baby in Gerry's empty arms. 'Ye can? That'd be brilliant, lads. Ah'll buy ye a pint next time we're doon the club.'

The door closed as Clare left. Her shoes could be heard clattering down the street and then disappearing round the corner. 'That's great, just great!' moaned Gerry, going into the kitchen and laying the baby on the table. 'How are we supposed to come up with our great idea carting a babby aroond with us?'

'Ha'way, man,' said Sewell, picking up the baby himself and bouncing her gently. 'Have a heart. The bairn'll be nee trouble. Besides, we've got Rusty, kids love dogs y'kna.'

'Where is he then?'

'Eh?'

'Where's the mutt?'

'Hold her a second,' said Sewell, handing the baby over to Gerry. He ran upstairs. A minute later he came back down. 'He's gone.'

'How?'

'Just gone. Must have slipped oot behind Clare.'

Taking back the baby from Gerry, Sewell glowered over her head at his friend as he rubbed her back.

'Divven't look at us like that, man,' protested Gerry.

'It's because ye didn't want him. He could sense it. And noo he's oot and aboot again. Ah've got to save 'im from the dog boy, man Gerry.'

'It'll be ye that needs saving, if he knas ye've had his hoond.' Gerry scratched under his armpit, then let his arms fall to his sides. 'Ha'way, Sewell. We've enough on wor plate with entertaining this babby and coming up with the great idea.'

Delivering a strong kick at its lock and then turning the key three times, Gerry opened the coal house door. 'This'll dee the job,' he announced, and bringing out the Tesco shopping trolley, they placed the baby in it. 'It's a playpen on wheels.'

Pushing the trolley before them they squeaked down the road. The baby lay on a cushion, looking up at her uncle and his friend with impassive contentment. 'Geronimo or what?' quipped Gerry.

'Gan roond the shop first,' said Sewell.

'Nee way, man,' said Gerry. 'We're supposed to be saving money, not spending it.'

'Have a heart, man,' said Sewell. 'It's for the bairn.'

'Aye areet,' said Gerry in a tone of voice bordering on the snap. 'Ah'll wait oot here for ye, but ah'll tell ye this just once, divven't gan deeing any of that emotional blackmail.'

Sewell came back with a penny chew and handed it to the baby. 'What ye deeing?' demanded Gerry.

'Thought the babby looked hungry.'

'It cannet eat one of these, man. It doesn't know how to unwrap them.'

'And this is for when it gets thirsty,' added Sewell, taking out a can from the pocket of his bench coat. 'Not a bad price eh. One chew and a can of Tango for a penny eh?'

'Aye, areet,' said Gerry, taking the can with a smile. 'We'll give her it when she starts crying. That's them trying to tell ye they're thirsty.'

'Or that they've done a shite,' added Sewell knowledgeably.

Halfway down the street the baby started crying. The boys looked at each other. With a shrug, Gerry opened the can. 'Here ye gan, babby,' he said, holding the can out. The baby knocked it back with a flailing hand and began crying even harder. 'Ha'way, youngster, take a drink,' he pleaded. But she wouldn't and when Gerry poured some directly into the baby's mouth she spat it out, nearly choking. 'This is nee good,' said Gerry, wiping his hands on his tracky bottoms. 'We need one of them spout things.'

'Mebbes she doesn't like Tango,' Sewell volunteered. 'Ah'll gan and nick some Vimto. Bairns love that.'

'She needs a bottle, man Sewell,' said Gerry disdainfully. 'Where can we get a one o' them?'

'Why divven't we gan roond your Clare's?'

'Na. Me mam's . . . me mam wants some peace, man.'

'Has she gorra gan back to hospital?'

'Divven't kna,' said Gerry evasively. 'Mebbes.' He paused by the window of a house. 'It's 10.17,' he informed Sewell, squinting in at the green light of the video clock. '10.17 on a match day and what are we deeing? 10.17 on the day of our geet mega plan and what are we deeing? Trying to find a bottle for the babby.'

'Mebbes the clock's wrong.'

'Eh?'

'Mebbes the clock's wrong. Mebbes it isn't 10.17.'

Gerry sighed. 'Doesn't have to be exact y'kna. All ah mean is that instead of getting all excited about the match, we're trailing roond with a whelp in a shopping trolley.'

'Oh na,' moaned Sewell, waving a hand before his nose. 'Ah think she's shat herself an' all, man.'

'Quick, get doonwind!' exclaimed Gerry.

They pulled the shopping trolley and baby behind them back to the house. 'Reet,' said Gerry, lifting away the unwashed plates and cups on to the kitchen table and placing his little niece in the kitchen sink. 'Get all the windows open and breathe through your mouth.' Turning on the tap, he pulled off the soiled disposable nappy and threw it out the window. He lifted the baby up to the tap.

'What ye deein'?' asked Sewell.

'Ah'm washing the shite away, man.'

'Under the tap?'

'Aye.'

'Ye cruel get!'

'What's got into ye, Sewell?'

'Wait for it to run warm at least, man. Where's the Tango? Ah'll put it in this,' said Sewell, finding a baby's bottle in the cupboard.

'And ah'll stick this on that,' said Gerry, pulling a tea towel out from underneath all the dirty dishes on the table and tying it around the baby's waist in a bow.

'Not too tight, man,' urged Sewell solicitously.

Out on to the streets of Gateshead rolled Gerry, Sewell and the baby in the Tesco trolley. 'Ha'way,' said Gerry, leaning down and picking up an empty can of Viborg lager from the pavement. He put some pebbles in the can and, rattling them in front of the baby, put it in the shopping trolley with her. 'That'll keep her interested. Babbies love rattles y'kna.' The baby stared at the green Viking ship that sails across the yellow Viborg can.

They skirted the football pitches which the trotting-pony

was still circling. A flock of pigeons flew overhead, changing direction abruptly. Trotting-ponies and pigeons are familiar sights in Gateshead. Pigeon lofts ring the edges of the estates in Gateshead like vast shanty townships; and trotting-ponies endlessly circle the borough as though constantly setting and reaffirming the metropolitan border lines.

'Have you thought yet?' began Sewell after a while. 'The big idea?'

Gerry paused for a moment, Sewell craned his head over to him in anticipation. 'Na,' began Gerry. 'Not yet. Give wor a while longer, man, cannet ye?'

Sewell looked at the trotting-pony. 'What aboot getting a one o' them? They put big bets on the trotting-ponies y'kna. Ah've seen them up Swalwell.'

'Na,' said Gerry dismissively. 'Who'd drive it? Ah cannet stand horses, and nee disrespect to ye, Sewell, but you're awer heavy. The rest'd be finished lang since and wor poor nag would still be struggling roond the first lap.'

Another flock of pigeons rolled over the sky. 'Pigeons,' Sewell said. 'We could catch them and sell them.'

Gerry snorted angrily. 'Just leave the thinking to me, will ye?'

Leaning down distractedly into the shopping trolley, Sewell rattled the Viborg can in front of the baby, who cooed happily.

The River Team flows through Gateshead on its way to the Tyne. Where it bubbles through the waste ground on which the travellers sometimes camp, it is the width of a road. Industry, long since disappeared, has created a mini gorge through which the water runs, and a platform of concrete remains as a bridge. There are trees, willows, alders and sycamores, and small inlets for mallard ducks to breed. Grey wagtails land on stones. Kingfishers whirr their kaleidoscope through the monotonous Gateshead grey. Gerry led Sewell and his baby niece that way. They stopped on the bridge. 'What we need is summink like last year,' announced Gerry, sending a stone into the water below. He looked significantly at Sewell and then crossed to the other side of the bridge.

Sewell looked up from the water gushing below them. 'Eh?' he called, pushing the baby after his friend.

'What an idea that was,' crooned Gerry appreciatively. Sewell looked at him questioningly. 'Y'kna,' urged Gerry. 'It was when me mam had the wheelchair.'

'Oh aye, we went into British Home Stores in toon,' returned Sewell slowly.

'We put all the gear under me mam's blanket. What a belter idea. Would have worked an' all if the daft coo hadn't dropped everything in front of the security guard.'

Recrossing the bridge, Sewell pushed the trolley over the waste ground, lifting it over the bricks and rubble and fording the puddles which lay in the depressions of ancient concrete. Reaching the wire fence, they passed through an opening the size of a doorway. Back on the football pitches the trotting-pony was gone. They walked on to the houses. Passing an uncurtained window, they peered through it. The green light of the video clock said 12.01. 'Noon on the match day,' intoned Gerry bleakly. 'And we're tramping the streets with a bairn in a Tesco trolley. We're knackered. Hungry an' all.'

Immediately Sewell perked up. 'Ye can say that again. Let's ger wor dinner. Ah'll dee the honours.'

Pulling his bench coat to the exact angle, Sewell stepped inside the Spar. He walked up one aisle and then down another. Someone had already put silver foil over the lens of the video security camera. He smiled to himself. Slowly he browsed through the pie section. 'Scotch pie? Cornish pasty? Mebbes even a stottie,' he said to himself, straying to the ready-made sandwich section.

'Areet,' greeted Gerry, smiling conspiratorially from behind the crisps.

'Gerry?' Sewell stammered. 'What are ye deeing in here?'

'Giving ye a hand.'

'Ye cannet leave the babby ootside, man.'

'Why not like?'

'Someone might take her.'

'Take her? With a shitty nappy an' all?'

'Aye.'

'Well stone me.'

With two quick movements a chicken pie and a Scotch pie disappeared into Sewell's bench coat. As a diversion Gerry took a packet of crisps to buy. 'Twenty pence,' said the woman behind the till, her permed hair falling over large glasses through which she tried to peer.

'Eh!' exclaimed Gerry as he put the crisps back. 'Daylight robbery!' he told her, careful not to crunch the two packets lying up his sleeves.

Outside Sewell was bending over the trolley, cooing at the baby. 'How could ye leave her by herself, man?' he demanded angrily.

They walked down the road past the bus stop. When they had turned the corner Sewell opened his bench coat. 'Chicken or Scotch pie?'

'Scotch,' said Gerry, and produced the crisps from his sleeves like a conjuror. 'Plain or pizza-flavoured?'

'Pizza.'

They sat on a wall. Gerry broke off a bit of his pie and gave it to the baby. Opening the crisps, they ate in silence. 'She doesn't seem very hungry,' remarked Gerry, chewing.

Sewell finished his pie with a lick of his fingers and, tilting his head back, funnelled the last crumbs of the crisps into his mouth. 'Belter,' he burped. Looking at the baby he saw her holding a crust of pie up to her mouth and sucking helplessly at it. 'She's got nee teeth, man Gerry,' he said. 'She cannet manage it.' Taking the pie from her he shoved the lot into his mouth.

'Ye greedy get,' said Gerry, trying to grab a crumb for himself.

'Keep back, ye,' Sewell warned him. Having chewed on the

pie for a while Sewell then spat it out on to the palm of his hand. Bringing it over to the baby he scooped a bit up on the forefinger of his other hand and put it to the infant's mouth like a spoon. Gurgling happily, she took bite after bite. When she had eaten as much of the pie as she wanted Sewell topped up her bottle with more Tango.

'Should see your face, Sewell man. Ye look like a lass.'

'Do ye want this bit?' Sewell asked, holding out the crust of pie that the baby had not wanted.

'Na,' said Gerry.

Sewell pushed it into his own mouth, chewed once and then swallowed. They sat on the wall for a while, deep in thought. 'What we need is an idea like the wheelchair one,' mused Gerry. 'But ah just cannet think.'

Dejectedly they trailed into the park which had been built when Gateshead had played host to the International Garden Festival. The flower beds and walkways were gradually sinking back into the general dereliction of the area but they still retained some of the original grandeur and design. The Dunston Rocket tower block rose above them, its top floors beginning to disappear with the closing weather. It started to rain.

'Just what we need,' cursed Gerry. 'What ye deein', Sewell?' Sewell had taken off his bench coat. Gerry watched him open-mouthed as he attached the garment to the trolley. It formed a roof for the baby.

'Cannet have the bairn getting wet,' said Sewell simply.

'Ye look naked withoot that coat,' Gerry told him. 'Like a plucked turkey. Still fat y'kna, but all plucked.'

The rain was growing harder. The moss which flourished on the neglected paths of the park was slippery underfoot. The trolley's wheels seemed to be squeaking louder than ever as Sewell pushed it carefully through the rank shrubberies and weed-filled flower beds. Under her special canopy the baby smiled widely. 'She's happy anyway,' remarked Gerry.

But the rain showed no sign of relenting, and Sewell shivered like a pony when the drops went down his neck.

'Ha'way,' said Gerry. 'Let's take shelter.'

Turning round, they headed for the Low Teams shops, that thin, tumble-down, semi-paralysed parade. Drawing the shopping trolley under the grey concrete awning of the parade, Gerry stood a milk crate on its end and sat on it. Sewell sat beside him. Mutely they watched the rain coursing down, dripping rapidly from the edge of the awning.

The door to one of the shops opened and a girl came out.

'Areet, Gemma,' said Gerry.

'Areet,' said Sewell.

'Ee areet, lads,' Gemma replied, smiling widely. 'Haven't seen ye at school for ages, Gerry man.'

'Well, y'kna . . .' smiled Gerry. 'Other fish to fry.'

Gemma smiled again and passed a hand through her hair, an unruly explosion of blonde peroxide with the roots showing dark. In height she stood two or three inches above Gerry, but she was so thin, arms, legs, even hands, that she looked tall, like a weed which grows between concrete slabs alone on derelict ground. Despite its lean, almost pinched look which gave her the appearance of someone much older and more knowledgeable than she actually was, her face held the beauty of the wild, wasteland flower. Her tracksuit was black and white, she wore it zipped to her throat in protection from the rain. Seeing the baby she was filled with transports of delight. Leaning down to the shopping trolley she lifted away the bench coat and blew little kisses. 'Ah didn't kna,' she said to Sewell, handing him his coat.

Sewell blushed frantically, hiding his embarrassment in the job of putting his bench coat back on. 'It isn't mine.'

'Oh,' said Gemma. 'Is it yer sister's babby, Gerry?'

'Aye,' replied Gerry.

'Ee canny!' cooed Gemma. 'She's got a rattle an' all.' Shaking the Viborg can, Gemma laughed delightedly, then, picking up the baby, she bounced her in her scrawny arms. The baby giggled back. 'What's she called?'

'Keegan.'

'Well, ah wish she was mine.'

Sewell cleared his throat, and spat the phlegm away awkwardly.

'Have ye got the time, Gemma pet?' Gerry asked.

'Half two,' replied Gemma, the thinness of her arms apparent as she lifted her sleeve up to see her watch. Reluctantly she handed the baby back. 'Ee, yous two are brilliant,' she enthused. 'Dead good with the bairn.' Sewell took the baby from her and laid her tenderly back in the trolley. 'Ye've really got the knack,' Gemma told him. 'Ee, ah've gorra run. See yous later.'

And with that she ran off into the rain.

'Canny lass,' said Gerry. 'Why've ye gone all red, man Sewell?'

'Said she wished the babby was hers,' replied Sewell dreamily.

'Aye, but not yours an' all,' laughed Gerry. He turned to Sewell, but Sewell was still staring after Gemma. 'Forget it, man. She's seein' a mental ice hockey player from Sun'lun'.' They waited. Slowly, the rain slackened. It looked like it might stop. The drops continued dripping heavily from the edge of the concrete awning as the water drained off, but beyond it only single droplets landed on the pavement. Gerry sighed heavily. 'Half two,' he said. 'Half two on a match day and what are we deein'?'

'It's not that bad,' said Sewell after a short while. 'Ah divven't mind looking after the babby.'

'Eh?' Gerry asked, suddenly looking up at his friend.

'Ah said lookin' after the bairn, it's not too bad like.'

Gerry's eyes narrowed to a slit, a smile grew on his mouth. 'Ye've cracked it!'

'Eh?'

'Sewell man, ye've cracked it.'

'Cracked what?'

'Wor great idea. Ye've cracked it. Think aboot it. Ye've said it yerself. Ah divven't mind lookin' after the babby. That's what ye said. Then Gemma, what did she say?'

Sewell scratched his head in thought. 'That she wished it was her babby.'

'Not that, man. She said we were naturals at it. That we had the knack.'

'What are you talking aboot, man?'

Gerry rubbed his hands excitedly. 'Child care, man. Ah'm talkin' child care.'

'Why?'

'Are ye on this planet or what?' snorted Gerry. 'There's money in child care. Especially roond here. There must be because they start so young. There's bairns everywhere ye turn. We'll offer a service. Call it Breaks for the Babby. Or Bring wor yer Bairns.'

'Ah get ye!' exclaimed Sewell nodding his head. 'One o' them crashes.'

'Crashes?'

'Aye, where people leave their bairns to crash oot.'

Gerry grew suddenly serious. 'The word's crèche, man,' he said, and then placing a finger over his lips to keep Sewell quiet, raised an eyebrow in deep thought. 'We'll have to get more trolleys oot o' the river. They'll be wor basic resource. With the wheels on, they're prams; withoot the wheels, they're a playpen. Then there's that auld paddling pool we found last summer. It's still in the coal shed. All we have to dee is to patch up the hole, blow it up, fill it with tennis balls or summink and we've got one o' them ball pools.'

'And ye could make more rattles,' added Sewell, kicking an empty can of Yeoman bitter out from under the awning on to the road beyond. 'And for extra we could feed them. Like we did with this one.'

Something began to dim in Gerry's eyes. Not noticing it, Sewell carried on. 'And we could take them on trips, gan doon the river an' that. We could get the nappies from Boots. Y'kna they've got mother and babby rooms in the shops with free nappies. We could just gan in there and help worselves. Take a different babby in each time so they cannet say owt in the shop. Take all the big nappies so they last longer. We could . . .'

'Mebbe it's not such a great idea,' interrupted Gerry, shaking his head dubiously.

'Why not?' demanded Sewell. 'It's foolproof.'

Gerry stared down at his niece. Somehow she had emptied the can and was placing the stones in her mouth. 'There's all that health and safety y'kna.'

'Health and safety? What ye gannin' on aboot, man Gerry? Who could be healthier than this bairn, and as for safety . . .' Sewell delivered a resounding blow to the metal cage of the trolley. 'It's solid, man. All ye need dee is put on a roof and there's nee way a babby is gettin' oot of there.'

'Ah just don't think we'd get away with it. Ye need tae dee courses these days.'

Sewell was sceptical. 'Courses bah!' Worriedly he stared at his friend. 'Areet,' he urged. 'We divven't need to register officially. Not to begin with like. We could start off just roond here. Build up gradually.'

Leaning down into the trolley, Gerry slapped the baby firmly on the back. Sewell let out a cry. 'Calm doon,' Gerry told him, and the baby spat out three stones, one after another, on to Gerry's outstretched palm.

'See,' said Sewell admiringly. 'Ye're a natural.'

'Na, man.' Putting the stones back into the Vigorg can, Gerry was adamant. 'This isn't wor great idea. We're back to square one.'

'Ah just divven't understand ye!' blustered Sewell. 'Just when ah hit on the way to make wor money . . .'

Putting up a hand, Gerry silenced him. A young mother was pushing her baby along the parade of shops. 'Areet, pet,' Gerry greeted her. 'Leanne, isn't it?' Leanne nodded. Gerry smiled.

'Gannin' oot the neet?' Leanne nodded again. 'Bet y'are an' all,' he said. 'Whose gonnae be lookin' after the babby as ye drink yerself mortal doon the Bigg Market? Ah'm only asking because me mate Sewell here is deein' a course at Gateshead College in child care. It's for his survey.'

'Ah leave him with me mam,' replied Leanne simply.

'Thanks a lot, pet,' Gerry returned.

Leanne stared at him. 'Is that all?' she asked. 'Divven't ye write it doon?'

Gerry pointed at his friend's head. 'Keeps it all here. Phenomenal memory but. He could win competitions.'

After Leanne had gone into the chemist's, come out again, and disappeared round a corner, another baby buggy came into view, this time pushed by an older man. The baby was fat and complacent, the man wore his thinning hair greased down in the style of the nineteen fifties. A smoker's cough preceded him like a sonar. 'Excuse me, sir. It's Mr Armstrong, isn't it?' began Gerry.

Mr Armstrong wheezed his affirmative, just managing to add, 'It's the Macartens' youngest lad, eh?'

'Aye. Me mate here, Sewell, Billy Sewell's lad, is deein' a course at Gateshead College on parenting roles. As part of a survey, can ah ask ye, Mr Armstrong, is it your babby?'

Mr Armstrong took out a cigarette, coughed, struck a match, coughed, lit the cigarette, coughed a lot, and then shook his head. 'It's me grandbairn. Ah'm looking after him for the weekend. Me daughta works weekends.'

'Thank you,' intoned Gerry.

'What ye deein'?' Sewell demanded when Mr Armstrong had disappeared.

'Ye'll see,' replied Gerry mysteriously.

They didn't have to wait long before a third example came in search of the chemist. It was a woman in an imitation leather miniskirt and jacket, buttoned open to reveal a deep cleavage. A home perm bounced on her head as she approached. The buggy she pushed was designed for two infants, but three were squashed into it. At the woman's legs a further four children followed closely. Gerry stepped out to her. 'Areet, Audrey.'

'Areet, Gerry. Areet, big lad.'

'Areet.'

'Areet.'

'Me mate here, big lad Sewell,' began Gerry fluently, 'has been accepted on a child care course at Gateshead College.'

'Congratulations, big lad,' smiled Audrey.

Sewell blushed. 'Ta.'

Gerry coughed lightly to get her attention. 'But before he begins his course he needs to collect some data. Y'kna, information like. Ah wonder if ye could tell wor aboot yer child care arrangements, Audrey.'

Audrey nodded her head and, reaching out, placed a finger on the smallest infant in the baby buggy. 'This one's Elliott,' she said, tickling him under the chin, at which Elliott swiped furiously. Then in a rapid recital, each name accompanied by a tickle under the appropriate chin, Audrey went through the names of her brood. 'Then Caitlin, Hannah-Jade, Dolly, he's Keegan and so is she.'

'We've got a one o' them an' all,' smiled Gerry. 'They're not all yours though, are they?' he prompted gently, with a significant glance at Sewell.

'These two are me daughta Stacey's,' she said, picking the backs of two heads from the crowd. 'At least ah think sae,' she added, trying to turn their restless faces towards her. 'Aye, and this one's Peggy's, these two belong to me sista's daughta Kelly, this one's me stepbrotha's grandbairn, and this one's . . . this one's . . .' Licking her hand she rubbed roughly at the face which had been staring up at her, monitoring her every word with the utmost gravity. 'And ah divven't kna who this one is. Ee, who are ye, pet?'

The child, aged about four years old, blinked passively, washing his massive blue eyes even brighter. Sniffling mightily, he wiped his nose on his sleeve, leaving a dark smear on the freshly cleaned face. 'Ah'm Dalton O'Brien.'

Audrey smiled. 'Oh aye. Ah'm looking after him for a while for his mam.'

When Audrey and her charges had toddled on their way, Gerry turned to Sewell. 'See? It's nee good. Who'd pay wor to look after their bairns roond here? It's the family, man. What they call the extended family.'

Beyond the shelter of the awning, the rain had reintensified. It drilled Gateshead, drumming the roofs and thrumming the glass of car windows and houses. Sighing, Gerry picked up the baby. Carefully Sewell took her from him and, unzipping his bench coat, he placed her carefully inside. 'Gerry?' he said after a while. 'We still haven't got that idea, have we? We're not gonnae get wor tickets, are we?' Gerry did not reply. Streams of water gushed down the road, carrying with them all the fag ends and sweet wrappers of life, before gargling mournfully into the drains. Suddenly there was a bark from out of the rain. Sewell looked over with a puzzled air. There was another bark. 'Rusty,' Sewell announced. 'Rusty's come back.' Shivering in the downpour, his body made thin by the water, Rusty lifted an uncertain paw and whined imploringly. Sewell looked over at his friend. Almost imperceptibly Gerry nodded. 'Here, boy,' shouted Sewell delightedly. 'Here!'

Cringing and snuffling, Rusty threw himself at Sewell. 'This is Rusty,' said Sewell, leaning down so that the baby in his bench coat could also touch the dog. 'He's a friend of mine.' The baby laughed and stretched out a hand. She stared and stared, seemingly mesmerised by the way the dog's tail curved over its back. Obligingly Sewell manoeuvred the baby so that she could grasp the tail.

'Pity Rusty couldn't come up with wor idea,' Sewell chuntered. 'Ah mean we could run a dog-walking service but all the hoonds roond here walk themselves. Still, he's such a bright spark. Cleverest mutt ah've ever known. There must be summink he can dee.' Sewell probed the pockets of the bench coat, eventually bringing out a packet of biscuits. 'Thought ah'd got wor a pudding,' he mused. Taking out one of the jam rings, he held it out to Rusty who had been licking the baby. Taking it gently, the dog lowered itself to the ground and ate the biscuit between two paws. 'Look at that,' Sewell said. 'Like he's got hands.' Waiting for the dog to finish the biscuit, Sewell took out another two; eating one himself, he tossed the other to Rusty. The dog caught it deftly, and again lowered itself to eat it from between its front paws. 'Good dog,' Sewell said, and then wandered a few yards down the awning. He took out two more biscuits, swallowed one down whole and held the other one up. 'Want a one?' he asked Gerry.

'Aye, hoy it awer.' The biscuit flipped through the air like a stone. Gerry put out a hand, and was just about to catch it when Rusty flew out in front of him, snout-first. Intercepting the biscuit, Rusty landed skilfully, and again settled down to eat it from between his paws. 'Stone me!' said Gerry. 'D'yus see that?'

'Here, have another,' said Sewell, this time sending the biscuit spiralling just below the level of the awning. Again Rusty hurled himself up, leaping impossibly high. The biscuit crunched, as the dog consumed it from between his paws.

'Ah cannet believe it,' said Gerry. 'Here, give me them.' Walking over to Sewell, he took the biscuits. Taking one out, he threw it high and hard. Rusty caught it. Flexing his arm, Gerry threw another as hard as he could. A few moments later, and the dog was calmly munching the biscuit.

'He's like a goalie,' Sewell remarked proudly.

'Eh?'

'Bet even Gazza couldn't get a penalty past Rusty.'

Gerry's eyes darted from side to side. 'Ah think ah've got it.'

'Got what?'

'Wor idea. Beat the dog. Ye pay to beat the dog.'

Sewell bristled. 'Neeone's gonnae touch him while ah've a breath in me body.'

Gerry laughed wildly. 'Not that kind of beat. Beat, as in penalty beat. Y'kna, score.'

'What ye gannin' on aboot, man Gerry?'

Gerry closed his eyes in thought. 'Ah've worked it all oot. This is wor idea. Ye pay to take a penalty against the dog. For a prize. Ha'way, man, ye've seen yersel' what he's like. And a ball's easier to stop than a biscuit. We'll make loads.'

'Nee way,' said Sewell.

'Nee way?'

'Nee way. It's cruel, man. Kicking a ball at a dog.'

Gerry furrowed his brow. 'Aye. Cannet hurt wor prize asset. Need summink softer.' Staring around, Gerry suddenly darted out from the cover of the awning and stooped into a gutter. He plucked up a mass of dripping paper and, still standing in the rain, began to roll it into a ball. 'We need a snazzy name,' he called out. 'Summink to catch attention. Beat the dog, ten pee. Ten pee, score against the dog. One dog, one ball, get it roond the hoond. Na. It's nee good. We need summink purely belter.' Coming back under the awning, Gerry threw up the ball and volleyed it forcefully. Rusty leapt across to save it.

'Two bob, beat the dog,' said Sewell.

'Say that again,' said Gerry, freezing to the spot.

'It's auld money. Me auld man telt wor.'

'Not that bit.'

'What, two bob, beat the dog?'

Solemnly Gerry walked up to Sewell and shook his hand. 'We've done it, bonny lad. That's wor idea.'

'A bob's five pence. Two bob's ten.'

'Aye, better make it: three bob, beat the dog. Or even four.' Gerry punched the air triumphantly. 'We could dee him oot in a toon top, and a scarf roond his tail.'

'Na,' said Sewell, suddenly serious. 'We're not turning him into a circus dog. He's wor business partner.'

'Aye, aye, whativver,' said Gerry airily. 'The thing is, we need a stall. A pitch. Y'kna, a place to dee it. Cannet dee it on grass, the day, it's pissin' doon.'

'Dee it here,' said Sewell simply.

'And then we need a sign. Geet big letters. We shouldn't have sold all them Biros we twoced.'

Sewell knelt down to stroke Rusty. 'Ask Ally five-bellies.'

'Big Al?'

'He did that sign above his shop with a geet black pen. Ye kna the one: Big Al's Fruit and Veg has moved doon the Road.'

Gerry pondered this, and then began to talk excitedly. 'Aye, we'll dee that. A huge sign. Bigger than Al's. The biggest sign ever seen this side of the friggin' Tyne. A real five-bellies of a sign. We'll hoist it on top of the Angel, so people'll see it from miles aroond. Ah can see that Season Ticket noo. Four bob the day; five, six bob tomorrow. There's nowt that dog cannet stop, and y'kna what people are like roond here. Everyone thinks he's a Gazza.' Gerry's eyes suddenly widened. 'We could organise competitions, take bets. We could even get Gazza to try it. Think of the publicity. The papers'd come. Even the telly. Friggin' hell, Sewell. We're on to a winner.' There was a hushed awe in his voice. Suddenly he began to shout: 'How! Ye chavers, come awer here.' A group of boys approached. Bedraggled in the rain, their sodden T-shirts stuck to their thin ribs. 'Got to think of a prize,' said Gerry. 'How aboot, four bob, win the dog?'

'Nee one's winning that dog.'

'That's the point, man Sewell. Neeone will win. Ye've seen the hoond. He's belter. We've just got to have it as a piece of cheese in the trap.'

'What aboot the shopping trolley?'

'Some prize that,' replied Gerry. 'We need summink decent.'

'A pair o' Season Tickets,' offered Sewell.

'Are ye taking the piss?'

'Ah thought ye said it had to be summink halfway decent.'

'But the whole point o' deeing it, is so that we win them. What'd be the point in getting them just so we can give them away? Na. We need summink irresistible. Unless we use the psychological approach.'

'Eh?'

'Con them, man.' Gerry smiled to himself. 'Yous like footie?' he asked as the boys joined them under the awning.

'Aye,' they replied.

'Ye any good like?'

'Why aye, man.'

'Are ye really, really good like?'

'Better than ye.'

Gerry laughed. 'It's not me ah'm thinking aboot.'

'Who is it then?'

'Sewell,' said Gerry, 'prepare the challenge for wor young-sters here.'

'Have yous been smokin' tac?' a boy in glasses asked, as Sewell guided Rusty ten yards down the parade.

'There ye gan, hot-shot.' Gerry lobbed the bundle of papers to the boy wearing glasses, who caught it on his foot and, flipping it up, took it with a bemused hand. 'If ye're any good then let wor see yer.'

'Are ye mental or summink?'

'Thought ye were supposed to be a good player. Ha'way, there's yer ball. Beat the dog.'

'The dog?'

'That dog there. The posts are the pavements and the shop. The crossbar's the roof. Here ye, hold this for a minute.' Gerry lifted the baby from the trolley and handed it to one of the boys, who took her with a sigh.

'And mind ye keep her well oot o' the way,' added Sewell, kneading Rusty's legs like an athlete's.

The bespectacled boy shrugged, and then, scarcely bringing back his foot, he drilled the ball of papers at the dog. Rusty stepped neatly to one side and caught it. Prancing over to Sewell, the dog dropped the ball. 'Gis that ball,' demanded the shooter.

'Yus want another try?' asked Gerry, with a smile at Sewell.

Scrunching the papers more tightly together, the boy took a run at the ball. Rusty soared through the air, the tip of his snout deflecting in on to the road. The boy ran over, and picked up the ball, dripping from a puddle. This time he took a full run-up. Without seeming to move, Rusty caught the ball. 'What are yous laughin' at?' the penalty-taker screeched at his laughing friends. 'Ah bet you cannet dee any better.'

'Why divven't yus try?' offered Gerry. One after another, they tried to beat the dog. The ball, knocked out of shape, had to be replenished by some stray pieces of fish and chip paper. 'Reet,' said Gerry. 'That'll be five poonds twenty.'

'Eh?' replied the boys.

'Five poond fifty,' put in Sewell. 'Four bob a shot.'

'Nee way.'

Gerry tutted seriously, and took a step towards the boys, who bunched on the edge of the pavement like a nervous flock of sheep. 'Me mate Sewell here doesn't like being conned. In fact he gets angry. Especially when his dog's involved. Divven't ye, Sewell?' Sewell nodded his head seriously. 'Ah kna for a fact he'd get well pissed off if someone owed his dog money and wouldn't pay it.'

'It's not his dog,' piped up one of the boys.

'Eh?'

'Ye heard him,' another said. 'It's not his dog.'

Gerry frowned. 'That's not a very nice thing to say. Ye'll hurt Sewell's feelings. And y'kna what that means.'

'Ah kna somebody who'll dee more than that if they find oot aboot this,' said the boy who had scored on the pitch.

The bunch of boys stirred uneasily. 'The dog boy,' they whispered as one.

'Sewell's the hardest in Gatesheed,' boasted Gerry.

'Aye, but Matthew's off his heed,' one boy said.

'He's mental,' said another.

'He's a psycho radgie,' they intoned together.

'Aye well,' began Gerry, 'the thing is . . .' Suddenly the boys scattered. The one holding the baby deposited her in Gerry's confused hands. They ran through the pouring rain, two of them falling, but immediately picking themselves up again and taking to their legs. 'Who rattled their cage?' mused Gerry.

'Him,' said Sewell, pointing.

Gerry followed Sewell's finger. 'The dog boy.' For a moment he stared at Matthew who was rounding the derelict area of a playground; he had not seen them yet. 'Run for it!' he shouted. When he had sprinted ten yards, he suddenly stopped. 'Ha'way, Sewell. Yus cannet just stand there. He's a psycho radgie.'

'Ah'm not scared of anyone, me.'

Gerry stared wildly down at the playground. Having paused to spin the merry-go-round wheel, Matthew was nearing the parade of shops. 'If not for yersel', then for the dog. Ye saw for yersel', the life ye rescued him from.'

With reluctance, Sewell lumbered after Gerry. Rusty's nails tapped against the wet Tarmac as he joyously chased them.

When they reached the safety of the Spartan Redheugh factory, Gerry stopped to face Sewell. Drops of water ran down their faces. 'We cannet gan on like this,' said Gerry miserably. 'At this rate we wouldn't even get in to watch the friggin' Beddlington Terriers.'

'Ye'll think of summink, man Gerry.'

Gerry grimaced with thought. 'Aye, ah will, but until then . . . until then ye better leave wor alone.' Sewell stepped forward in protest. Gerry put up a warning hand. 'It's the only way. Ah need to concentrate. Non-stop. Full brain power. Ah'll get in touch when ah've worked it all oot. Here, ye take the babby.'

4

Gerry saw the siren light, its bright cobalt blue dazzling the gloom of the grey Gateshead afternoon. He began to sprint. Reaching the flats, he saw that the ambulance was parked in the courtyard. Paramedics were carrying a stretcher down the stairs. The blanket of the stretcher was red as blood.

He arrived at the bottom of the steps as his mother was being carried down them. 'Ha'way, son, oot the way,' one of the paramedics told him. But Gerry could not move. He seemed to have lost the use of his legs. 'Ha'way, son, we need to get her away,' the paramedic repeated.

A woman in a towelling dressing gown appeared on the steps above the stretcher. She was holding a can of LCL Pils lager. 'She just conked oot, didn't even finish her drink.'

'Do you know if she's on any medication?' a paramedic asked.

'Ah'll gan and get them.'

The paramedic's voice seemed far away. 'Oot the road, lad.'

Mechanically, Gerry shuffled aside to let them past.

The woman who had brought the can of lager ran past him with a bowl full of pill bottles. 'Ah just took what ah could see,' she said. 'Ah live next door, ye see. Ah'd only popped roond for five minutes.' The paramedics lifted the stretcher into the ambulance. Gerry walked over. 'This is her lad,' the woman told them.

'Ha'way then, get in the back, lad.'

Gerry stared without understanding. 'He doesn't kna what's gannin' on,' the woman said as she helped him into the ambulance. 'Ah'm Audrey, pet. Ye kna me,' she told him, speaking the words loudly and slowly. 'Your mam's took a turn. Ah rang an ambulance. Clare and them are oot in the toon. As soon as they come back, ah'll tell them.' The paramedic's radio flared, Gerry flinched from the distorted feedback. 'She's having difficulty breathing, pet,' Audrey explained.

The wail of the sirens echoed hysterically against the enclosing walls of the flats. The rain lanced the roof of the ambulance as it sped away. Gerry stared at his damp tracksuit, and then at his mother's face. Raindrops clung to her hair like small, valueless gems. The ambulance drove through a red light, its siren shouting.

The ambulance lurched its way through Gateshead, cars pulling up on the pavement to let it through, pedestrians staring after as it drove past them. The younger ones were mesmerised by the speed, the older ones grimly thankful that they weren't the cargo. The religious ones crossed themselves. The ambulance rolled over the consciousness of Gateshead like a wave on a beach, leaving, when it had receded, its flotsam of fear, its indentation.

'Is she . . . is she gonnae be areet?' asked Gerry at last.

'We'll do the best we can,' said the paramedic non-committally.

Gerry didn't seem to hear. Again he asked the same question. 'Is she gonnae be areet?'

The ambulance drew up at the hospital. The paramedics lifted Mrs Macarten out. Gerry followed the progress of the small body swamped in a red blanket. Underneath the breathing apparatus, her face was bleached by the stark lights of the sirens. 'Ye cannet come in here,' said a nurse as he tried to follow his mother into the casualty ward. 'Ye'll have to take a seat in reception.'

Gerry looked at the nurse. 'Is she gonnae be areet?'

'We'll do the best we can, pet.'

The waiting room was half full. The chairs were placed in rows facing the reception desk. Gerry sat down. Scattered about were men in football strips nursing various injuries, twisted limbs, dislocated fingers and blood-soaked heads. In front of him was a little old man who hugged himself and rocked gently back and forward. The old man wore a raincoat and a flat cap, both of which dwarfed him as though he had recently shrunk. Directly behind Gerry sat a little girl holding her bandaged hand gingerly; she was pale. Beside the child was a man, his arms folded, grim, staring straight ahead. Gerry stared at everyone but he could not focus.

'Ah'm sorry, Mr Storey,' a nurse was saying as she brought out a patient on a trolley and pushed him against the wall in the corridor. 'If ye can wait here we'll get ye a bed as soon as possible.'

'Thank you, nurse,' said Mr Storey pleasantly, but he flinched in pain when the trolley knocked against the wall.

'Nurse,' called Gerry, getting up and going over. 'Is she gonnae be areet?'

'Who?' asked the nurse.

'Me mam,' replied Gerry. Searching for the right words, he seemed to find them. 'Mrs Macarten. Ah'm her son.'

'The doctor will come and and speak to you about it.'

'Can ah gan in and see her?'

'Just take a seat please.'

Gerry sat down. For the next half an hour he remained motionless. More people came in and sat down. Nobody left. Gerry held his hands out and examined them. He could not see properly. It was as though the flashing light of the ambulance was still dazzling him. 'The toon are two up,' one young man in a football strip said to another.

'How d y'kna?' replied the other.

'Him awer there, he's got a radio.'

'How long's left?'

'Ten minutes tae gan.'

The voices reached Gerry like distant, muffled, meaningless murmurs. Half-heartedly he searched the waiting room for the radio.

There was a sharp shriek of pain from the ward. The little old man rocking himself back and forth began mumbling to himself. 'Ha'way, hinny,' he said to no one who was present. 'Ye'll be areet, man hinny woman. Ha'way, hinny. Buck up. Ha'way, hinny.'

'Where's the radio?' said one of the injured footballers. 'Cannet ye turn it up, mate, so all of wor can hear?'

'Oh, hinny man. Ha'way,' grieved the old man, almost disappearing into his hat and coat, as though searching there for the person he was addressing.

The little girl behind Gerry whimpered a little and stared at her bandaged hand. The grim man beside her glowered. Some more people came in. Still no one left. It was growing hot. And noisy. 'Hinny,' the old man implored into the peak of his cap. 'Hinny. Keep a haad.' The little old man began to sing, as though the charm of melody might bring to him the one he sought. 'Hinny, thoo shall have a fishy on a little dishy,' he sang.

There was a shout from the footballers who had all gathered in one place around the radio. 'Three nowt,' one of them said.

'Nurse,' said Mr Storey as a nurse flashed by his trolley.

'Uhuh?' said the nurse, slowing for a moment.

'Ah divven't want to trouble ye, but do y'kna when me bed'll be ready, pet?'

'Eh?'

'Ah haven't got a bed, ye see. Ah was told ah'd get a bed.'

'No. Sorry.' She looked at the clipboard attached to the end of his trolley. 'Ah can't tell ye when the bed's going to be ready, Mr Storey.'

'Oh, reet. Canny,' said Mr Storey. 'Ah just thought ah'd ask.' And closing his eyes he tried to sleep, but his face was crumpled like an empty bag.

There was another scream of pain from the ward, then a rush of white as nurses and a doctor ran to a bed. A curtain was pulled quickly. Gerry got up and stretched his legs. Someone was smoking a cigarette near the back of the waiting room. 'Put that tab oot, man, it's nee smoking!' someone remarked.

'Who's gonnae grass on wor like?' replied the smoker,

smiling at the supportive murmurs which rose from the majority of those waiting.

'Hinny, thoo shall have a salmon,' sang the little old man.

'Top of the league now, aren't we?' said one of the men around the radio. 'Toon army! Toon army!' chorused the others.

Gerry took out some crumbs of tobacco from his pocket and a rolling paper. Lifting a hand, he pressed it against his forehead to still the words that were swirling in his head. 'Top of the league?' he muttered incomprehensibly. With a shaking hand he rolled the cigarette and lit up. He breathed the smoke in deeply and wreathed it out through his nose, but the cigarette had not been rolled well and, having flared briefly, it was quickly out. Gerry ground it under his heel. The little girl with the bandaged hand looked over. 'What are you in for?' she asked Gerry.

The man beside her shuffled down and whispered something in her ear. The girl whitened. The man got up and went over to the toilet.

'It's me mam, pet,' Gerry told the little girl when the man had disappeared, even his own voice, though soft, reverberating around his head.

'Is she going to die?' the girl asked.

Gerry stuttered and looked in puzzlement at the girl. 'Ah . . . ah divven't kna.'

'My mum's dead already,' said the little girl whose eyes were brown with huge pupils. 'I live with my dad and his girlfriend.' Cautiously she nodded in the direction of the toilets. 'That's my dad.'

Gerry looked to take a long drag on his cigarette, but realised that he had already put it out. 'What's the matter with your hand?' he asked abstractedly.

'Nothing,' said the girl, adding anxiously. 'I'd better not talk to you any more.'

'Hinny, thoo shall have a little fishy on a little dishy,' sang the old man, rocking himself further into his coat.

'Toon, Toon, Toon army!' shouted the footballers.

'Nurse,' called out Mr Storey, his voice as pained and sad as a gull on the Tyne. The nurse didn't hear him and hurried off. 'Can ah have a bed?' Mr Storey said to himself. 'Me wound's giving wor some gip.'

'My dad told me to say that it was an accident,' said the little girl, speaking out of the corner of her mouth.

Gerry suddenly blinked and, doubling up, threw his head into his hands. The emergency of the siren pounded in his skull, distorting every other noise in the hospital, until those in the waiting room seemed to be speaking in rhythm to this flashing, wailing urgency, forming a litany of desperate anxiety.

'Hinny, thoo shall have a salmon.'

'Geordies, Geordies top of the league, top of the league, top of the league!'

'If ah could lie in a bed.'

'But it wasn't really an accident.'

'Hinny, when the boat comes in.'

'Top of the league, top of the league!'

'Ah've paid me stamps all me life. Can ah not have a bed?'

'You see, my dad's girlfriend . . .'

'When the boat comes in, hinny. When the boat comes in. But there's nee more boats, man hinny. There's nee more boats to come.'

Speaking all at once, with equal insistence, the voices built to a crescendo in Gerry's head, and then, crashing, fell silent. For a long time he could hear only his own heart beating.

The hours in a hospital pass slowly. Outside it might be night-time but inside the bright strip-lights reveal everything, searching those who wait, seeking out the seeds of their pain, and relentlessly germinating them. The trolleys clatter like cattle stalls as they are lined up against the wall. Now there are three patients waiting in a corridor for a bed. Now there are four. One of them will die there before the night is out. Mr Storey will die there. His blood will remain unwashed on the wall for twenty-four hours. Pain and fear fill the air. People arrive to wait in the waiting room, but no one seems to leave. Extra chairs are brought in. These are filled. People have to stand at the back. There is nothing to do but wait. 'Me mam,' said Gerry. 'Will she be areet? She's having difficulty breathing. What's the matter with her? Ah've been here for hours, man, and they won't let us see her. Can she breathe areet now?'

At about seven o'clock a drunk staggered in. He was small. His age was difficult to determine. He could have been anything between fifty and seventy. A nurse confronted him and pulled out a bottle of vodka from his jacket pocket. The drunk man stared at the nurse. 'Ye're a canny piece of cracknell,' he said. 'What ye deein' later?'

The nurse looked at him. 'Ee, do ye think ah'm desperate?'

'Ah divven't kna, hinny,' replied the man. 'Are ye?'

Unsteadily the man walked up and down the waiting room scanning the seats. When Gerry turned to see him, his face drained pale. He looked wildly about, as though searching for an exit. Then he dropped his head. Heedless to the pain, he clenched his fists until the nails embedded themselves into his palms. The drunk stopped abruptly as though he'd found what he was looking for. 'Gerry!' he shouted, stumbling through the seats. 'Gerry!'

Reluctantly Gerry raised his head. 'What are ye deeing here, man dad?'

'What d'yus mean?' Mr Macarten swayed unsteadily on his feet; his voice was also swaying between the morose and the belligerent.

Gerry held out his hands. 'She won't want to see ye, man dad.'

Mr Macarten fell heavily on to the chair in front of Gerry and with a great effort was able to twist himself round to face him. 'Ha'way, bonny lad, a man's got a right to be interested in his friggin' wife, hasn't he?' he demanded. 'Or would ye take that away from wor an' all?' As though suddenly shoved, he fell forward, his head bouncing on to his knees. Pulling himself up in his chair, he twisted round and stared at his son, breathing deeply as though he had just accomplished a feat of outstanding energy. 'Ah love her,' he said when he had caught his breath. 'Always have . . .' His words dissolved in a beery belch. Sighing, Gerry looked away. Swatting this disapproval from him with a flick of his wrist as though it were a fly buzzing in his face, Mr Macarten plunged his hand into his pocket. But he couldn't find the bottle and his hand came back empty. Flopping heavily, he craned his neck down to the pocket, and prising it open with his fingers he peered in. Straightening up he scratched his head puzzledly. 'Have ye got a drink, hinny?' he asked.

Gerry did not reply. There was a pause. Staring intently at his son, Mr Macarten struggled to his feet and, knocking the chairs out of the way, came to slump beside Gerry. Gerry stiffened. Shrugging, Mr Macarten crossed his arms and leant back so that the chair tipped on to two legs. 'So what is it this time?' he asked. 'Tried to top herself again to get a new hoose?' Gerry did not reply. Mr Macarten looked around challengingly. 'Where's the rest of them like?'

'Clare was in toon. Gran was oot at bingo, ah think,' he replied mechanically.

'The auld bitch.'

'They'll be coming along later.'

'What aboot wor Sean?'

'He's still inside.'

'Oh aye. So who's lookin' after the friggin babby?'

'She's areet,' replied Gerry softly.

'How is she? Ah haven't seen her for ages, Gerry man. Ah miss her. She's me grandbairn y'kna.' There was a long pause as Mr Macarten searched his pockets again. 'Have ye got a drink, Gerry pet?' Gerry shook his head. 'What aboot Bridget then, boy?'

Gerry tensed. 'Divven't kna.'

'Eh?'

'Ah divven't kna where she is. She's disappeared.'

'Aye well, make sure ye tell us when she comes back. Reet? Reet?' His father thrust his face into Gerry's and spoke menacingly softly, 'What's the matter, lad? Why cannet ye look wor in the eye?'

Suddenly his father grabbed hold of Gerry's arm. 'Ah want to kna where me daughter is. What's wrang with that?' He tightened his grip. 'Divven't ye say ye believe in them lies yer sister and mam's been spreading?' Gerry flinched under his father's intensity, turning his face away just in time to hide the sudden flash of rage. He began to twitch as the terrible anger built. He could feel it gathering in his heart like flood waters building at a dam. 'Ha'way then, look at wor,' his father challenged. Yanking his arm free from his father's grip, Gerry raised a hand and clenched it into a fist. Red-faced and sweating, he slowly stood. Looking down at his father, he felt his breathing quicken until it became almost physically unbearable, and a great sickness filled him. His legs gave way. Collapsing into his chair, he tried to catch his breath, his chest rising and falling convulsively as though he were retching. When he looked over, he saw that his father was watching him with drunken incomprehension. With a rush of relief, Gerry realised he had been able to hide his anger. 'Ye divven't believe it. What they say, ye divven't, do ye?' chuntered his father. 'Of course ye divven't. You're me bonny lad eh? Eh?'

'Of course,' whispered Gerry.

Laughing suddenly, Mr Macarten looked about the waiting room as though searching. Slowly he brought his eyes back to Gerry. 'Give us the address, pet, tell us where your mam and them are living.'

Gerry looked away. 'Who told ye where ah was the neet?'

'Bumped into that Audrey doon the club, man,' replied his father laughing lewdly. 'She's a reet Bobby Dazzler in her mini-skirts that Audrey.'

After a strange, silent moment, Mr Macarten abruptly got up. He pushed past the people sitting waiting. Staggering and tripping, he found a way down a corridor choked with the trolleys of ill and dying people. 'Where you going, sir?' asked one of the nurses as Mr Macarten barged his way into the emergency ward.

'Ah've come to see me wife.'

'Ah'm sorry, sir, but ye've got to wait in the waiting area.'

'Divven't ye start,' he shouted. 'See that lad there?' he yelled, pointing in the general direction of the waiting room. 'He keeps me wife and bairns away from us. Evil he is. An' ah love her. Jesus Christ knows how much ah love them all. She's me wife. They're me bairns.' The nurse tried to lead him away. 'Haddaway,' he warned. 'Before ah bite ye.'

Gerry got up to follow. He almost fell. The nurse was saying something, but he could not hear her. All the faces in the waiting room blurred. Stumbling around the trolleys, and through curtains, he found his mother and father in the second but last booth.

'Mam, are ye areet, Mam?'

Mrs Macarten looked thin and drawn. Tubes led in and out of her arms. Her hair was damp against her forehead. She was staring blankly at her husband. When Gerry arrived, she turned to him. 'Ah think ah'm knackt this time, pet.'

'Ah'll gan and get ye a drink then, man,' said Mr Macarten, lurching round. He fell, but grabbing hold of the curtain was able to steady himself, his weight pulling the curtain round the bed.

'Ah didn't tell him, Mam, honestly,' whispered Gerry hoarsely. 'Ah didn't breathe a word.'

'He'll find oot where we live. We'll have to move again,' said Mrs Macarten, managing to talk between deep breaths. Then she began to cough. The nurses ran in and bustled round her, they were all wearing sterile gloves and paper masks round their mouths. A doctor wearing similar protection strode in.

'What the hell are you doing in here?' he demanded.

'She's me mam,' gasped Gerry. 'She's having difficulty breathing. Is she gonnae be areet? Tell her ah didn't tell him.

Ah promise. Ah didn't tell him. He won't find wor. Ah'll nivver tell him. And if he ever hurts any o' wor again, then ah'll kill him. Ah swear doon, ah'll kill him.'

Staring bemusedly at the nurses as they bustled him away, Gerry became dimly aware of a commotion at the reception desk in the waiting room. 'You can't come in here,' he could hear someone saying. 'Dogs are not allowed.' Slowly he focused. Over at the desk Gerry saw a large figure standing his ground determinedly. The figure held a baby in one hand and an improvised lead in the other. Attached to the orange twine was a dog. A white dog with rusty spots. When the dog saw Gerry it began scrabbling to get to him. His nails tapped enthusiastically on the linoleum of the waiting room. 'Areet,' said Sewell. 'Been looking everywhere for ye. Met Audrey ootside the club, she told us you were here.' He lowered his head to smell the baby and crinkled up his noise. 'Ee man!' he gasped. 'Is there a one o' them mother and babby rooms, ah think the tea towel needs changing again.'

Gerry stood on one side of the concrete slab bridge. Under him the Team splashed through its small gorge on the waste land where the travellers camp from time to time. 'Ah said close your eyes, man Sewell. Divven't peep. And stop squinting. Ye look like a bloody Eskimo. Ha'way, start crossing now.'

'Eh?'

'Ha'way, close your eyes an' walk towards me.'

Sewell stared uneasily down at the river. He felt for Rusty who was obediently waiting at his heel. 'There's a river doon there, man.'

'It's only the Team, man. Ha'way, close your eyes. This new idea is the best ah've ever had, ah swear doon it is. Came to us last week when we were shiftin' hoose, but if it's gonnae have a chance of working ye've gorra trust us.'

'What is it, this big idea, man Gerry?'

'Ah telt yus, ah'm not telling ye until ye're ready.'

'Ready?'

From across the bridge Gerry beckoned Sewell. Sewell looked around him, scanning the waste ground as though searching the rubble and vegetation for help. Unwillingly he returned his eyes to the concrete slab which lay across the two high banks of the river.

'Ye've got Rusty there,' cajoled Gerry. 'Reet. Walk over to me with your eyes closed.'

Gripping the length of orange twine which served as Rusty's lead and wrapping it tightly round his taut fist, Sewell closed his eyes and took a step on to the bridge. Glass crunched under foot. 'And ye've promised to tell wor if ah gan near the edge?'

'Aye, aye.'

'It's funny,' Sewell said when he was halfway across. 'The water's geet loud, kind of speaks to ye. Ah can make oot which bits are deep and which bits shallow.'

'Ha'way, Sewell, ah told ye to cross the bridge not build it. And divven't gan any more to your left, you're only a fly's fart from the edge.'

Feeling every inch with the toe of his trainer before taking a step, Sewell moved painstakingly across the bridge. Leaning down he felt for Rusty. Reassured by the dog's cold nose, he pushed on. 'That's it. Just carry on,' urged Gerry. 'You're gettin' the hang of it.'

Sewell's face was white when he reached Gerry. A bead of sweat ran from his forehead down his nose. With great relief he opened his eyes. 'Ye've done it,' said Gerry, offering him his hand.

Sewell shrugged. 'Are ye gonnae tell wor what it's all aboot noo, man?'

'What it's all aboot, Sewell, is money. What it's all aboot, Sewell, is wor Season Ticket. What's it all aboot, Sewell, is this.' Gerry looked about him suspiciously then, satisfied that no one else was near, drew Sewell closer to him and cleared his throat. 'We need a pair of dark glasses, a stick and the dog.'

'Eh?'

'You're going to pretend to be blind, and Rusty's yer guide dog.'

Sewell stepped back. 'Na.'

'Why not?'

'Ah said na.'

'But why?'

'Ah'm just not gonnae dee it.'

Gerry stared archly at his friend. 'Ye divven't even kna why yet. Anyway, yus've got to give a reason. Ye cannet just say na.'

Scratching his head, Sewell stared back through half closed eyes. 'Well . . .'

'And it's got to be a good reason an' all.'

There was a pause, then at last Sewell said, 'Why cannet you be the blind man, Gerry?'

'And when was the last time ye saw a blind man my size?' shot back Gerry immediately.

There was another even longer pause. Rusty yawned and flopped in a contented heap at his master's feet. Sewell tried to speak, opened his mouth a few times, but to no avail.

'This'll do as yer stick,' decided Gerry, breaking a slender branch from an alder tree growing from a clump of bricks built into the river bank, and handed it to Sewell.

'It's supposed to be white,' remarked Sewell petulantly, declining to accept the stick.

'We'll paint it, man.' Gerry inhaled meditatively. 'Wor plan is simple. We'll gan to the Metro Centre. Once there ye gain in the shop carrying a bag awer your shoulder, y'kna the type that blind people have for all their things. Well, ye're going to fill it with CDs and videos and that. We can put one of them coats on Rusty, y'kna one of them tartan coats, an extra large one, and stuff the coat with gear an' all.'

'Ye could put one of them barrels roond his neck an' all,' said Sewell, warming to the idea. 'Like one of them what-d'ye-call-'ems.'

Gerry spat dismissively. 'Let's try and keep it sensible, man. A young chaver like ye with a blind dog and a tartan coat is stretching things, a mongrel dressed up as a bloody great St Bernard would be taking the piss. Rusty's perfect as he is. He's so docile.'

'Docile?'

'Like ye, Sewell. Now, ye'll have tae get used to him leading yus aboot. The key is to look realistic y'kna.'

Sewell sunk his head deep into his bench coat and then lifted it out again. 'Ah can dee it,' he said. 'Me and Rusty can dee it, but what aboot Matthew?'

'We'll just have to be careful, man. Practise doon here, and behind the Spartan Redheugh. Places where he cannet see wor,' planned Gerry. 'Practise for aboot a week or . . .'

'Ah think ah can dee it noo,' Sewell interrupted Gerry proudly.

'Eh?'

'Gerry man, ah think ah could dee it the day.'

A broad smile spread over Gerry's face. 'Now you're talkin'.'

Sewell looked down at the dog fondly. 'We've developed one o' them bonds. He knows what ah want before ah even ask. Ah'd trust him with me life. All ye need dee is get us a better white stick.' And so saying Sewell grabbed the alder branch from Gerry and cast it into the Team. The river took it, twisting it under the bridge, bouncing it on its grey current, until it passed out of sight, bound for the Tyne.

'Reet,' smiled Gerry. 'Gan through yer paces again. Get yersel' back awer the bridge. And nee more Eskimo squinting.'

An hour later, a blind youth was winding his way through the streets of Gateshead, in one hand half of a snooker cue painted a kind of cream, in the other a length of orange twine attached to the collar of a white-and-rusty-coloured dog. Reaching a busy road, the dog stopped the youth dead in his tracks and tugged at the bottom of his bench coat with an insistent paw. 'That's his way of talking,' said Sewell, tickling Rusty under the chin.

'Belter,' whispered Gerry as they crossed.

They walked under the Newcastle to Carlisle railway, and over the pedestrian bridge strung above the main road to Edinburgh. 'Can ah open me eyes for a minute, Gerry?'

'Nee chance. Ye're blind for the rest of the day, man.'

Sewell sighed heavily. 'But we divven't seem to be gannin' in the reet direction.'

'Secrecy,' whispered Gerry. 'We're gannin' the least conspicuous way y'kna.'

'It'll take us all day to get there at this rate.'

Gerry stopped dead. 'Sewell?' he snapped. 'Who's the brains? Divven't mumble. Just tell us who the brains is. Eh?'

'Ye are.'

'Who is?'

'Ye.'

'Clamped! So shut yer trap, and dee as ah say.'

They climbed Lobley Hill, to run a decoy through Whickham. 'This is miles longer,' whimpered Sewell. 'It's areet for ye, ye haven't got to be blind.'

'It's all part of the plan, man Sewell,' Gerry told him. 'This way we'll throw off anyone who might be following us. And keep tapping that snooker cue oot in front of ye. Ye're blind, man, it's supposed to be your antennae y'kna.'

On Whickham Highway, Gerry suddenly laid a hand on Sewell's arm to stop him. Behind them, in the distance, the huge statue of The Angel of the North could be seen embracing Gateshead. Sewell exhaled slowly. 'Face the twocing angel and say yer prayers,' said Gerry.

'Ah cannet even see it,' grumbled Sewell.

'Doesn't matter, y'kna what it looks like, just face it,' ordered Gerry, bundling his friend round to face the Angel. 'Metro Centre, here we come!' he exclaimed as they moved off again.

Walking the length of the Highway, they came down Dunston Bank. 'Gazza's mam lives there y'kna,' said Sewell, pointing to a street which ran on the contour of the hill.

'Ah kna that, man.'

'An' his brother's an' his sister's is awer there.'

They passed the swimming baths and then the Thorns Comprehensive. Through the steamy windows of one of the classrooms a teacher could be seen sitting at his desk in despair as thirty-odd teenagers, muffled in coats and all yelling in loud voices, sat and stood and swore around him. Gerry was going to shout something, but just in time recalled the mission. He checked himself and spat with purpose. 'Almost there, bonny lad,' he said. 'Almost there.'

Reaching the Thorns themselves, a piece of land owned by the council and part of the Great North Forest, they left the road and took a path. The path was muddy and waterlogged with the recent autumn rain. 'Divven't let us stand in any dog shite,' said Sewell. Squeezing through a fence they walked into the meadows. The meadows were on a hill. In summer the grass grows past the waist here and the fox raises a litter. Two partridges flew up at their approach. 'What the hell was that?' demanded Sewell, his painted snooker cue uprighting itself like a club.

'Nowt,' soothed Gerry.

'Canny big nowt,' Sewell pointed out sceptically. 'Ha'way, let us open me eyes, man. Neeone'll see wor here.'

'Divven't be so nervous,' countered Gerry. 'Ye've got to start trusting us, man Sewell.' They walked down through the meadows, surprising a heron into its ponderous, ancient flight. 'There she is!' exclaimed Gerry, pointing to the Metro Centre that lay visible beneath them now. 'There's wor Season Ticket.'

The Metro Centre sprawls over the flat, drained, marshy ground by the Tyne. It is unbelievably vast. It has many roofs and towers and buildings. It is like an immense cathedral with vast precincts. It is like a city. Thousands of people work there, millions meet and talk and shop. It is like a gigantic hive of bees. In all weathers the glass of the Metro Centre seems to gleam.

Sewell and Gerry worked their way to the bottom of the hill. There they met with the underpass which forms a stinking cavity under the A1 dual carriageway to Edinburgh. 'Littlewoods, C and A's, Smith's, Boots, HMV, Marks and Sparks, the Disney Store,' reeled off Gerry as they walked into the underpass.

'Everything's A Poond,' put in Sewell, opening his eyes.

'Why aye!' laughed Gerry.

Sewell screwed up his face. 'Ah'm being serious, man Gerry.'

'Divven't be stupid,' said Gerry.

The walls of the underpass were daubed with graffiti. Viborg Lager and Omega Cider cans littered the ground. They walked to the middle and then Sewell stopped dead, the slightest of tugs on Rusty's twine being enough for the obedient dog to obey. 'Stupid?' Sewell asked.

'Stupid,' reiterated Gerry. 'And keep them eyes closed.'

'How am ah being stupid?' said Sewell, blinking his eyes open.

'Everything's A Poond, man, why aye!'

'What d'ye mean?'

'Everything's a Poond!'

'What's wrong with that like?'

'Aye, what's wrong with it?'

'Well aye, what's wrong with Everything's A Poond?'

Their words echoed in the underpass, the natural characteristics of their voices exaggerated by the concrete walls so that Gerry sounded even more clipped and busy than usual and Sewell droned more slowly; like a bee and a wasp trapped under glass.

'We've come here to steal, man Sewell,' buzzed Gerry sharply. 'What we steal we sell. We sell to make money. Money for wor Season Ticket.'

'Ah know that but . . .' returned Sewell, being cut off in mid-sentence.

'Tell me how much exactly d'ye think people are going to give wor for things stolen from Everything's A Poond then eh?' demanded Gerry, speaking the whole sentence without pause for breath.

'Em . . .'

'Remember they'll give us less than they would if they bought them in the shop.'

'Em . . .'

'Think.'

'Ah can't say exactly, man Gerry.'

'Have a guess.'

88

'How can ah know the price of everything?'

'Ye divven't need to be exact. Have a guess. A wild guess.'

'Ah divven't kna.'

'Aye ye do.'

'Ah divven't.'

'What's the shop called?'

'Ha'way, Gerry.'

'Na. What's the shop called?'

'Emm . . .'

'Here, ah'll help ye. It's called Everything's A . . . Go on tell us the rest of its name. Everything's A . . .'

'Ye kna yersel' what it's called.'

'But ah want ye to tell us. Everything's A . . . ? Everything's A . . . ?'

Sewell rolled his eyes as though being tortured. 'Everything's A Poond, man!' he exclaimed. 'It's called Everything's A Poond.'

Gerry sighed heavily with hard-won satisfaction. 'So how much is the most expensive thing in that shop? And how much is the cheapest?'

Sewell knelt down to stroke Rusty who was waiting patiently. 'Good dog,' he cooed. Rusty wagged his tail and barked. 'At least one of wor is making sense,' Sewell told him, bringing half a biscuit from the pocket of his bench coat and feeding it to the dog.

'Divven't feed him too much, man,' said Gerry. 'Ye've got to keep him keen today. Y'kna, a bit hungry. A bit lean. Ye'll have him as fat as ye.'

'Whose dog is he?' replied Sewell in a voice as near as he would ever get to thundering. 'When you're a dog handler ye get sensitive to an animal's needs. And let me tell ye, ah kna for a fact that he wanted that biscuit!'

'Areet, areet,' coaxed Gerry, reading the graffiti on the walls. 'Tell us this then, Sewell man,' he continued when Sewell had calmed down. 'How many things d'ye think ye could fit into that bench coat of yours? In all the pockets and that? How many things from Everything's A Poond?' Instinctively Sewell reached to feel the zips on his many pockets, he blew out his cheeks and narrowed his eyes as though an estimate was scarcely possible. 'Y'kna the type of gear they sell,' prodded Gerry. Sewell shook his head. 'Ye divven't kna? Well ah'll tell ye. They make a lot of small things. Some big. But lots of small. So ah would say ye could fit aboot twenty or thirty things in your bench coat. Reet? Do ye agree?' Cautiously Sewell nodded his head. 'Good,' continued Gerry, now taking a step towards his friend with every point of his argument and holding him in a relentless, unblinking stare. 'So between us we get mebbe fifty things from Everything's A Poond. Fifty things from Everything's A Poond adds up to fifty quid. That's why it's called Everything's A Poond. Not Everything's A Tenner, or Everything's Got A Different Price, but Everything's A Poond. Halve it for selling roond the doors. Twenty-five quid. And with fifty things wor coats'll be chocker. We'll have nee room for owt else. So a whole day's work, the idea of the guide dog used and then days spent gannin' roond the hooses and we've made twenty-five quid.' Gathering momentum, Gerry's voice speeded to its climax. 'Twenty-five quid at best. A Season Ticket costs more than twenty-five quid, much more. We need much more. THAT'S WHY WE'RE NOT GANNIN' TO EVERYTHING'S A POOND!'

'Divven't shout. Ye're frightening Rusty, man,' said Sewell after a pause.

Gerry spat and rubbed his hands meditatively. 'Ha'way. And . . .'

'Ah kna,' interrupted Sewell, closing his eyes with a sigh. 'And keep them eyes closed.'

In Gateshead all roads lead to the Metro Centre. But no pavements do. Slip roads, interconnecting roads, freight roads, car park roads, overflow car park roads, Green Quadrant roads, Blue Quadrant roads, any colour under the sun Quadrant roads, Retail Park not quite within the actual Metro Centre roads, Metroland roads, Harry Ramsden roads, Asda-and-

IKEA-the-pool-destroyers roads. Roads everywhere, where once there was a wild wet land. Gerry and Sewell emerged from the underpass and, half slipping, half skiing on the mud down a steep tree-lined bank, were spilt on to one of the Shopping and Leisure Complex's many roads. A car zoomed past them. 'Bloody Hell!' moaned Sewell, waving his stick feebly.

A constant stream of traffic swirled past their toes, the dampness of the terrain mixing with their exhaust smoke to form a poisonous smog. Rusty sneezed twice. 'We'll cross after this next blue car,' said Gerry.

'Which blue one?' questioned Sewell. 'Ah'm blind remember.'

'Now!' shouted Gerry, grabbing Sewell's elbow.

They only just managed to make it to an island of soil between roads. The cars drove past them in a thick current. The vegetation on this island was stunted and rendered austere by the pollution. Sewell stubbed his toe against the stump of a shrub. 'That's it,' he swore. 'Ah'm not deein' this any more.'

'Yes ye are,' replied Gerry. 'Right, now!'

Road by road, bleak island of land by bleak island of land, they inched towards the Metro Centre. For a while they had to leave the safety of the verges and walk directly into oncoming traffic. The cars beeped and blasted their horns. 'Get lost!' shouted Sewell, shambling and growling like a great bear, remonstrating with his cream snooker cue at the disappearing eddies of noise. 'Are ye blind or what?' Sewell yelled at another car as it blasted its horn at them. 'Ah'm blind, ah'm friggin' blind!'

The drivers and passengers in the cars turned to stare at the strange sight coming towards them. 'Bang gans the element of surprise,' mumbled Gerry.

They went in through the entrance to Marks and Spencer. 'Nee dogs allowed,' read Gerry with a smirk.

'Oh bloody hell,' moaned Sewell. 'We cannet even get in the door.'

'Guide dogs excluded, man,' Gerry informed him as calmly as he could manage. 'Guide dogs excluded.'

They walked slowly through the vast atrium of Marks and Spencer. 'Divven't start with that whistling,' said Gerry, beginning to separate from Sewell. The carpets were soft, the lights bright white. 'Reet,' whispered Gerry. 'Let's get into action. Ah'll see ye after in Metroland, as planned. At the kiosk. And remember. This is wor big idea. This is wor Season Ticket.'

'Ahhh me lads,' whistled Sewell breathily, moving off with Rusty into the deep heart of the shop. 'Ye should have seen us gannin'!'

Feeling the thick material on a pair of men's trousers, Gerry looked about him for a security camera. He grunted with satisfaction on seeing one trained on him from a mirror pillar. Through the corner of his eye he saw the peaked cap of a security guard lowered menacingly over his forehead. Taking a man's jumper from the rack, Gerry stepped in front of the mirror and held the garment out in front of him. He looked about himself as suspiciously as possible. In the mirror he saw Sewell and Rusty pass the security guard. The security guard's eyes followed them. Ostentatiously Gerry pulled the jumper over his head. Taking another jumper, he held it up as though he were examining it. But still the security guard did not turn to look at him. 'Ha'way,' he hissed to himself, 'Sewell's the one who's supposed to be blind.' Looking about himself as guiltily as possible, he pulled on the second jumper, and admired himself in another mirror pillar. This time he saw that the security guard was looking at him. He spoke into a walkie-talkie. When he put the walkie-talkie down, the security guard began walking towards Gerry. Gerry moved off. The security guard trailed Gerry. Gerry's face relaxed into a smile.

Gerry took the security guard through the whole shop. He browsed behind the bedding, appeared light-fingered at the lingerie, stopped too long at the shoes, eventually making for the exit through the Hosiery and Ladieswear sections. By the time he reached the door, there were four security officers zeroing in on him. Gerry put his hand on the door handle. Without a glance of recognition Sewell and Rusty walked casually by. Gerry opened the door for them. 'Excuse me, son,' said a young security guard. 'Would ye mind accompanying us back to the store?'

'Ah wouldn't mind,' said Gerry, calmly, 'except ah haven't left yet. Ye see ah haven't finished me shopping.' And doubling back on his circuitous route Gerry once again led them between the Hosiery and Ladieswear sections, through the shoes, the lingerie, the bedding and back to Menswear. The security guards watched with opened mouths as Gerry took off the jumpers and replaced them on their hangers having smoothed out the creases. 'Awer thin,' Gerry told them. 'The material y'kna. Ah was trying them on for warmth. Chilly north-eastern winds y'kna!' With a smile he turned and left. The security guards looked at each other helplessly as Gerry bounced towards the exit. 'Ah told ye not to confront a suspect until he's totally outside the store,' the original security guard was saying to one of his younger henchmen. 'We've got nowt on them until they're outside, man. Outside. D'ye understand?'

'Ootside,' replied the admonished young man, staring wistfully after Gerry.

Where once countless watercourses threaded their way through reed beds and quagmires, people now flow down the main channels or trickle in and out of shops and cafés, bearing with them the driftwood of their purchases. Gerry was still laughing as he eased himself into the busy drift. He stared in the windows of the shops, pausing occasionally to glance at the interior of one of them with a professional eye. From the shops music blared, people's voices hummed. Climbing on to the next level he nipped through the Roman Forum with its mock marble exteriors and columns, and cut into the Antiques Village. The roofs of the little make-believe Victorian houses and the fake cobbled streets reflected the lurid glare of a midnight constellation, strings of electric lights set in the papier-mâché sky. A bearded mannequin standing by the mill wheel and bridge in a top coat and a bowler hat burst into guttural life as Gerry passed him. 'Welcome to the Metrrro Centre,' the mannequin cried, rolling his r's right down in the back of his throat as though he were bringing up phlegm. 'Have a grrreat Northumbrrrrian day!' Gerry relaxed. He'd never stolen anything from the Antiques Village before. He was safe here. He looked at the people sitting in the café beside the water mill. They were drinking coffee and eating huge scones. Gerry's stomach groaned. He made a mental note to stop in at The Sweet Factory before going home.

Passing from the fabricated, starlit world of the Antiques Village, he re-entered one of the malls and turned left. It was quieter here. A backwater. Gerry slowed to a meditative stroll. Curious, he stopped to examine the windows of a bookshop. Inside people were browsing at the shelves, steadily moving from one book to another the way the travellers' ponies graze on road verges. Gerry edged into the shop. Feigning interest in a stack of calendars on the counter, he watched a customer bring a book to buy. The shop assistant took up the book to look for its price and then punched the digits into the till. 'Nineteen ninety-nine please,' the assistant said in a singsong voice. The till whirred. Gerry watched the customer take out a brand-new twenty-pound note and hand it over. Its violet colouring gleamed brilliantly under the lights as it was passed for the transaction. Gerry narrowed his eyes. 'Nineteen ninety-nine,' he repeated to himself. 'Who would have thought it?'

Pausing to spit outside the Sunderland AFC shop, Gerry swung his upper body over the safety railings and hung upside down to look into the window of the shop directly below, the Newcastle United shop. Shirts hovered upside down. A video showed players running on their heads. Uprighting himself, he set off again. Out of the quietness he could already hear the screams building.

Metroland, the funfair within the Metro Centre, can be heard long before it is reached. As the shoppers near it, they are met with the eerily echoing screams of the rollercoaster and the many other rides. It is like approaching a slaughterhouse. Or the scene of a massacre. And the noise grows steadily louder until on the very threshold of the indoor amusement park, it is a bloodcurdling din.

Gerry looked for Sewell by the fast-food kiosk at a crossroads of stall-lined alleys under the rollercoaster. There was no sign of him. The screaming grew to a crescendo and the metal girders supporting the segment of the ride above began to creak. The rollercoaster flew by. In the din Gerry thought he heard his own name. 'Gerry! Ha'way Gerry!' He looked about, but saw nothing. Wandering down one of the alleys he heard it again. 'Ha'way man Gerry! It's belter!' Gerry walked on, stopping by a smaller ride that involved sitting in a carriage at the end of a metal arm and spinning around. 'GERRYYYYY!' someone shrieked. When Gerry listened carefully he was sure that he could make out the barking of a dog too. His heart dropped. The rollercoaster came round again and the smaller ride began to decelerate until the passengers became individually identifiable from the spinning whirl. 'Areet?' said a voice much closer now, followed by a definite bark.

'Sewell man, what ye deein'?' moaned Gerry.

Sewell waved. When the ride came to a stop he climbed out from behind the flimsy safety bar. Rusty scuttled out behind him, his nails clattering on the metal base of the ride. 'What the hell are ye deein'?' demanded Gerry.

'Ah'm celebrating, man,' replied Sewell, grinning.

'Ye're supposed to be blind.'

'Divven't give wor that prejudicism stuff.'

'Eh?'

'Even the blind are allowed to enjoy themselves.'

Gerry looked at Sewell and blinked hard. He drew him within the lee of the rollercoaster rails as the ride clattered overhead again. 'Yer eyes were open again, man. Ye looked like a friggin' fish. We're supposed to be professionals. Y'kna what ah mean by professionals? It means that if ye're pretending to be blind then ye keep your friggin' eyes closed!' Gerry turned away for a few seconds, his face screwed up with frustration. 'Anyway, what d'yus get?' he asked, turning back to his friend whose eyes were now clamped tight.

Sewell whistled self-importantly. With a nonchalant shrug he unzipped his bench coat and delved a hand within. 'Three ladies' shirts, two skirts, some bras and knickers . . .' he counted, his fingers feeling the fabric closely.

'Oh aye!' laughed Gerry.

'Ah just took what was to hand, man. A scarf, a . . . ah divven't kna what this is . . . some sort of material anyway, two pairs of gloves, a bag of soaps, a rubber duck and . . .'

'Eh?'

'Three ladies' shirts . . .'

'Just them last three things.'

'What? A bag of soaps and a rubber duck.'

'And that last thing.'

Sewell took a step back defensively. 'They're for yer mam, man. Noo she's oot o' hospital. Ah saw the soaps and thought she might like them. The duck's for the babby. Bathtime y'kna.'

'Thanks,' said Gerry. 'Sewell,' he added.

'Aye?'

'What's the third thing?' Gerry held his hand out and grasped Sewell's. Sewell placed a spray can in it. 'Not another air-freshener for the netty?' smirked Gerry.

'Na,' said Sewell in an injured tone. 'It's body spray. Perfume. See on the label.'

Gerry rolled the can in his hand. 'Oh aye?' he asked.

Sewell blushed. 'It's for Gemma.'

Gerry shook his head. 'See sense, man. She's engaged to a cracker.'

Sewell balanced on the outsides of his feet like a child. 'It's just a present,' he mumbled.

Gerry inhaled as though he were about to speak. Then, sighing, he expelled all the air. 'Ha'way,' he urged, taking out two carrier bags from his pockets and holding them out. 'Hoy the stuff in here.' Sewell placed the stolen goods in the bags. 'That'll leave room in yer bench coat for wor next target, and remember ye're blind. Follow me at a distance of twenty paces.'

'Does it have to be exactly twenty?' Sewell asked. Gerry grunted affirmatively. 'Well, how can ah dee that if ah cannet see?'

The rollercoaster creaked overhead as Gerry negotiated the alley of stalls. The smell of burgers from the kiosk dizzied him for a moment. Suspicious, he waited for Sewell to catch up with him. When Sewell and Rusty were abreast with him he spoke out of the corner of his mouth like a ventriloquist. 'What else did ye take from Marksies?'

Sewell jumped a little. 'Nowt, man Gerry, and divven't sneak up on wor.'

Gerry put his hand out. An object was placed on it. As he walked on he looked at the object. It was an empty plastic package. The words Bacon-lettuce-tomato Best Quality Sandwiches were written on a disc of paper stuck to the empty package.

'Ah couldn't resist it,' explained Sewell lamely. 'Marksies dee the nicest stuff. Ah always like to pop into their food hall.'

'Fat get!' Gerry seethed under his breath. 'And for the last time KEEP YOUR EYES SHUT!'

'How d'ye kna ah was . . .' mumbled Sewell, closing them.

They had left Metroland and were just walking through the Food Court, whose fast-food counters and tables ring the amusement area like vultures, when some voices hailed them from the tables of Wok and Roll, a Chinese fast-food outlet. 'Gerry! Sewell! What ye deein'?'

Gerry swore and carried on. Through the corner of his eye

he saw Sewell and Rusty approaching the voices, the snooker cue tapping loudly on the tiled floor. The voices burst into laughter. He could hear Rusty bark suspiciously. Unwillingly, Gerry turned round. There were three of them.

'What ye deein' with that dog and yer eyes closed?' one of the voices asked loudly.

'Areet, Jimmy,' greeted Gerry when he had reached the Wok and Roll seats. He sat with the others, resting his elbows on the litter-strewn table.

'Areet, Gerry,' replied Jimmy, as small as Gerry himself, but with a disproportionately large head, covered thinly in wispy, fair hair.

'Areet, Mally.' Gerry nodded to the one whose face was covered in spots.

'Areet, Gerry,' replied Mally.

'Areet, Darren.' Gerry raised his eyebrows to the third one.

'Areet, Gerry,' Darren returned in a nasal voice.

All three of them had their short hair slicked down so that it lay over their foreheads in thin, greasy fingers. From time to time, and always at the same time, they flicked their foreheads to ensure that their comb-teeth fringes still hung perfectly vertical.

'What are yous up to?' demanded Jimmy, who resembled nothing so much as a five-foot-high baby.

'We're . . .' began Sewell excitedly.

'Deein' nowt,' finished Gerry. 'What are yous up to, waggin'?'

'Nicked off from school like ye,' all three of them replied simultaneously.

'What's Sewell deein' keeping his eyes closed?' questioned Jimmy, leaning over and spitting.

'Ah'm . . .' began Sewell.

'Deein' nowt,' finished Gerry.

'What's with the dog?' Jimmy asked, his huge face leering with infantile derision.

'It's . . .' began Sewell.

'Nowt,' finished Gerry.

'Did ye hear aboot that Matthew kid?' said Mally. 'Lost one of his dogs. He threw a radgie. Gonnae kill whoever took it.'

'What's with the snooker cue like?' asked Darren who, having cleared his nose by closing one nostril at a time with a forefinger and blowing the other strenuously, merely sounded even more nasal. 'And what's in them carrier bags?'

'We're late,' explained Gerry, cutting in before Sewell could even begin his answer. 'We'll have to get off, lads.'

'Ha'way, we'll come with yous,' decided Jimmy.

'Na . . .' Gerry replied uneasily, standing up. 'Ye cannet.'

'Why not?' demanded Jimmy. He got to his feet and stepped towards Gerry threateningly.

'Em . . .' said Gerry thoughtfully.

'Got a problem like?' Jimmy menaced, scratching his infantile head.

''Course not,' replied Gerry. 'It's just that . . .' Darren, Mally and Jimmy had formed a ring round Gerry. Their faces pressed in on him. The fingers on their hands played restlessly. 'It's just that . . .' Gerry floundered.

At that moment Rusty raised his gums over his teeth and suddenly lunged at the ring of lads, his snapping bite a hair's breadth away from them. 'Rusty,' admonished Sewell. 'Calm doon, Rusty!' But Rusty leapt up at them, growling, making the twine lead taut as a guitar string.

'It's geet vicious,' approved Jimmy, his baby face puckering with pleasure.

'What a monster,' admired Mally.

'It wants to kill wor,' intoned Darren.

'What a belter hoond!' all three exclaimed.

'Aye well, as ah was saying,' said Gerry smoothly. 'We'd love ye to come along with wor but the dog wouldn't let ye. See ye later then, lads.'

'The dog boy'll want to kna where ye got the hoond from,' Jimmy called out as Sewell and Gerry and Rusty were walking away.

'Bought him,' replied Sewell. 'From Marks and Spencer's.'

As soon as they were out of earshot Gerry began explaining the next job to Sewell. 'So,' he concluded, 'Ah'll see ye there. It's called Waterstone's. Ah'll gan roond looking and then ah'll leave the books for ye to take popping oot of the shelf. Ah'll whistle softly to guide ye, so nee Blaydon Races, and Rusty'll dee the rest. Areet?'

'Reet,' agreed Sewell. 'Good lad, Rusty,' he added, kneeling down to pat the dog and bury his face in the animal's flank.

'Divven't get too fond of that mutt,' warned Gerry. 'He's a working dog, remember.'

Classical music was playing in the shop. 'This'll dee me heed in,' moaned Sewell under his breath as he walked in through the open doors. There was a blast of heat from some vents. Sewell listened closely. The smell of the books was sickly. The carpet was soft under his feet. He sighed appreciatively. 'Now this is what we could dee with twocing,' he whispered to Rusty. 'A nice bit of carpet. Can ye tell me what he wants with books?'

There was a sharp cough from over his shoulder. Rusty pricked his ears and tugged Sewell over to where a moment ago Gerry had subtly but pointedly replaced the book he had been reading halfway out of the shelf. Sewell felt his way over the books, stopping at the one that protruded. He passed it once and then doubled back. With a tentative hand he reached for it. It was hard-backed. The corners were sharp and the dust jacket smooth. It was deceptively heavy. As he slid it into the recesses of his bench coat he staggered, nearly dropping it. Deeper into the shelves Sewell found another book left for him by Gerry. This one was just as heavy. The two together were like millstones in his bench coat. It was hot. He began to perspire. A fat bead of sweat plumped down his forehead.

Following a jaunty whistle from Gerry, Sewell followed Rusty past some more shelves over to the far wall where the dog stopped. As he searched the shelves Sewell could hear

Rusty licking his lips with satisfaction. Kneeling down to the dog he felt the shelf at this height. The book was there. He had secreted this third and the heaviest of the books when he became aware of Gerry making furtive but fervent whistling signals. Gerry's abrupt appearance at his elbow made Sewell jump. 'After ye, sir,' Gerry said in a loud voice, adding quietly, 'they're on to ye, gan doonstairs and browse.'

Led by Rusty, Sewell negotiated the stairs. 'Ah'm completely in yer control,' Sewell whispered, his stick clattering uselessly down the stairs. On the lower level of the shop he headed feverishly for the shelves nearest the doors. 'Can I help you?' a sudden voice from behind him enquired. He was about to turn and answer when he remembered that he was blind. Instead he looked up in the opposite direction.

'No thank you,' he said, deeply pleased with himself for his cunning.

'That's an unusual guide dog,' the voice persevered, its calm tones slightly discomfiting Sewell. 'Where was he trained?'

'Em . . .' said Sewell. 'In Whickham.'

'Whickham?' The voice had a faintly sceptical one.

'Whickham,' Sewell repeated. His mind had gone blank.

'It's an unusual choice for a guide dog. They don't usually use Heinz ones, you know, fifty-seven different varieties.' The voice seemed to sharpen itself. 'Whereabouts?'

'Whereabouts?'

'Yes, whereabouts was your dog trained in Whickham. I'm something of a dog handler myself, you know, strictly amateur.' A distinct chill fell on the voice as it added, 'So whereabouts in Whickham?'

'. . . in the fields and that . . . Y'kna, Washingwell Woods,' Sewell stammered.

'Washingwell Woods?'

'And all them fields roond aboot.'

There was a short pause. 'Strange,' remarked the voice at last.

Sewell's throat filled. He tried to clear it. His voice was at its slowest. 'Why?'

'They usually train guide dogs for the blind in towns and cities, on streets, where people live, you know.'

'They do?'

'They do.'

'Well ah live in woods, divven't ah?'

'In Washingwell Woods?' quizzed the voice with an unpleasant and growing hint of mockery.

'No,' stumbled Sewell. 'Not Washingwell Woods. Just woods. Trees y'kna.'

'Where?'

Sewell swore under his breath. The heat was getting unbearable. He felt like a piece of bacon spitting under the grill.

Unnerved, Sewell was actually beginning to feel blind. Panic surged over him. What if keeping his eyes screwed so tightly closed for so long had somehow really deprived him of his sight? He moaned. He could certainly feel a burning sensation in his eyes. Perhaps it was just the sweat which was now dripping freely from him, but then again . . . Darkness seemed to stretch ahead of him like a terrifying cavern. 'Atishooo!' As he sneezed he threw up a hand to his face, and, shuddering, glanced through a gap between the fingers. Euphoria gripped him when he realised that he was not blind. But the glimpse totally disorientated him and he staggered drunkenly. He seemed to be trapped in an endless corridor, the walls lined with black shelves full of shimmering books whose pages were sharp as razors. The carpet which had felt so generous under his unseeing feet was revealed as a garish, dripping blood-red. And the shop assistant facing him had, with her long, lank, dark hair parted at the centre, and her huge black fingernails, the look of a vampire. He put down his hand and resumed his pretend blindness.

'Ah live in Kielder Forest,' he hazarded wildly, the words flowing unchecked from his mouth. 'Miles from anywhere.

With ponies and huskies; them Newfoondland dogs an' all with the webbed feet y'kna,' he added recklessly. 'Snows most of the year. Big castles.'

'What are you doing in this bookshop, sir?' the shop assistant insisted, her tone now brutally blunt.

'Ah'm um . . .'

'Yes?'

'Ah'm . . .' Sewell desperately searched his memory for the word Gerry had used. With a rush of relief he recalled it. 'Ah'm broowsing.'

'Browsing?'

'Having meself a quick broowse y'kna.'

'A quick browse?'

'Just a quick one like.'

'Really?'

'Really.' Sewell began to relax a little. Relief buoyed him like a drowning person who finds some wreckage to float on. 'Ah love books me but. Well, ye need them when ye live oot in the wilds man.'

'Remarkable!' exclaimed the assistant.

'Not really,' smiled Sewell almost complacently.

'No. That's really remarkable.'

'Eh?'

'You see, I thought you were blind.'

Sewell opened his eyes. He looked directly at the assistant. Her face was cold. Then he glanced down at Rusty. The dog whined imploringly. After this he looked over for Gerry who was standing a few yards off, hiding behind the cover of an immense tome. 'The thing is,' he began. 'The thing is . . . RUN FOR IT!'

6

In Gateshead, when October drips into November, the nights grow desperately long and often the days never seem to even begin. The sun peaks, if seen at all, just above the horizon. The rain is ceaseless; in the houses the lights burn constantly. The tower blocks rise like icebergs in a frozen sea. Flocks of seagulls gather around vast puddles, their wings flashing arctic white. People wander forlornly across rain-swept wastes like wolves. Scavenging desperately for comfort, they hole up in the den of their homes, gathering around television sets where they will snack and sleep for the next six months as though the glowing screen were the carcass of a great kill, or a never-dying fire.

'Gerry!' shouted his grandmother one November morning towards midday. Being deaf, her spoken words were unshapely, more approximated than fully-formed. 'Gerry, get up.'

'Nana,' moaned Gerry, pulling the pillow over his head. The rain drummed monotonously against the window like fingers of a waiting hand. The pane was steamed up with condensation.

'Gerry!' his grandmother urged.

'Areet, areet!' Gerry called down. Leaning out of bed he banged his fist against the floor.

'Gerry, doonstairs noo!' Her words thudded up against the bedroom floor.

'Areet!' shouted Gerry again, but then he quietened. There was no point in shouting. His grandmother would never hear him. Getting up, Gerry shivered in the dampness. He threw his clothes on, jogging bottoms and an old yellow sweatshirt, and hurried downstairs. The stairs creaked. His grandmother did not look round. He walked over and tapped her on the shoulder. 'Down in a minute,' he signed with his hands. 'First I wash.'

His grandmother frowned. 'But school?' she returned with her hands.

Without answering Gerry retreated to the stairs. He turned before climbing back up. 'Cup of tea,' he requested with his hands.

In the bathroom, the cold water lanced his face and hands. Shivering, he dried himself on his sweatshirt. The wallpaper above the toilet had unpeeled again. He took up the yellowed ends and stuck them back against the wall. It held for a few moments and then crashed down. Gerry left it. He searched half-heartedly for the toothpaste and then gave up. Entering Bridget's room he made for the cupboard. On his knees he felt for the jar. With a deep breath, he brought it out.

There was a thickish wad of notes, but there were still too many coins. Painstakingly he counted the money into piles. In total two hundred and thirty-five pounds. He stared at it slowly and carefully, his lips parted slightly.

Gerry was scooping the money back in the jar when he heard the floorboard creak behind him. He looked round to see his grandmother standing there watching. 'I'm coming, I'm coming,' he told her with gestures which were also trying to conceal the money.

When he came downstairs, she was waiting for him, sitting on the settee. Although the gas fire was on full, she wore her duffel coat. Her head was very round with short, thick, grey hair. Her body was thin. Her eyes, although set deep in her skull, were quick and knowledgeable. She had a snub nose. The skin of her face was wizened, each wrinkle brutally counted by the starkness of the unshaded lightbulb. A steaming cup was waiting for him on the arm of the settee. 'With milk,' she signed.

'Thank you,' he replied, sitting down beside her. For a long time he stared at the tea. With his hands on his lap he scrutinised the mug, cocking his head at different angles, examining its precarious balance. Picking up the mug at last, he sipped carefully as though each taste had an individual value that could be measured. 'Milk and sugar too, good.'

For a while they sat drinking their tea without any more communication. Then Gerry heard his grandmother click her tongue with annoyance. He looked over at her. 'Why aren't you at school?' her hands asked.

Gerry did not reply. The delicious liquid slipped smoothly down his throat, warming and comforting him. The gas fire gurgled peacefully. 'It's good,' his hands thanked her. 'This sweet tea is good.'

The rain could be heard rapping against the bricks. 'Your mam is back in hospital,' his grandmother signed after a while. Gerry nodded with a sigh. A few more moments of tea drinking slipped past. 'Go to school today, Gerry. For your mam.' Gerry stiffened slightly and looked away. He shook his head tersely. His grandmother grabbed hold of his shaking head and stilled it. 'Yes,' she moaned loudly, speaking the word aloud in her frustration. 'Be like Bridget. Bridget is a good girl,' she signed.

Gerry shook his face free. 'Bridget is gone.'

A silence followed. Gerry, cradling the warmth of his cup in the palms of his hands, put it down so that he could sign, 'Where is Bridget?'

She shook her head.

Going into the kitchen, his grandmother came back with a plateful of digestives. She offered him one.

She sat back down on the settee, putting the biscuits between her and her grandson. Shrewdly she watched him eating for a while. 'Why were you looking in her wardrobe, Gerry?'

Gerry's face dropped. He shook his head. 'Nothing.'
'You lie.'
'Nothing.' His bottom lip came out.
'You are always in Bridget's wardrobe. I watch you.'

Gerry sighed. His eyebrows knotted as though he were thinking deeply. 'Money, Nana. Money.'

'You steal?'

Gerry looked away.

His grandmother repeated her question. 'Gerry, you steal?' Without looking back in her face Gerry nodded.

'Ahh!' she growled, her disgust freely showing. Re-establishing eye contact, Gerry inched towards her, lifting up the plate of biscuits and resting it on his knee. She shook her head. 'You are a man, a bad man. You are like your father. You steal from everybody, even your own sister . . .'

Gerry tried to explain. 'I do not steal from Bridget,' he signed quickly.

His grandmother's hands whirred quicker and quicker. 'You are like your father. Go and live with him,' she told him. 'When your mother comes home, you will move to live with your father. When Sean comes home he will live with you and your father.'

Desperately Gerry tried to interrupt his grandmother but he was too unskilled in the language with which they communicated to compete. Gripping the plate of biscuits, he sank back and watched the blur of her hands, which violently grappled the air about her, as though she were wrestling an invisible and detested adversary. With a final, choking growl, she seemed to gain a telling grip and throw her opponent aside. Then, falling still, she held her hands out, and stared at them. Gently he put his own hand on hers for a moment. Then he reached out for his mug, but it had gone cold. The dregs of his dunked biscuits scummed the surface of the tea.

Gerry was not sure how long they'd been sitting together like that when there was a knock at the door. He sat through it. There was more knocking, this time louder. Reluctantly Gerry got up. Going to the window first he peered out furtively. Seeing no danger he opened the door. It was a middle-aged woman dressed smartly in a multicoloured jacket and black trousers. She carried a briefcase in her left hand and wore pendulous earrings in both ears. Her hair was cut short and shaped into a bob. In its brief exposure to the rain it had been flattened against her head. 'Oh it's ye, Maureen,' Gerry said, letting her in.

'Hello, Gerry,' the woman replied in tones of weary complacency.

Gerry went through to the sitting room and sat back down on the settee. 'Social worker,' he signed to his grandmother.

She replied with a raised thumb, then signed, 'She'll tell you to go back to school.'

'OK?' thumbed the social worker, entering the room and standing there awkwardly for a little while. Gerry's grandmother pointed at one of the armchairs. 'I'm not stopping for long,' the social worker said, shaking her head and remaining standing. 'I have another meeting. I just popped in here to have a quick word with Gerry.' Gerry's grandmother signed something. The social worker tried to understand her, got her to repeat it. 'No, sorry. I don't understand,' she admitted finally.

'Nana says', translated Gerry, 'that ye're always welcome . . .'

'Thank you,' signed the social worker, a smile making her earrings jiggle.

His grandmother slapped Gerry on the arm. '. . . Especially if ye can get us gannin' to school,' he finished.

'Well, that's why I'm here,' said the social worker, her beaming and nodding teasing her earrings into a full dance. 'I have something very good for you, Gerry. I will give you something very special; if you agree to do one thing.'

'Aye?'

'If you go to school.' Gerry shook his head. 'For just two weeks. You don't even know what I'll give you yet.'

'Maureen man, ah'm not gannin' back to school.'

The social worker sniffed and held up her head triumphantly. 'I bet you will,' she said.

'St Jude's? Nivver. It's a hell-hole.'

'Gerry,' said his grandmother, who had been reading the conversation like a tennis match as she followed each volleyed shape from the lips. 'Gerry! School!' Her spoken words were loud in the confines of the small room.

'You should listen to your nana,' said the social worker.

'Gerry! School! School!'

'Your mother won't be in hospital much longer,' said the social worker. 'Just think what it would mean to her if you were at school.'

'There's nowt in this world that could get us back into school,' explained Gerry calmly.

His grandmother threw her eyes and hands up to heaven. The social worker began chuckling. 'Are you sure about that?' she asked.

'Totally.' Gerry was adamant.

'Are you willing to make a bet?'

'How much like?'

'Sportsman's.'

'Ah'll bet yer owt you want that ah'll never gan back to school.'

'You're on. Because I know you'll be going there today. I've got you the uniform. Even a new coat.'

'Ah'm not gannin' to school for any poxy uniform, me.'

The social worker raised a hand. 'What about if I give you two tickets for the football?' she asked.

'Eh?'

'It's a cup match. If you go to school for two weeks then I will give you them.'

Gerry blinked. 'Was it for two weeks you said, Maureen?'

'Starting today.'

Giving out a little cry his grandmother hugged Gerry, got up and then hugged the social worker. 'Maureen! Good!' she said, her deafness again distorting her spoken words.

Gerry followed the social worker outside. Water was gurgling loudly down the drain. 'Hold on,' he said, leaving her on the threshold. He came back carrying a large cardboard box. 'Ah couldn't find an umbrella,' he explained, leading Maureen to her car under the protection of the box. He had to stand on tiptoes to hold it above her head. The rain dotted noisily on the cardboard. Climbing into the back seat she brought out the school uniform still in its cellophane wrappers. And the coat.

'It's a swot's jacket,' said Gerry, holding out the coat at arm's length. 'A pure boffin's.'

'Then you'll have to be a swot,' laughed the social worker, getting into the driver's seat and starting the engine. 'I'll give you the tickets when you've done the two weeks. Oh yes, there's the bus fare for school. Both ways. Don't spend it.'

His grandmother was standing by the settee when Gerry came back in. 'Beautiful clothes,' she signed.

'The coat is shit,' he mouthed.

'So you go to school now?'

Gerry nodded. 'But only for two weeks,' he muttered.

His grandmother smiled. 'Perhaps you are not like your father. You can live here.'

There was a pause. The rain harried the house with thrusting gusts. Somewhere, incongruously, an ice-cream van played The Blaydon Races. Its notes, seized by the wind and distorted by the rain, were scattered eerily over Gateshead. Gerry knelt down by the fire, and cupped his hands around its warmth. He turned when he felt his grandmother's hand on his shoulder. 'Please, put on your new school clothes,' she signed.

'Why?'

'I want to see you in your school uniform.'

'OK,' Gerry agreed after a moment. 'But not the coat.'

Gerry got up, his cheeks glowing from the fire. Smoothing off the raindrops which still clung to the cellophane wrappers, he brought the clothes into the kitchen. Looking over his shoulder he could see his grandmother sitting stock-still, as though in a trance. He opened the packets. Even socks and underwear had been included. Stripping off his jogging pants and sweatshirt, he stood there naked. He flexed his arms and then his legs. He was shockingly thin, like a plucked starling. Goose bumps pricked his flesh. Shivering, he pulled on the socks and then the underpants. They were far too big. The trousers and shirt fitted much better. There was even a tie. With a fixed grimace of concentration he tied the tie. He could sense his grandmother's excitement as she shifted positions on the settee, turning her body towards the kitchen. Searching under the kitchen table he found his trainers and then put them on. He looked at the uniform and the trainers. He tied the laces in meticulous bows, but there was still something wrong. He took the shoes off again and, spitting on them, scrubbed vigorously with a sodden tea towel. Then he lathered a small sliver of soap and washed the trainers, drying them with the sweatshirt. When he put the trainers back on he smiled. They were spotless.

Just as he was about to go through to the sitting room there was a tap on the window. Gerry turned to see a song thrush on the window ledge, looking into the kitchen, with its head leaning to one side, and then the other.

'Gerry!' shouted his grandmother. Gerry did not move. He watched the bird shake the droplets of water from its feathers, fluffing up its body. 'Gerry!' Cupping his hands, he held them out to the bird. The thrush began to sing. Gerry walked over to the window and opened it. For a moment the kitchen was filled with the notes of the song. Gently, he stretched his cupped hands through the open window. 'Ha'way,' he whispered. 'Ha'way.' The bird, once again putting its head on one side and then on the other, examined Gerry minutely, as though considering the hand. But then suddenly taking fright, it flew away, leaving Gerry's hands empty on the sill.

Gerry walked through into the sitting room. On seeing him, his grandmother burst into applause. Gerry smiled.

'Good!' she thumbed, and reached down for her old brown handbag beside the settee. Scrabbling inside, she pulled out a dirty pink comb. Beaming with joy, she beckoned Gerry, who came over and sat down beside her. Her face was mesmerised as she licked her fingers and damped down Gerry's hair. Gently the comb smoothed away the teeth of his fringe in a sideways sweep. Gerry gritted his teeth. The old woman crooned happily as she groomed him. When she had finished, she cupped his whole face in her hands and smiled.

'Nana,' signed Gerry sharply, pulling back. 'Listen. I do not steal from Bridget. It is my money. I put it in the wardrobe because it is safe there. Sewell and me are saving it. We want . . .' again he had to finger spell, 'Season Tickets. Do you understand? We want Season Tickets for the football.' He stared urgently at his grandmother's face, which stared back at him blankly. 'Season Tickets to watch the football,' he reiterated. 'A Season Ticket means . . .' In frustration his eyes tightly closed in the attempt to find the words. 'It means we watch every game. We never miss a game. It means we belong . . .' But when he opened his eyes, he saw that his grandmother was not reading his signs. She was sitting back on the settee staring into the fire, her eyes lifeless and exhausted. And all at once she seemed shrunken and used-up. Only her eyes sparkled as though seeing things that no one else could. 'Nana.' He came over and kissed her on the cheek. 'School now.' She nodded and then went back to the fire. Taking his hand, she gave him a faint, almost imperceptible squeeze.

Gerry ran upstairs and burst into his room. He threw the coat on to the bed, and getting on to his knees ran a hand under the bed. 'Two birds with one stone,' he said, pulling out the books he had stolen from Waterstone's with Sewell. Putting them under his arm he descended the stairs. His grandmother was still absorbed by the fire, the pink comb lying inert in her lap. Foraging inside the kitchen he found a plastic bag. But the material was too thin and when he put the books in the bag its flimsy plastic gave way. Under the sink he found a Co-op bag. This held the books. 'Textbooks,' he signed to his grandmother. But she did not seem to see him.

He closed the front door and left her to whatever it was she saw in the glowing gas fire.

Outside the rain was still coming down, squeezing itself over everything like a wrung cloth. The grass on the football pitches shone green, patches of dog muck gleamed. On the roads the puddles deepened by the kerbs. A newspaper, hidden by the wind in the corner where two walls met, was slowly disintegrating into a sodden, illegible pulp, its stories lost for ever. There was a woman at the bus stop, the curls of her hairdo protected by a transparent rain-mate. 'Areet, pet,' she said. Gerry nodded. 'Late for school, aren't ye?'

'Half-day off,' Gerry replied, then to cut off the conversation looked straight ahead.

'What ye got in that bag?' she asked, but Gerry ignored her. 'Ye want a coat on a day like this,' the woman continued after a while. 'Ye'll catch your death mind,' and with a morbid gesture the woman pointed over to the doctor's surgery whose new orange bricks stood out against the grim grey of the estate.

Gerry narrowed his eyes shrewdly. 'Ye lookin' to buy a coat like?' he asked. 'Brand-new, top-quality.'

In the distance the bus appeared. It lumbered to a halt at a stop in the distance and then lurched off again, belching smoke. 'St Jude's,' said Gerry, placing the coins the social worker had given him down on the driver's black tray.

'Ye're nice and early, hinny!' laughed the bus driver. 'A real prize-winner ye. Eh! Ah'll drop ye at the bottom mind. Ah'm not gannin' up the bank.'

Gerry took the tear-off ticket and climbed the stairs. There was no one else on the top deck. The bus' engine roared into life and, riding the rocking rhythm of its movement, Gerry finally made it to the back where he sat down. The match flared as he struck it and the cigarette glowed into life. It was one of his grandmother's. He had only taken three. The bus bumped as it negotiated the traffic-calming hump laid on the road to slow the joy-riders. Gerry blew out the smoke and, having wiped away the heavy condensation with the sleeve of his jumper, looked through the window. Gateshead flashed by. The waste ground where the travellers sometimes camp, the Dunston Rocket tower block and the parade of shops, Swalwell of the sodden trotting-pony fields, Shibdon pond where water rails peep from the reeds. And finally Blaydon. Gerry got off at the precinct, and began to climb the bank. The church clock struck one. The rain grew harder. The drops coursed down the nape of his neck, disappearing into his shirt collar and tracing their way down his back. Near the top, he waited in the brick bus shelter, reading the obscenities on the wall, until the rain slackened, and then stopped altogether.

'Afternoon, Gerry!' called Mrs Moore the lollipop lady, her ruddy face glowing. She was a round, inquisitive woman who bounced towards people like a ball. 'Didn't think ah'd ever see ye up this way again. Ye're a bit late, pet mind. Ah'm just gannin' mesel'. Mr Caird won't be too pleased.'

'Cairdy can please himself, man Peggy,' replied Gerry.

Peggy chuckled. 'Worra've ye got in that bag?'

Gerry shifted the bag of books under his other arm, shielding them from Mrs Moore's beady eyes. 'PE kit,' he told her.

'Oh aye,' she said, craning round to get a better view.

St Jude's is a shanty town of impermanent buildings straddling a hill. The school sign is small and undemonstrative, as though ashamed of what it represents. The main entrance is narrow, the doors heavy to open like the portcullis which is the symbol of Gateshead Metropolitan Borough. The yard is a flat piece of scarred tarmac terraced from the hillside; rubbish lies on it, in some places three or four inches deep. Stray dogs wander between the temporary huts which make up the English department, so that often the pupils baffle over Shakespeare to the iambic pentameters of canine copulation. During interminable afternoons when teachers cling to order by the very tips of their fingers, the motor-bikes arrive, throttling up the football pitches and spraying mud against the crumbling walls. Crazed, helmeted faces appear at the cracked windows, stirring up the pupils into vehement rebellion.

Reaching a side door, Gerry slipped inside the main building. With the heavy bag under his arm, he wound his way up and down interminable corridors, passing classroom after classroom in which the faces of children were savage with boredom or derision. Mounting a final, hidden staircase right at the back of the school, he reached the dining room. Looking through the perspex window in the door, he saw that the tables had been moved to one side, and he recognised his classmates gathered in an uneven circle on the floor. The teacher was perched above them on a plastic stool. Breathing deeply, Gerry entered the room. The whole class turned to look at the newcomer at exactly the same instant as though their heads were on the same neck. 'Ah, Gerry,' said the teacher, a middle-aged woman, in a surprised but kindly voice. 'I don't think we've seen you for a while?'

'Ah've been off for a while, Miss,' Gerry explained, looking about.

The whole class erupted into laughter. 'Areet, Gerry! Where've ye been? Thought ye were deed!' their voices called.

'Settle down, settle down,' soothed the teacher. 'Well, come and join us then.'

The circle of bodies opened up for him momentarily before closing again like the electric door on a bus. He squeezed in and sat down, concealing the books between his legs. Gemma smiled at him. He smiled back. Grabbing hold of Mally's shoulders, Jimmy levered himself up too. 'Walked any dogs lately, Gerry?' he hooted. The class exploded.

'We were talking about experiences,' the teacher explained, speaking over the buzzing hilarity. Holding her hands over the class, she raised her palms inclusively. Her deeply wrinkled face was heavily but inexpertly made up. Two rouge spots dotted her cheeks like an Aunt Sally. There was something elfin about her as though she were permanently poised to understudy a performance of *A Midsummer Night's Dream*. 'Experiences,' she said, rolling the word on her tongue. 'Before you came in, Gerry, Lindsey had told us about the time she thought she'd won the lottery.'

'Ee, summink like that happened to me, Miss,' began Gemma.

'Go on then, Gemma,' encouraged the teacher.

'Me mam thought she had the numbers.'

The teacher leant forward, and, resting her face on her hands, nodded vigorously. 'What was it like?'

'It was really good like, but then terrible.'

'So yours was an experience that started off as good and then deteriorated?'

'Aye.' Gemma twiddled meditatively with a strand of hair that twisted up through her red scrunchie. Half the length of the hair was dark, while the other was the yellow of custard. 'Everything sort of went quiet. Ah couldn't hear anything. Ah couldn't even hear the telly or the music from next door. It was like . . .'

'Yes, Gemma, what was it like?'

'Em . . . like being wrapped up in cotton wool.'

Like a heron darting for a frog the teacher lunged forward at Mally who had pinioned Jimmy's arm behind his back. 'Malcolm, I'm not telling you again,' she said.

'He started it,' said Mally, reluctantly dropping the arm like a hungry dog relinquishing a bone.

'Y'kna, Miss, it was the best moment of me life. Me and me mam just stared at each other.' Gemma gave Mally a haughty look.

'Areet, swot?' smirked Jimmy, feeling the thick material of Gerry's new school jumper.

'Fuck off,' whispered Gerry.

'What was it like when you found out that you hadn't won after all?' said the teacher.

'Well, ah watched it again, me and me mam always video

the lottery, ye see, Miss. It was then that ah saw that the balls . . .'

'The balls?' butted in Jimmy with a hyena grin on his baby face.

Gemma drew herself up straight and stared at Jimmy coldly. 'Ah saw that we hadn't won. No more than a tenner anyway. Ah didn't kna how to tell her. Ah just rewound the tape again, and pointed. When me mam saw, we just hugged each other. That was it.'

Suddenly Mally cried out, his yell reverberating throughout the room. 'Right, that's it!' snapped the teacher, her face taking on the anger and menace of a pantomime villain. 'Malcolm Liddle, out! Out now!'

'But, Miss.'

'But Miss nothing,' she retorted. 'You've done nothing but mess about since you got in.'

'Ee, shocking!' said Mally, hauling himself to his feet as though he were a seventy-year-old man. 'It wasn't me.' The rest of the class watched him stumble towards the door like a decrepit Captain Oates heading reluctantly for the ice. Jimmy's face was contorted with rat-like triumph. 'Y'always pick on me, Miss. It's purely shocking.'

When Mally had gone, the teacher thought deeply for a minute, wagging her head airly from side to side. 'Did you think that winning the lottery would make you happy?'

Gemma stared at the teacher in disbelief. 'Divven't ye, man Miss?'

The teacher put out her bottom lip as though thinking and then turned to the rest of the class with a flourish of her head. 'What does everybody else think?'

The question dropped into the class like a match on a pile of damp gunpowder. For a while they sizzled and smoked. Eyes looked up to the ceiling. Faces were contorted. Heads shifted positions on to different hands. Then they exploded with answers.

'Course it would, Miss.'

'Why aye.'

'Nee point in asking.'

'Ye could do owt with the lottery, man Miss man.'

The teacher bobbed up and down excitedly on her seat. Gerry looked round the class. He smiled at Gemma again who smiled back. Then he squirmed further into the circle of bodies, knocking Jimmy's hand away as it made a grab for the books. 'Ye like reading, Natalie?' he said to a bovine-looking girl wearing glasses. She nodded. Surreptitiously he peeled back the bag to reveal the books. 'Three quid each. Fiver for a pair.'

'Haven't ye got any horror?' the girl asked.

'What do you think about it all, Gerry?' the teacher suddenly asked.

'If ye ask me these are horrifying enough. Feel the weight o' that. They're monster.'

'Gerry,' repeated the teacher.

The sounds of the kitchen could be heard through the thin metal partition which separated the Drama class from where the cooks toiled over steaming water. Pans and trays were being rattled in sinks, and cutlery counted out on to tea towels. 'Ah'm sorry, Miss, didn't quite catch that.' At that moment Mally fell through the door. Pretending to be injured, he hauled himself to his feet.

'It was Jimmy Walsh!' he called.

'It's no good. You won't get Jimmy or anyone else to go out with you like that,' warned the teacher in a friendly but firm voice.

'Eh?' said Jimmy, his face knotting aggressively. He glared at the teacher like a child assassin. 'Ah'm not a puff, man Miss.'

The teacher looked at him uncomprehendingly. 'I never said you were.'

The reply was terse, hummingly aggressive. 'Aye, well ye'd better not.'

'What are you talking about, Jimmy?'

'Saying that ah go out with Mally. Ye stupid auld cunt.'

Instantly the teacher scanned the class, measuring the situation as though with a precision instrument. 'I'm not sure what you just said but if I think I hear it again then you will be in serious trouble. Do you understand?'

'But ye called us a puff,' mumbled Jimmy.

'Oh, for pity's sake shut up!' said the teacher.

'Aye, shut yer face,' said Gemma.

With relief the teacher saw the class subside into passivity again like a low fire that is stirred into a few flames by a poke, only to die down after its brief flare.

The teacher smiled at Gerry like an ally. 'Carry on then,' she said.

Gerry's face twisted in thought. Gingerly he fingered the carrier of books. Mally was now doing press-ups, and every time he rose up on his wrists, he struck the door so that it opened. 'D'ye dee the lottery, Miss?' he asked.

'Yes, I do,' replied the teacher.

'Does everyone else?' asked Gerry.

Those who were listening thought again and then began calling out, their voices attracting the attention of those not concentrating. One by one the slumpers dragged themselves into more upright positions.

'Ah put three on.'

'Ah put on four.'

'Five.'

'Some weeks ah put ten on.'

'Ah've put on more than that.'

'There's Wednesdays now, an' all,' added Gemma.

'Why do you ask, Gerry?' the teacher said.

Gerry looked at them all and then stood up. 'Waste o' money, man,' he said. Most of the faces followed his, even those who had been watching the dismissed Mally pulling faces through the window in the door.

'Not if ye win, it's not a waste o' money,' growled a youth with heavily pitted skin.

'Ye nivver dee though. Do ye?' The class exchanged

glances. 'How much does it come to in a lifetime? Think of how much ye'll spend putting the lottery on. How much have ye spent so far, and how much will ye spend on it until ye die? Is there anyone who can work that oot for wor?'

The class began the calculation on the abacus of their thumbs and fingers.

Gerry looked at the teacher, she smiled him on. 'Let's say we spend a fiver a week on wor lottery. Five times by, how many weeks are there in a year?' he questioned.

'Hundred and twenty,' called a voice.

'Fifty-two,' shouted another.

'That's the one,' said Gerry.

'Can we get paper, Miss?' requested Gemma after a few moments of silent calculation. Avoiding slipping on a stray chip, the teacher walked over to the filing cabinet with poise, as though she were crossing the stage at the play's most dramatic moment. With a faintly tragic air she distributed paper and pencils. The pencils chewed at the paper, teeth chewed at the end of the pencils as the multiplication chewed at the class. 'Haven't ye got a calculator, Miss?' Gemma asked.

'Ah could gan to a top set and lend a one, Miss. Them swot kids have got them,' offered somebody.

'We'll just have to work it out for ourselves,' said the teacher.

'If ye want to buy a dozen calculators ah could get them for ye. Top-quality mind.'

'No, thank you, Jimmy.'

A profound, active, unusual silence ensued. No one noticed Mally who, having grown tired of flicking V signs through the window, had now pushed the door open and was simulating masturbation.

'What was the sum again, Miss?' came a voice from the middle of the class, its tone monotonous with lack of understanding.

'Fifty-two weeks in a year. Times that by how many tickets

yus put on. Then times all of that by how many years ye'll live.'

'Thank you, Gerry,' said the teacher.

'How do ah kna how many years ah'm gannin' to live?' someone else asked.

'Got a nana?' Gerry asked.

'Na. She's deed.'

'Use her age, and add five years. Advancement o' medical science an' all that.'

The class worked steadily.

The teacher stared at the teenagers before her. 'We'll really have to do some Drama soon,' she said.

'This is Drama, Miss,' Gemma told her with a smile. 'We're finding out about life. We could make a play about it. Call it: *The Dream*. Or summink.'

'*The Price of a Dream*,' added Gerry.

'Ah've got it!' exclaimed a voice excitedly. 'One million, two hundred and twenty thoosand.'

'Well, aye!' the class was outraged.

'Divven't talk rubbish.'

'Ye thick bastard.'

'Ha'way, concentrate,' ordered Gerry.

Another silence ensued, broken at last by a triumphant exhalation. 'It's thirteen thousand.' Gemma's voice was calm but certain.

'Are you sure?' The teacher smiled.

'Ah'm sure, Miss. You spend thirteen thousand poond on the lottery in a lifetime.'

The class were stunned.

'Think what yus could dee with that.'

'Ee, and ye nivver win either.'

'It's a friggin' shan.'

A bell pierced the outrage. Immediately, the class jumped up and began heading for the door. 'Jimmy, would you and Malcolm collect in all the pencils and paper,' decided the teacher.

'Na,' bristled Jimmy. 'Why should ah? Why divven't you get Gerry to dee it? He was late.'

Gemma came over to Gerry. 'Ah thought yus'd given school up,' she said.

'D'ye kna anyone who wants to buy some books?' he smiled.

'Because I want you to do it,' the teacher said to Jimmy.

'That's shan!' replied Jimmy.

'That's life.'

'Up yours, Miss, ye lesbo.'

'Ye'll need a top-setter, Gerry,' said Gemma. 'Ee, but it's canny funny to see ye withoot Sewell.'

'Aye well, it's to dee with him why ah'm here. Business, y'kna.'

Gemma laughed. 'What yous two scheming aboot noo?'

The teacher had grown serious. 'What was that, Jimmy?'

'Ah said it's not fair.'

'I hope that's all you said.'

'Oh, fuck off.'

Side-stepping the challenge like a rugby player, the teacher again relied on her reputation for deafness. 'Yes, all right. You can get off. But collect the papers in first. Now, Gerry,' she said, turning to Gerry.

'Ah've got Food Technology next,' said Gemma.

'What ye making?'

'Pizza.'

'Canny.'

'Better gan. Ye have to get the oven on reet at the beginning. Nowt much else to dee after that mind.'

'Ah'll see ye later then, Gemma,' Gerry said.

'Good luck with your plans.' Gemma seemed to blush slightly as she left. 'And say hello to Sewell for us, will ye?'

'That was interesting, Gerry,' the teacher began when Gemma had gone. 'What you were saying about the lottery.'

'Ah nivver put it on, me, Miss. Got better things to dee with me money,' he said.

'Aye, spending it on drink and tac,' said Jimmy, thrusting the papers and pencils he had collected at the teacher.

'Off you go,' she said.

'Ah divven't dee them either, man Miss,' added Gerry. 'Nee drink. Nee tac. Nee nowt.'

'What do you spend money on then?'

There was an explosion of derision from the door through which the last few people were now leaving. 'Thems divven't have nee money. His auld man pisses it all doon the side of the wall.'

'Goodbye, Jimmy!' ordered the teacher. 'Don't listen to him,' she added.

'Ah divven't, man Miss. He's a prick.'

'You were telling me about money.'

'Ah'm trying to save it, Miss. For summink special. For summink ah really want.' Gerry looked around to make sure there was no one left in the room. 'D'ye kna Sewell, Miss?'

'Sewell? Small lad?'

Gerry laughed. 'Na. Got expelled. Wasn't his fault but. Mr Caird had him cornered. Well, it's me and 'im, Miss. We're saving for wor dream. Not the sort of dream yus have when ye're sleeping. But when ye're awake. Except ah dee dream aboot it at neet an' all.'

'We all need dreams.'

Gerry nodded. 'That's what gets to us aboot the lottery. People dee it 'cos they got nowt else. Kna what ah mean? Ye'll meet them somewhere and they'll say, ah well, mebbes ah've won the lottery. It keeps them gannin', ah suppose. Summink to distract themselves. But it's not a real dream. It's not theirs. D'yus kna what ah mean, Miss?' The teacher nodded. 'Could be anyone's. Ah'm not saying that my dream is any better. But it's mine. Couldn't be neeone else's.'

The teacher's eyebrows knotted with interest. 'What do you dream about, Gerry?'

Gerry shrugged evasively. 'D'y'ever watch the toon, Miss?'

'Newcastle United?'

'Aye.'

'I have done. What about you?'

Gerry coughed uncomfortably. 'Aye, course ah have. Whereaboots in the ground did ye gan, Miss?'

'Oh, it's all changed now. What about you?'

'They've changed since ah used to gan an' all.'

'Really? You must have been young.'

Looking away, Gerry paused for a moment. Then he looked back. 'Ah was a pure bairn. What do they say? Knee-high to a grasshopper.'

Bodies for the next class were beginning to congregate at the door. 'Just wait outside, thank you,' the teacher called. 'I suppose it's hard to get in nowadays,' she said.

'Ye've got to have a Season Ticket.'

The teacher narrowed her eyes thoughtfully. 'Who in that Drama class goes to watch them then?' Gerry shook his head. 'You mean not one of you goes to the football?'

Gerry lowered to the ground the books which he had been holding behind his back. Flexing his muscles, he smiled. 'Neeone. Some of the top-setters gan.'

'But you used to?'

'Aye. Course ah did.'

'What was it like?'

'Eh?'

'What was it like when you did go? You said you were very young. Did your father take you, or an older brother?'

'Aye. It was me auld man, Miss.'

The new class was growing noisy at the door. 'Ah nivver fuckin' wanted to gan oot with 'im in the first place,' a girl was explaining to some friends. 'Skinny bastard. Nee arse on 'im.'

Gerry shuffled uncomfortably, nudging the books edgily with a toe. 'Ah cannet remember it that well really, Miss.'

'What do you remember?'

Gerry thought deeply for a few moments. 'It was geet noisy.'

'I bet it was.'

'And there were people everywhere. Ah divven't remember

who won.' Gerry seemed to examine his hand for a while as though he might read some words written there. 'What ah remember best is me auld man's coat. He used to always wear it when he took me to the Toon. Ah can see that coat clearly even noo.'

'Did he take you often?'

Gerry grinned. 'Aye. Every week.' He narrowed his eyes dreamily. 'We always used to get a cup o' tea at half-time. Ah was too small to get to the hatch, but me dad, why, he lifted wor reet up. It came in polystyrene cups. That tea. It was too hot for me. So me auld man held it for wor. Ah was awer young, you see, Miss. He looked oot for us. Made sure neeone pushed wor, or owt. He stood over wor, Miss, looking after wor, like, well like the statue.'

'The statue?'

'Y'kna. The Angel. The way its arms are oot. Sounds mental, eh?' Gerry blushed.

'No. It doesn't sound mental.'

Gerry blinked and prodded the books as though to orientate himself. 'Ah'll nivver forget it, man Miss. Ah'll nivver forget it.'

'Why did you stop going?'

'Ah divven't kna. Just did.' There was a pause.

'Is that your dream?'

'Eh?'

'Your dream, Gerry. Going to the match with your father. Is that part of your dream?'

Gerry looked down at his feet. 'Ah divven't kna. Mebbes.'

'We could continue this theme next week if you like.'

'How d'ye mean, Miss?'

'We could all choose a memory. Dramatise it. Then talk about how we feel about it.'

Gerry shook his head. 'It's private. Ah divven't want to dee that.'

The class was crushed at the door. 'In you come,' said the

teacher, then turned back to Gerry, talking to him over the din of the entering throng. 'How's Bridget, Gerry?'

'Ah divven't kna,' said Gerry, beginning to move off. 'She's done a runner.'

The teacher grimaced lightly. 'Pity. She was doing so well. Is she not staying with your nana?'

'We're staying with her noo.'

'Well, tell her we're missing her.'

'Aye.'

'And how's Sean?'

Gerry blushed with embarrassment for a moment. 'We haven't got his release date yet.'

'You should think about coming to school more often, Gerry.'

'Aye.'

With one last smile, the teacher stared at the class who were grouped in an untidy circle.

'Ah divven't want to dee owt the day me, man Miss,' challenged a girl.

'And why is that, Lucy?'

''Cos ah'm fucking pissed off, that's why.'

The corridors were deserted. Looking for his class, Gerry wandered freely through the depths of the school. He stared through the little windows of classroom doors, searching for familiar faces. 'Gerry man! Gerry!' welcomed the inmates of Year Eight Set Seven as he passed them. Getting up from their seats they thronged to the door. The teacher got up too. Through the window Gerry could see his lips moving, but he couldn't hear his voice. He walked on. Heads poked round the corner of the opened door calling him back. 'Areet, Gerry!' they shouted. 'Been takin' any more dogs for a walk roond the Metro Centre lately?'

'Get back in,' the teacher begged. 'Get back in please.'

'Get back in,' the class responded, parodying their teacher's soft voice into a lamb's bleat. 'Get bbbbaaaack in please. Baaa!'

On the top floor of the main building Gerry encountered a boy and a girl sitting on the step outside one of the Science rooms. He had already walked past when he stopped and came back. 'Areet,' he offered, smiling uncertainly.

'Hello,' the girl replied stiffly.

'Been hoyed oot?' started Gerry pleasantly.

'No. We were feeling ill,' the girl informed him coldly. The boy looked up and then dropped his head into his hands with a groan.

'Ah see,' considered Gerry. 'Top set, are ye? Both from Whickham?' The girl and boy looked at him and nodded. Gerry glanced up and down the corridor surreptitiously before pulling out the books. 'D'ye want to buy a book?' he asked.

'No thanks,' the girl responded.

'Ha'way, look at them first, man,' coaxed Gerry. Unwillingly the girl accepted the books. 'Now that's beautiful,' he breathed, fingering the cover of the first book. 'Just what ye need, man.'

'Why should I want a Complete Spanish dictionary when we don't even do Spanish?' The girl handed back the dictionary.

Gerry took it with an injured air. 'Well, hinny, ye might want to gan to Spain on yer holidays. How ye gannae pull the Diego lads if you divven't kna the lingo? Anyway, have a look at this, d'yous dee Art?' he asked, thrusting another volume under their noses.

The girl turned the pages of the immense History of Art book. 'Not like this,' she replied, frostily scanning the gaudy pictures. The boy began coughing loudly, looking up at the door behind them.

'Hold on,' soothed Gerry. 'One last one. Here, it's a hardback. A classic. See, it says Everyman's Classic, *A Sportsman's Notebook.*'

'What's it about?' asked the boy, taking it.

'Em . . . football,' replied Gerry. 'Kev Keegan wrote it before he left the toon.'

'It says Ivan on the spine.'

'Ivan?'

'Ivan Turgenev.'

'O aye. He helped him. They all have helpers when they're writing books. Y'kna Ivan Turkeyoff. Used to play for Bulgaria. Or was it Romania? One of the two. Y'kna the gadgie. Canny player, looked like a fish but.'

'How much?' asked the boy.

Gerry smiled brilliantly. 'What ye got, bonny lad?'

'I'll give you five dinner tickets.'

'Ha'way, ah can get them free, man.'

'Well . . .'

Just then the door behind them began to open. Quick as a flash Gerry gathered his books back into their plastic bag and disappeared down the corridor. 'How are you two feeling now?' asked a sympathetic voice. Gerry scuttled through a little-used fire door.

After searching for the class for about a quarter of an hour, Gerry found a chair at the end of a long corridor. He sat down. A class could be heard chanting in a foreign language. Somewhere in the distance, a teacher was screaming dementedly. Gerry stared at the walls of the corridor, reading posters about the harmful effects of cigarette smoking. Listlessly, he drummed his fingers on the books, which he rested on his knees. From time to time he smoothed the new material of his jumper, feeling its texture uncertainly. Suddenly a door was flung open at the far end of the corridor, and a figure emerged. The figure began walking towards Gerry with a steady, certain step that echoed loudly in the corridor. It was squat and thickset. Jumping to his feet, Gerry bolted. But the plastic carrier bag gave way with the sudden movement, and the books clattered the ground. In the quiet that fell after the books, Gerry could hear the footsteps quickening behind him. Feverishly he gathered up the books, but it was too late. When he straightened, Mr Caird was standing over him. His face was puce. 'Gerard Macarten, get into my office now!' he barked.

Gerry looked up and down the corridor. 'Ha'way, man Sir.'

'Don't you man me, Gerard Macarten!' Mr Caird spluttered.

Wearily Gerry set off. Mr Caird was directly behind him. His steps bore down on Gerry like machine-gun fire. 'Right,' Mr Caird told him, sweeping him into his room. 'Let's get this clear before we begin. You still owe me a ten-page essay from last term. Have you done it?' Sitting behind his desk Mr Caird stared up imperiously at Gerry, his heavy hands poised before him like two crabs.

Gerry searched his memory. 'Yes,' he replied.

'What?'

'Aye, ah've done it.'

'Yes, Sir. Sir. Yes, Sir,' corrected Mr Caird, his hands inching sideways and then back again. 'Let's try that again. Have you done the essay?'

'Yes, Sir.'

'That's better. Have you got it with you?'

'It was last term.'

'I'm not interested in when it was. Have you got the ten-page essay you owe me with you now?'

'No. No, Sir.'

Mr Caird's fingers tensed threateningly like claws. 'Then I must remind you that it's a school rule that you cannot attend normal lessons when there are punishments outstanding. Bring it tomorrow morning. Is that understood?'

'Yes.'

'Let's try that again,' said Mr Caird his hands suddenly scuttling a few inches over the desk towards Gerry. 'Do you understand what I am telling you?'

'Yes, Sir.'

'That's better. Now. I need hardly remind you about the school's policy on uniform. Your uniform is incorrect.'

'It's new, Sir.'

'I don't care about that. Are you aware that your uniform is incorrect or must I run through the school's policy on uniforms for you?'

There was a soft, uncertain knock. A few seconds later the door opened and a spectacled face popped round it. A tie and shirt collar followed the face, then a jacket, then the rest of the suit. 'Sorry to bother you, Mr Caird,' began the intruder, smiling obsequiously. 'I've got the three copies of that list you wanted.'

'Right,' allowed Mr Caird grudgingly, not taking his eyes from Gerry.

'Can I give them to you please? It's an amendment of the earlier lists I made.'

'Put them in my in-tray then, Mr Brown,' Mr Caird snapped, gesturing irritably, his fingers catching at the in-tray and sending it flipping over on his desk top.

'Right then, Mr Caird,' replied the intruder nervously. He placed his carefully word-processed pieces of paper beside the dislodged in-tray and then, having backed away to the door as though he feared Mr Caird might lunge at him if he turned, he left.

Without looking away from Gerry's face, Mr Caird's hands considered the pieces of paper. They approached them cautiously, dabbing at them with an index finger. Abruptly, they scooped them up between the pincher of thumb and forefinger and, having considered them for a while, dragged them down into the lair of a drawer. 'What are we going to do with you?' Mr Caird began again. 'Despite people like you, this is the best school in the area. We've received recommendations. Just look at the walls in here!' he exclaimed. 'Look at all those lists. They're not just here to paper the wall, you know. Each list covers a different Year group Set, their Subject and Agreed Teacher Action Plan. It's taken months to work it all out. Do you know what that means? Do you?' Mr Caird's hands reappeared on his desk, emerging from the drawer as though from under a rock. 'It means that I won't have the likes of you spoiling the smooth running of this school. Do you hear? I won't have you ruining my lists.'

Suddenly stopping, Mr Caird drew breath, gulping at the air, his teeth working around his lips as though he were trying to swallow himself. Gerry looked at his face. He was getting even redder. 'I know what you're like, Macarten. Oh yes. Make no mistake.' Without warning, his voice dropped to a whisper: 'Where were you on the evening of June twenty-first? Well then?' His eyes hardened. 'I know it was you, man. You and that fat kid I expelled. I cannet prove it, but I can make yer life here a misery!' Mr Caird launched himself out of his seat and towered over Gerry. 'It's kids like you who give us a bad name. Give the whole area a bad name. I need you to conform. I need something which will hurt you enough to get you to conform to our rules. But what will that be? What can I use as a lever to keep you in place? You've been away for months, owing me a ten-page essay, and now, and now . . . YOU TURN UP IN TRAINERS!'

Gerry looked past Mr Caird's anger to see a familiar face at the window. He gasped with shock. Mr Caird sat down again, sinking into his chair, and his hands flopped on the desk like crabs found dead on the sand at the ebb of the tide. He sighed heavily. Closing his eyes he played his hands into taut fists again, re-animating them. Gerry took another glance at the window. Rusty's face suddenly appeared beside Sewell's as the dog jumped up. 'Why did you come back?' began Mr Caird again.

Gerry hid the smirk on his face. 'To learn things, Sir.'

'You expect me to believe that?' Mr Caird scoffed. 'Anyway. I don't want you here. I don't want you ruining our position in the league tables of achievement. What do you say to that?'

Gerry checked himself. Through the corner of his eye he saw Sewell bouncing into view, followed by Rusty, as though they were on a trampoline. 'Ah want to be here, Sir. Just for a little while. Two weeks mebbes.'

'What on earth do you mean by that?'

'A trial period, y'kna, Sir. Ye could give wor a trial period of two weeks.'

Mr Caird blinked craftily. 'You like Drama, don't you?'

Gerry nodded.

'Well, what if I had you out of every Drama lesson to write out the school rules? Just the relevant ones, the ones that you can never seem to remember. Would that hurt you?'

Rusty barked. Sewell laughed. Mr Caird stared speculatively at the lists on the wall. 'Well, don't just stand there looking out of the window. Would it hurt you?'

Gerry bit back his laughter. 'No, Sir. Ah mean yes, Sir.'

'What's so fascinating through that window?' demanded Mr Caird, swivelling round. Gerry nodded urgently at Sewell, who disappeared just in time. 'Well? What's so interesting there?' Mr Caird added just as Rusty bounced into view.

'There's a dog jumping up and doon ootside, Sir.'

'I can see that,' barked Mr Caird, lowping up out of his chair and banging his fat knuckles against the window. 'Clear off,' he ordered. 'Dogs are not allowed on the school premises.'

Mr Caird went back to his desk and sat for a whole minute as though deep in thought. 'Right then,' he said with an air of finality. 'You go home now. Come back in the proper uniform, with the ten-page essay plus another four pages for wearing trainers . . .'

'Eh!'

'Plus another two pages for answering back.'

'But these are the only shoes ah've got.'

'The school rules state that pupils must wear regulation black shoes. It's all in here.' Mr Caird reached down for a huge file, fat with word-processed documents. 'Uniform, pages four to six,' he crowed triumphantly, hammering his thumbs against the pages. 'All pupils must wear regulation black shoes.' His face glowed with triumph. 'So off you go then. I have some lists to see to.'

As Gerry turned to the door Mr Caird coughed for his attention. 'What do you say to the conditions attached to my allowing you to return?'

Gerry bit his tongue. 'Yes,' he nodded. 'Yes, Sir.'

Exhaling with satisfaction Mr Caird began sorting through a mountain of paper.

Sewell and Rusty were waiting at the school gate. Rusty launched himself up at Gerry, barking excitedly. 'Caird dee yer heed in?' Sewell asked. Gerry handed him the books with a shake of his head.

'The next two weeks are gonnae be the longest of me life,' he said. 'But when ah'm in this hell-hole, ye'll be oot earning money.'

'Deein' what?' asked Sewell.

'Owt. But if ah'm gonnae be suffering, then so are ye. Besides, Sewell, ah cannet wait any longer. We've got to get wor Season Ticket in the bag. Ah swear doon. What else is there withoot them?'

7

Winter arrives over Gateshead with a vengeance. The rain falls day after day, saturating even the concrete. The wind, sharpening itself on the jagged masonry of boarded-up houses and broken bottles, wields itself across the borough, slashing at the stunted trees and wire fences, harrying plastic carrier bags and people up the streets. Nothing can keep out the wind and rain. No hat. No coat. No walls. Then one night it stops blowing, the sky clears and the pavements become sheets of ice. Breath spumes like car exhausts. The whole of Gateshead freezes and grows brittle and white. Then after three days of ice, the rain and wind come back, churning the ground into deep clarts of mud and whetting the air into a razor again. December: Rain. Wind. Rain. Wind. January: Ice. Wind. Rain. Wind. Rain. February: Snow. Wind. Sleet. Wind. Rain. Wind. Wind. Wind.

And there is nowhere the winds blow quite so much as the once-wetlands around the Metro Centre. They rail at the invasion of buildings, ghosting over the two concrete platforms of the railway station, which lie there, parallel to the tracks, like a pair of fallen monoliths from an earlier era.

'Ha'way, man Sewell,' said Gerry as the train pulled in. 'This is us.' The electronic doors shuddered open. Sewell followed Gerry on to the train. 'Ah telt yus not to bring the hoond,' said Gerry.

'And ah telt ye, where ah gan, he gans,' replied Sewell. Prowling down both carriages, they took up the last table. Sewell sat opposite Gerry. Rusty jumped into the window seat. 'He likes the view,' explained Sewell. Then he sighed.

Gerry snorted with frustration. 'For the last time, will ye cheer up?'

Sewell crossed his arms. 'Well, aye,' he growled at last.

'Well aye what?'

'It's bad enough getting chilled to the bone standing on that friggin' platform, but then this . . .'

'Then what? Say it, bugger lugs. Ye've been twining aboot it all bloody day. Anyway, at least ye had a bench coat and a layer o' fat to keep ye warm.' Two electronic pulses sounded, and the train began to move off.

'It's not that, man.'

'What is it then?'

'Ye kna, man Gerry man.'

'Tell wor then.' The guard had begun collecting tickets. 'And ye'll have to pay a half for that dog's fare.'

Sewell pursed his lips with a superior air. Then, taking off his bench coat, he clapped his hands. 'Gan to groond,' Sewell whispered to the dog. Immediately Rusty jumped under the seats, and crawled into the place for luggage. Sewell concealed him with his coat. Then sighed again.

'Ye're deein' me heed in ye are,' said Gerry.

'Ah cannet help it.'

'Just tell wor what is it!'

'It's . . .'

'Aye.'

'It's aboot today, man.'

'What aboot it? Ah thought ye'd have liked to gan to a cup match.'

'Aye, ah would.'

'Ah did two weeks in that hell-hole for this, man Sewell.'

'Aye, ah kna, but . . .'

'But what?'

'It's not that it's a cup match. It's where the match is, man Gerry. Anywhere else. Ah mean anywhere else in the whole world.'

'Tickets please,' put in the conductor, who had arrived at their table.

'Two returns,' said Gerry. 'To Sunderland.'

'Sun'lun'!' Sewell moaned as the conductor walked away. 'Why aye, man! Sun'lun'.'

Gerry scowled. 'It's not my fault me social worker knas nowt aboot football. Ah mean d'yus think ah would have suffered for two whole weeks if ah'd knan it was to gan and see the friggin' Mackems? Well and truly bloody stitched up. Two tickets to gan and watch Sun'lun'.'

The train lurched over the railway bridge. Gerry leant over to look down. A hundred feet below, the river ran over its muddy bed. Behind them the massive span of the Redheugh road bridge joined Gateshead and Newcastle in a vast platform of concrete. And between the Redheugh and the colossal steel arc of the Tyne bridge, the low-lying swing bridge stood like a pontoon. Rusty began to bark. 'Who shook his cage?' Gerry asked.

'Doesn't like being shut oot o' things,' replied Sewell. 'He's awer sociable.' He clapped his hands. 'Coast's clear.' Rusty emerged and, wagging his tail, jumped back into his window seat.

Rolling into Newcastle station, Sewell suddenly tutted.

'Look,' snapped Gerry. 'It's not as if we're gonnae watch them play or owt. We're only gannin' to Sun'lun' to sell the tickets to get money for wor real ones. Divven't look at us like that, man. Anyroad, what were ye deein' when ah was sweating in that school? How much did ye earn? Eh, tell wor the grand total.'

'Neeone wants their back gardens cutting in winter, man.'

'Well, ye should have come up with summink else then.'

'Ah did!' Sewell suddenly burst. 'Ah'd like to see ye shift one hundred and twenty pot ponies in two weeks. Couldn't give them away, man. Specially since these had friggin' three ears! Like summink from a freak show. Then when ah chipped the extra ear off, why ah had to take fifty pence off the price, 'cos noo ah was dealing with shop-soiled, wasn't ah?'

Gerry bit his lip. 'With or withoot three ears, they look aboot as much like ponies as ye dee, Sewell man. Divven't kna what they are me. Just lumps o' pot. Aye well, divven't think they can stay in me room for ever. There's nee room to swing a cat there in the first place.'

'Divven't worry,' said Sewell. 'They're not knocked off. That Macca got wor them cheap from a porschelin factory.'

'Porcelain, ye daft get. Y'kna. China.'

'Aye well, wherivver it was, the mould was knackered.'

Gerry shook his head. Having filled a little with elderly shoppers, the train doubled back on itself over the bridge. Rusty barked again. This time the train turned left and trundled through central Gateshead towards the International Athletics Stadium. Sewell's bottom lip played out petulantly. 'Ah divven't kna why wor have to gan to Sun'lun' at all. Ah mean why divven't we sell them in Newcastle?'

'Because nee bugger'd buy them. And ah divven't want me heed kicked in.'

'We could have sold them in Gatesheed. There's some who support Sun'lun' here.'

'Aye, reet oot in the back of beyond. Leam Lane and up friggin' Stanley way.'

Wrenching itself from one window-rattling rhythm to another, the train pulled in at Heworth station. About a dozen people in red-and-white scarves and hats boarded. Sewell gestured in alarm. 'A load of Mackems have just got on,' he spluttered. Gerry slid in on the seat beside him.

'Reet,' he said, his eyes shifting about cautiously. 'If we want to get oot of this alive then dee as ah say. From now on divven't talk, divven't say a word, leave the talking to me.'

'Eh? Man alive man,' moaned Sewell.

'See? Ye speak pure Geordie. Open yer mouth in Sun'lun' and ye're dead meat.'

'Ha'way, man Gerry ah cannet . . .'

'Shh,' hissed Gerry, clamping his hand over Sewell's mouth. 'Ye stand oot like a sore thumb, man. Look aroond. They're all staring.' Sewell looked up and then down the carriage. 'And get rid of the hoond again. We divven't want to attract any attention.'

The train gasped to a stop. The sign on the platform read East Boldon. The train filled with more people garbed in red and white. 'Say nowt, man,' whispered Gerry, gesturing a cut throat with a forefinger. 'And divven't look so terrified, Sewell man, the Mackems are like dogs, they can sense fear. Wild dogs, man, not like Rusty. They'll turn on ye and rip ye to shreds. And afterwards all we'll find of ye is a few scraps of yer bench coat blowing alang Roker beach.'

When the train left Brokley Whins station it was full. Two Sunderland supporters took the seats opposite Gerry and Sewell. The aisles were packed with standing passengers. The guard tried to squeeze through to inspect the tickets but couldn't. A cigarette was lit, its smoke drifted over the heads of the people. The hum of voices joined with the piston-jolting of the train to create a din of growing expectation. The train stopped at Seaburn. Somebody got off, then hammered on the doors to be let back in. 'Auld habits die hard, man,' he said, squeezing his way back on along with three or four other shoppers. 'Ah keep on thinking we still play at Roker. Forgotten about the new stadium.' 'Ee pet!' laughed an old lady with a blue rinse. 'It's strange with the lads gone from Roker.' Displaced by the new arrival, the line of passengers standing in the aisle shifted down. Two girls came into view and stopped adjacent to Gerry and Sewell. Gerry nudged Sewell. Sewell nudged Gerry. The girls were dressed in short skirts and tracksuit Zappa tops, whose trademark logo of two figures sitting back to back ran down both their arms. The rain, falling freely on the lush slag-heap meadows where Tyneside gives way to Wearside, had soaked the girls. Their hair, trapped in red scrunchies, balanced on their heads like soggy pineapples. Gerry smiled at Sewell. Sewell smiled at Gerry.

'Want to sit doon, pet?' offered Gerry.

Sewell gasped. 'Divven't talk, man,' he hissed from behind a cupped hand.

'Divven't worry,' Gerry whispered back. 'Ah can speak Sun'lun' me. Will ye sit, pet?'

The girls looked at each other and giggled. 'There's norany seats, man.'

'Ah kna,' smiled Gerry, indicating his knee by tapping it with both hands. 'Ye'll find it very comfortable.'

'Ee, worra cheek!' the girls shrieked, turning their back on Gerry. But then the one with the higher miniskirt looked back.

'Got something there for us like?' she quipped, looking Gerry boldly in the eyes.

'Come and have a look, pet,' he offered. 'Mebbes ah've got a present for ye. Ye'll have to unwrap it first but.' The girl laughed. The other girl turned and laughed. Sewell snorted.

'What's the matter with yer mate?' the first girl asked, pointing at Sewell who was grinding his teeth together to keep them closed.

'Oh,' admitted Gerry tapping his head gently. 'He's a bit simple y'kna.'

Sewell choked.

'Ee! Is he mental?' asked the second girl, pulling a piece of chewing gum from her mouth and stretching it out a whole foot in front of her face.

'No, no,' replied Gerry. 'He's just a bit shy that's all.'

'Can he talk?'

'Not really. He can mumble though. And y'kna what?'

'What?' the first girl asked.

'What?' the second girl asked.

Gerry looked around with mock embarrassment and said in a quiet voice. 'Ye should see what he keeps in his bench coat.'

From somewhere under the seats, there was a bark. The girls jumped, giggling loudly. 'That's his way o' saying he likes yus.'

Gerry was suddenly interrupted by a voice calling to him from down the aisle. 'Gerry! Sewell!'

The two girls looked down the aisle and then back to Gerry. 'Looks like yer lass is calling for ye.'

'Ah haven't got a lass, not until ah met ye,' Gerry said, but the voice called out to him again.

'Gerry! Sewell! Areet! Are ye gannin' to Sun'lun'?' With the minimum required for the nodding of a head Gerry indicated that he was. 'Ah'll see ye both on the station then,' the voice added.

Gerry turned back to the two girls but they had turned their backs on him and transferred their attention to two lads dressed in red-and-white tops whose heads were completely shaved apart from a crest of hair that ran lengthways in a stripe. 'It's geet cold when the wind gets up me knickers,' one of the girls was explaining to them.

'Is it Gemma?' strained Sewell, looking up the carriage to where the voice had come from.

'Aye, it's Gemma.'

Sewell blushed.

The train pulled over the Wear bridge. To their left the river deepened at its mouth, and just beyond the Marina's shimmering of yacht masts, the sea chucked itself on to Roker beach in great white rollers. Disappearing into a tunnel, they pulled in at Sunderland station. The girls left escorted by the two lads in red-and-white tops. 'Divven't ye ever dee that to me again,' Sewell thundered, freeing Rusty from the luggage space and putting on his bench coat.

'Shh, man!' warned Gerry. 'We're in the heart of enemy territory.'

Sunderland station is underground; water drips disconsolately down its concrete slab sides. Gemma was waiting by a litter bin. 'Areet,' nodded Gerry.

'Areet, Gerry. Areet, Sewell,' she laughed.

Sewell nodded in return, adding a grunt to his greeting. His eyes scanned her dreamily.

'What are yous doing in Sun'lun'?'

'Well,' began Gerry, pausing to think for a second. 'We've come to visit somebody.'

'Who do yous kna in Sun'lun'?' asked Gemma smiling brightly.

'Em,' hazarded Gerry, pausing again. 'We've come to see Sewell's cousin. Why, a distant cousin y'kna.'

Clenching his fists, Sewell seemed inadvertently to bang into Gerry. Gerry was about to react angrily when some Sunderland supporters walked past. Gerry drew Gemma under the stairs. 'He's a bit upset the day, pet,' he told her. 'This cousin of his isn't too well.' Gemma tutted sympathetically. 'Matter o' fact, he's in a wheelchair.'

'Disabled, is he?' asked Gemma.

Confidentially, Gerry drew Gemma closer. 'Awer fat,' he whispered. 'Cannet get aboot.'

'What's that ye're saying?' demanded Sewell.

'Just explaining how yus're part Mackem,' Gerry explained with a wink. 'Divven't worry, Gemma won't grass on ye.'

Sewell smiled uncertainly and, meeting Gemma's smile, blushed.

'Not been back to school again, Gerry?' Gemma enquired.

Gerry laughed. 'Them two weeks were enough for me.' He fingered the collar of his sweatshirt uncomfortably. 'Anyway, lass, what ye deein' in this neck of the woods?'

Gemma drew herself up to her full height. 'Ah'm meeting someone.'

'Oh aye?'

'Me boyfriend plays ice hockey for Sun'lun'. Ah'm gannin' alang to watch.'

Sewell's face fell. 'Gannin oot with him, are ye?' said Gerry, glancing meaningfully at his friend.

Gemma's face was beatific. 'Today's wor sixth-month anniversary. Look at me ring, man.' Sewell's face fell even further as Gemma held out her engagement finger to show the band of silvery metal.

'Canny,' admired Gerry.

'C . . . Canny,' stammered Sewell.

'He's geet serious aboot it. Getting married the summer after next. Hello, Rusty!' exclaimed Gemma suddenly, bending to stroke Rusty's ears. Sewell brightened a little. Rusty rolled over on his back. Gemma scratched his stomach. Rusty kicked his hind leg out in appreciation.

Gemma smiled at Sewell. 'Ah love dogs me. D'yous?'

Sewell nodded. Gerry spoke thoughtfully, 'They're areet.'

'Ee!' exclaimed Gemma, shaking her head. 'That reminds wor. The dog boy's after ye, Sewell. Thinks Rusty's one o' his. Came roond the hoose asking aboot yus. Ee, is that the time?' Gemma asked suddenly, looking up at one of the digital clocks hanging from the low steel rafters of Sunderland station. 'Ah'd better be gannin'. Cannet keep me man waiting.'

Gerry and Sewell watched her as she smiled, waved and then mounted the concrete stairs up to street level. 'She's lush,' whispered Sewell.

Gemma paused at the top of the stairs. 'And thanks for the donkey, Sewell,' she called down. 'Ah love ornaments me.'

'D'ye really fancy her like?' asked Gerry, suddenly serious.

Sewell stood back in amazement. 'Divven't ye, like?'

'Gemma? Ah was at primary school with her and then St Jude's. Known her for ages, man. Nivver thought aboot fancying her. Dead canny lass but.'

'Na,' stuttered Sewell. 'She isn't a lass. She's a lady.'

Gerry looked at Sewell sympathetically. 'Ye've gone withoot too long, man, ye're getting desperate.'

Sewell exploded angrily. 'Nee wonder ah haven't had a lass for so long when ye've been keeping me at it night and day with the Season Ticket.'

Hushing him and looking around anxiously, Gerry whispered earnestly, 'Are ye regretting it like?'

'Of course not, man Gerry. Ah want the ticket as much as

ye dee. Ah'm just saying that ah haven't even had time to get me hands warm.'

'And ye want to warm them on this Gemma lass?'

'Shut up, man!'

'Eh?'

'Divven't be so mucky, man. Ah fancy Gemma.'

'Aye?'

'Not just for her tits . . .'

'Although ye wouldn't mind toasting yer pinkies on them eh?'

'But for, well . . . for her smile.'

Gerry hooted. His laugh disturbed a pigeon in the rafters. Then he grew serious. 'Forget aboot her in that way. She's hitched to a Sun'lun' ice hockey player. Any road, keep it zipped noo. Not a word, reet? And ye owe the kitty fifty pence for that pot donkey.'

They resurfaced from the station and walked through W.H. Smith's to the main shopping street. The wind hit them like a hammer of ice. Rusty cringed at their heels. Hugging himself, Gerry moved into a doorway by the Bridges Shopping Centre. He looked up at the tower block rising dizzyingly above everything. Tattered on the wind, herring gulls swooped at the overflowing bins on the pedestrianised area, gossiping and bickering, perching on the backs of the empty benches, their roving red eyes and bright yellow beaks gaudy and disconcerting. 'Plan two,' shivered Gerry. 'We cannet try and flog the tickets here. Gemma might see wor. We'll have to gan straight to the groond.'

'Where's that?' whispered Sewell. 'They divven't play at Roker any more, y'kna.'

'Ah kna that, man,' snapped Gerry. 'Ah'm not a total bloody moron. It's called the Stadium of Light.'

'Stadium of Shite more like,' quipped Sewell.

'Reet,' said Gerry clamping Sewell's mouth with his hand. 'From noo on not another word. D'ye hear? Any Mackem hears ye say that, hears a Geordie say that aboot their new stadium, and they'll tear ye from friggin' limb to limb. Ah'm not joshing, man. Ye're hard, Sewell, ah admit that. Ye could easily have me. Ye could easily have most of Gatesheed. But even ye wouldn't stand a flea's fart of a chance cornered by a couple o' hundred Mackems baying for yer blood. DO AH MAKE MESEL' CLEAR? Now get that dog on a lead.'

Red scarves and football tops flowed through the veins and arteries of the city centre towards the football stadium. Joining the general drift Gerry and Sewell soon found themselves re-crossing the Wear bridge. There in the distance they could see the mighty structure of the stadium. 'Wow,' gasped Gerry, involuntarily emitting a low whistle. 'Say what ye like, man Sewell, it's massive. Not as good as St James' of course,' he added quickly but without conviction.

Turning left after the bridge, they followed the crowd through a narrow, high-walled street, passing as they went a caravan with a board tacked over its open hatch with the words New Stadium Pie Shop painted on it in red letters. The letters were unsteady and varying in size as though written by the infant son of the corpulent proprietor. There was an electrical shop too, called New Stadium Appliances. And a sports shop, New Stadium Sports. The narrow lane fed into a vast open space at the centre of which stood the huge stadium like a high-sided island. The tributaries of many other alleys disgorged their people into the same place, flooding the car parks and walkways with red-and-white scarves and hats. The tannoy from the ground could be heard welcoming the crowd.

Gerry looked around uncertainly, standing behind a parked car where the flow of bodies wouldn't drag at them. He looked over his shoulder at the stadium. 'It's belter!' he murmured simply, mesmerised. Sewell said nothing, his eyes were fixed on the third tier of the North Stand which lifts itself up like a stairway above the city. The flow of people began to slacken as more and more entered the ground. Still Gerry and Sewell stood there, barely moving. There was a sudden almighty roar. It quivered on the air like a thousand guns being fired and then grew louder and louder. The guns fired nearer and nearer, until they seemed to be thundering at them from ten yards. 'Ha'way, man,' said Gerry, suddenly springing into life. 'Why divven't we just gan in and watch?'

Sewell nodded. 'Ye come back here at quarter to five,' he said to Rusty, letting him loose.

'Dogs cannet tell the time, man,' laughed Gerry.

Sewell gave him a withering look.

Handing over their tickets to the octogenarian turnstile operator, they began to climb the stairs at the back of the stand. Higher and higher they climbed. Each time a steward stopped them to consult their chitties they were told, 'Higher, lads.'

'How much higher can we gan?' mused Gerry. The teams had just kicked off when the two emerged on the North Stand. Neither of them had ever been so high up. It felt even taller than the top floor of the Dunston Rocket tower block. The players looked like Subbuteo pieces on the distant green baize of the pitch. Gerry and Sewell swayed momentarily with vertigo and then struggled over knees and flasks to their seats.

The stadium was filled to the brim. It rocked and lurched and oohed and ahhed, pulsing in and out of excitement like the waves that roll up the vast arena of Roker beach. The Sunderland centre forward took a shot and there was an explosion of shouted applause. The referee pointed for a corner. 'Not bad,' whispered Gerry, wide-eyed. 'Better than Gatesheed versus Woking anyway. Them red and white colours are deein' me heed in though,' he added, gesturing surreptitiously at the crowd around them.

'Fuck them all, fuck them all,' began the Vaux Stand as the opposing team surged towards it in a flowing, swelling attack, 'Dalgleish, McDermot and Hall.' The chant grew louder, spreading to the rest of the ground until the whole stadium was singing. 'We'll never be mastered by black-and-white bastards, 'cos Sun'lun's the best of them all!' Gerry and Sewell sank lower into their seats. The ball swung in from the corner; a straining group of heads rose to meet it.

'If ye hate Newcastle clap yer hands,' sang the crowd, clapping their hands to the tune of She'll Be Coming Round the Mountain When She Comes. 'If ye hate NEEEWcastle clap yer hands. If ye hate NEEEWcastle, hate NEEEWcastle, if ye hate NEEEWcastle clap yer hands!'

Everybody clapped their hands. Gerry nudged Sewell. Squirming, they clapped half-heartedly.

When Sunderland scored, the stadium erupted like a volcano. Grown men and women hugged each other. Pot bellies rubbed pot bellies. Skinheads danced arm in arm like morris dancers.

'Wise men say,' began the crowd, at its loudest now, 'only fools ruuush in, but ah can't helllp, falling in lurvvvve, wiiiith ye. Sun'lun'! Sun'lun'!'

It was almost half-time and the noise was deafening. 'Ah me lads!' began the crowd, moving from one song to another like a karaoke machine. 'Ye should have seen us gannin'!'

Sewell bristled. 'Ah kna,' said Gerry softly, putting a consoling finger on Sewell's arm. 'Ah forgot to tell ye. They sing that here an' all. Ha'way,' he said, getting up and leading Sewell back across the sea of knees, 'we'll get refreshments.' Sewell looked questioningly. Gerry smiled. 'We've worked hard. Canny hard. We're only halfway there, but that's better than neewhere. We're on course for next season. Anyway, ah want wor to enjoy this moment. Look aboot, Sewell. This is coming to us. Let's get a cup o' tea, bring it back to wor seats, and imagine that this is St James'. That it's next year. And that we've got wor Season Ticket.'

The whistle blew as they reached the refreshment counter that runs the whole length of the concrete concourse behind the stands. 'Give wor,' said Gerry running his eyes lovingly over the menu board, 'two cups o' tea please.'

'Regular or large?'

'Divven't kna, just two cups o' tea, man. Milk and sugar. Lots of it.'

'The sugar's there. And the milks,' the assistant told him,

pointing to a tray with little sachets of sugar and tiny cartons of long-life milk. Gerry took a handful of them and, beckoning Sewell, placed them in his bench coat pockets. He took a second handful. 'Sweet tooth, y'kna!' he smiled at the assistant who was staring at the emptied tray. They took their drinks and stood at the window. Below them the River Wear wound its way through the gaps left by defunct shipyards like a tongue lolling from the toothless mouth of a geriatric. Forlornly the lights of the city began to twinkle. 'Ha'way,' said Gerry. 'Let's take wor tea up.'

They climbed back up the concrete stairs, carrying their refreshments gingerly. 'Oww!' yelped Sewell, as the tea spilt over his knuckles.

'Here are your half-time scores,' announced the Tannoy.

'Here we gan,' remarked Gerry, subtly digging Sewell in the ribs with his elbow. There was an almighty cheer when it was announced that Newcastle United were losing.

'SHIT!' roared Sewell, as they re-emerged on the stand. Hundreds of eyes sought out the strange reaction just as the floodlights burst into life, mercilessly exposing Sewell's open-mouthed grimace.

Gerry scanned about him like a fox. 'Ah kna,' he said loudly, his elbow digging harder this time, 'ah wish they were losin' by more an' all.' Adding in a hissing whisper, 'Ye were within a flea's fart of your life then, man, ye daft get.'

For the next ten minutes the stand was half empty as the people battled their way to the toilets and stood beneath TV monitors in the concourse, supping pints and discussing the match. Gerry and Sewell sat down, the only ones in their row. Gerry shivered contentedly. 'This is it,' he determined, his breath pluming in the cold. 'Sitting here like this. This is it. Just the ticket.' Smiling, Sewell put his elbows out and wriggled to a comfortable position. Gerry edged under the protection of the bench coat sleeve. His eyes were dewy. 'Sewell me auld mate. Next season, this'll be us. Next season.' Sewell beamed as Gerry continued, 'Mebbes we'll even have a couple of seats like these. Of course the football'll be much better like, but still ye get a sense of it here.'

Sewell nodded.

'We're Season Ticket holders,' Gerry announced to an imaginary steward, tapping his breast pocket. 'These are wor seats. Would ye mind moving? We cannet see. Thank ye.'

Sewell laughed.

'Aye, Season Ticket holders!' exclaimed Gerry, raising his plastic tea cup as though it were a chalice. He took a drink, cherishing the mouthful lovingly. 'Listen, Sewell,' he began after a moment, 'ah counted the tin again this morning. We're gonnae get there, son.' There was an appreciative silence as they drank their tea, and gazed over the panoramic sweep of the ground. 'Ha'way, Sewell,' Gerry whispered at length. 'Tell us that thing again.'

Sewell looked puzzled.

'Ye kna, man,' encouraged Gerry looking about. 'Aboot the time yer auld man took ye to see Newcastle play.'

'Why d'yus always want to hear that, man?'

Gerry shrugged his shoulders. 'Nee reason. Ah just like it, that's all. Ha'way. We'll tret worselves to a tab as ye speak.'

'Well, it was years agan,' began Sewell, taking out a large pinch of tobacco from a crumpled packet, and rolling it in a paper. 'And ah was a . . .'

'Pure bairn,' interceded Gerry. 'Knee-high to a grass-hopper.'

Nodding, Sewell lit the cigarette and, cupping it in his hand, brought it towards his mouth between sips of his tea. Gerry sat back and holding his tea in both hands, nursed the polystyrene lovingly in his palms. Sewell spoke with uncharacteristic fluency. 'Ah remember the coat he used to wear. And the way he looked after wor. Once, y'kna, he even lifted wor straight up on to the tea coonter 'cos ah was too small. We always had tea. In polystyrene cups. He would hold mine for us. So ah didn't scald mesel'.'

Gerry turned to him dreamily. 'Was it the best day of yer

148

life?' They got up to let a man pass. 'Sewell,' murmured Gerry when they had sat down again and been undisturbed for a while in silence. 'This is me first match. Ah've nivver even seen the toon play, me.'

'Ah kna that,' replied Sewell softly. 'Ye daft cunt.'

The rest of the game flashed by them in a mystifying, dizzying swirl of noise and colour. Sunderland won two-nil. Rusty was waiting obediently at the exit gate, braving the current of shoes and legs flowing against him, sniffing out each pair for the right one. He rolled over in extravagant joy when Gerry and Sewell finally appeared. They wandered back over the bridge, three silent figures in an ecstatic horde. 'Gerry,' Sewell asked as they walked down the steps into an underpass, 'd'ye think the toon came back?'

'Shh!' Gerry hissed, taking the steps two at a time to get back on to street level. Picking up their pace, they fell in behind a woman who held a transistor radio crushed to her ear. 'Excuse me, pet,' said Gerry. 'D'y'kna the Newcastle score?'

The woman half turned and peered suspiciously over the transistor. Then she smiled. 'Two-one,' she said. 'YES!' she added, punching the air with her free hand.

'Yes!' agreed Gerry.

'Yes!' copied Sewell jubilantly.

Gerry pulled Sewell round a corner. 'What ye deein', man?' he demanded.

'Two-one, man,' breathed Sewell excitedly.

'Who to?'

'Eh?'

'Two-one, who to? Think aboot it. That auld wifie's a Mackem. She wouldn't be cheering us, would she? We lost, you daft get.'

Getting back on the train they continued to maintain a silence. Station by station, through the old colliery land, the train shed its blood of red-and-white Sunderland supporters. Brokley Whins. East Boldon. After Heworth there were none left.

'Canny good that,' said Sewell, safe at last from the dangers of his accent.

'Aye,' agreed Gerry.

'Terrible football, mind.'

'Shocking.'

'But still.'

'Aye.'

'Great ground like.'

'Not a bad atmosphere.'

'Nee football like.'

'All kick and rush.'

'Still.'

'Aye.'

'Ye lads been to watch Sun'lun'?' the man sitting opposite them asked. He was dressed in a titfer hat and mackintosh. Pushing back his glasses which had slipped down his nose, he repeated his question in mild tones.

'Aye,' admitted Gerry at last, having looked around to see that there was no one within earshot.

'Canny ground but.'

'It's areet.'

'Ah used to gan in the auld days with Len Shackleton, y'kna,' he told them.

'Oh aye?' remarked Gerry.

The man smiled to himself. 'Roker Park was always full then. Never any trouble though. Ye just all stood together. There was no home or away fans. All laughing and shouting together. If anyone swore ye just said: Hey, nee swearing, man, there's ladies present! And d'y'kna what? That soon shut him up.' Dreamily the man pushed back his glasses again. 'Them days are gone now but,' he added with a sigh.

Lurching drunkenly from side to side the train passed into the environs of Gateshead and then Gateshead proper. The streetlights threw their jaundiced tint over the streets and lower floors of the tower blocks. Gerry and Sewell stared out of the windows. Rusty stirred in his place in the luggage storage and shifted positions. 'Ye from Sun'lun', lads?' the man asked, taking his glasses off now and wiping them with a handkerchief. His eyes blinked feebly like a mole's.

'Na,' Gerry answered.

The man cast his smile over Gerry and Sewell. 'Cannet get in at St James' eh? Divven't worry, it'll be the same at Sun'lun' soon.' He put his glasses on again. Slowly they slipped down his nose. 'Ye've got to be Season Ticket holders to see them Magpies now. Ah divven't bother with football any more me. Not watching it anyway. Ah see who's playing at home. Sun'lun' mostly, Newcastle sometimes, Boro, Hartlepool, Darlington, even Carlisle now and again, then ah get the train and go to the ground and walk roond it during the match. Listening to the crowd and that. Following the game by the noise of the crowd. Ah get free rail travel, ye see. Worked for British Rail for awer forty years. Not called British Rail any more now but. Na. Ah divven't bother with watching football. Ah just wander roond and roond ootside.'

Having come to a shuddering stop, the train pulled away again. The man, having talked his head down so that his chin was nearly on his chest, pulled himself upright again. The glasses, balancing on the very tip of his nose, were pushed expertly back. 'Aye,' he continued, 'it's Season Ticket holders only at the toon. But that's not enough. Not even a Season Ticket's enough nowadays. Is that a dog I can hear under there, big lad?' the man asked, leaning under Sewell's seat to look.

'What d'ye mean?' asked Gerry, sitting bolt upright. 'A Season Ticket's not enough?'

The man looked at Gerry with a sympathetic and vigorous shake of his head that completely confused his glasses which were already anticipating the usual downward motion. 'There's a waiting list. Seventeen thoosand are on it. Ye cannet just buy a Season Ticket, expensive as that is, but ye've got to buy a bond too. And who knas how much they'll charge when there's this new Euroleague.'

Gerry's eyes widened with panic. 'Eh? What d'ye mean, bonds?'

'A bond, bonny lad. Ye've got to buy a bond. Otherwise ye'll be on the waiting list until kingdom come. Costs a packet mind. More than the Season Ticket itself. The thing is, they want ye to pay twice. According to them buggers it's so ye can guarantee yer place for ten year. Is it hell, man. It's to get ye off the waiting list.'

Creaking over the bridge, the train pulled in at Central Station. It wasn't going on to the Metro Centre. Sewell and Gerry got off. 'Ah thought ye had a dog there,' smiled the man as he wandered off down the platform.

They walked from the station down to the Quayside, the city's crumbling relic of a proud maritime past. 'Dog Leap Stairs!' remarked Sewell to Gerry, pointing at a narrow flight of almost vertical steps.

'Pack it in,' ordered Gerry grimly.

It had grown colder, and the wind was sharpening. They crossed over into Gateshead on the swing bridge, the cormorants, silhouettes hanging their wings out to dry on the wooden barriers, staring after them. They turned past the Ovoline Lubricants factory, sliding on the pavement down which the oil runs into the Tyne. They walked on silently, into the darkness. Every so often Sewell let out an immense sigh, but Gerry kept obdurately silent. As they crossed a piece of waste ground, the grass was already brittle with the frost. Following the river, they passed grimly under the bridges, hearing the redshanks jumping occasionally into their noisy warning flights. When they entered the Teams the orange lights of the lampposts were thick with falling sleet. 'Ha'way,' begged Sewell, at last shaking the flakes from his head. 'We can still save for a bond.'

Gerry stopped abruptly. His teeth were chattering. 'Na. We'll nivver be able to afford a one o' them an' all each.'

'Ye nivver kna,' offered Sewell, but his voice was feeble.

Gerry shook his head. 'It's over, man Sewell. Cannet ye see? It's all awer.'

They parted at the head of Gerry's street. 'See ye tomorrow,' Sewell waved.

'Aye,' replied Gerry without conviction.

'You'll see,' pleaded Sewell. 'Summink'll turn up. It'll be areet. You'll see. You'll make it happen. Ye always dee.'

Gerry watched Sewell and Rusty picking their way through the sleet, over the football pitches and on to the waste ground where the travellers sometimes camp. He stood there until his friend and dog had crossed the concrete bridge, and there was nobody left to look at. Then he turned and went his way. The clouds were lowering over Gateshead. In one of the houses a marriage was dissolving into drunken voices and threats. There was no one else on the freezing streets.

When he was still twenty yards away Gerry could see that his front door had been left open. He narrowed his eyes. There were no lights on in the house. Arriving at the door he realised that it had been forced, practically wrenched off its hinges. 'Clare?' he called out, pushing his face through the opening. 'Mam?' he added uncertainly. 'Sean?' he ventured, slowly entering the dark living room. The room was cold, with an unattended damp smell, as though no one had been home all day. 'Is Nana aboot?' he heard himself ask, his voice sounding strange in the empty house. He hovered cautiously at the doorless opening; a tap dripped, its drop echoing eerily in the basin which must have been slowly filling from this leak all day. 'Bridget?' he appealed. 'Bridie?'

In the kitchen, the sink taps waited in the gloom like skeletal hands; he went over and silenced their dripping. In the sitting room, the settee crouched in the darkness under the grey outline of the uncurtained window, slightly yellowed at its centre by a street-lamp, the only one not broken on the street. 'Bridget?' Gerry's voice was louder now. Then he stiffened. From upstairs there was a rustle, a slight noise as of the ceiling creaking under the pressure of a foot shifting position on a floorboard. He looked up. It was coming from Bridget's room.

He climbed the stairs silently, steadying himself by flattening the palm of each hand against the walls. All the doors were closed. Except for Bridget's. Hers was open a crack. He paused for a moment for his heart to quieten, but it pulsed even more. His head too seemed to throb. Losing his balance on the top stair, he just managed to stop himself from falling. He walked over to Bridget's door on the balls of his feet and gently pushed it open. The room was pitch-dark. It took him a while to get used to it. Gradually his vision returned. The cupboard was open and its contents scattered all over the floor. Suddenly there was the flare of a match from the bed and a puff as it was applied to a cigarette. Someone was sitting on Bridget's bed. For a while, all Gerry could see was the red tip of the cigarette. 'Ha'way, man Bridie, ah kna it's ye, man.'

'Areet, Gerry.'

Gerry froze. The throbbings of his heart and head stopped abruptly. An eerie, terrible, stifling silence took their place. Slowly, a silhouette was sketching itself around the glowing cigarette end. A head, shoulders, body. Gerry closed his eyes and then opened them again. The stale stench of alcohol and sweat lay heavily on the air.

'Come here, son, and say hello to yer auld man.'

Beside his father on the bed Gerry could see Bridget's box. The one in which she kept all her important possessions. A small container. A shoe box. Its lid had been pulled back, its few contents scattered on the mattress. A comic, a fan of magazines, a hairbrush, a bundle of school exercise books and, resting on his father's lap, a picture of the Sacred Heart of Jesus. The picture showed a brown-haired, blue-eyed Christ tenderly throwing his arms out for an embrace; sunlight seemed to stream through his body, a huge red heart beat in his breast. On the back of the picture these words were printed: To Bridget on Your First Holy Communion, love Mam and Dad.

Gerry took a step back and felt for the door. He stumbled on an unseen object. Fighting a feeling of awful foreboding, he looked down. It was his jar, standing where it had rolled into a corner. He touched it with his foot. It had been smashed. Among the pieces of shattered glass was the odd coin. 'Ye bastard,' said Gerry quietly.

The cigarette end glowed in the dark. 'Divven't be a prick all yer life, man,' his father said calmly.

Gerry rolled his hands into fists, clenching them until the knuckles whitened.

'Why didn't yus fuckin' tell us, man Gerry?' his father suddenly demanded, his voice thick and maudlin. Desperate. 'Why didn't none of yous tell wor where yus were living? Me own flesh and blood, and not a word to us. Nee wonder ah got a bit angry.'

Gerry took another step back as his father stirred from the bed. 'What's happened?' he asked.

'Yer mam's back in hospital, son.' Gerry watched his father slowly approach. The cigarette, glowing off and on as he exhaled and inhaled, reminded Gerry of the light of the ambulance which had taken his mother to hospital that dreadful day. His head began to throb as though a siren was wailing in the room. Gerry threw his hands over his ears to block out the insistent clamouring, but his father prised them off. The siren and light immediately faded, leaving him helpless to the invasion of a different, even worse din, the gravel of his father's voice. 'Divven't worry, it's not the usual thing. Not too serious. She's had a little accident. Fell doon the stairs or summink. Lucky ah did find the hoose actually. Otherwise she'd still be lying where ah foond her. Wouldn't she?'

8

When does spring come to Gateshead? March, April, May? Sometimes, never. Only a gradual gentling of the rain; a brief blunting of the wind's knife.

Around February and March the grey eyes of Gateshead yearn for better months, faces are ashen as concrete, and it seems that winter will last for ever. Then in the night, unseen, shoots begin to stir in the black soil of the municipal flower beds, and one morning, behind the Spartan Redheugh factory and on the waste ground, the sallow scrub is found burning with a green flame. It is from here that the fire of spring spreads, relighting the sun with the crackle of chiffchaffs and the willow warbler.

'It's great news but, isn't it? Eh? Isn't it?' garbled Sewell excitedly. 'Ha'way, man, isn't it great news?'

The metro train was speeding towards the coast. Its yellow body harmonised with the clear blue of the Easter day. It was one of those rare glorious spring days.

'Ah cannet believe it mesel' like,' Sewell continued to chunter delightedly. 'Just think aboot it, Gerry. They're building another tier on the Milburn Stand at St James'. Increasing the capacity to fifty-one thousand. Fifty-one thousand! We won't need a bond. We'll just be able to buy wor Season Ticket straight oot. Isn't that belter, Gerry? Eh? Eh?'

Gerry shifted in his seat uneasily, his elbow resting on one of the cardboard boxes stacked high around them. 'Got to get rid o' these friggin' pot ponies first.'

Sewell beamed. 'Easy money. Brainwave, wasn't it? Mebbes it's me that's the brains noo, man Gerry.'

'Divven't coont yer chickens before they hatch.'

'Eh?'

'We divven't kna whether they'll take them yet, Sewell.'

'Course they will, man. Whitley Bay's full of amusements and stalls. Stuff like this, why it's just what they want.'

'Who'd want to win a three-eared donkey?'

'They're ponies, man. And they haven't got three ears any more. Not all o' them anyway. Ye'll see. Someone'll take them as a job lot.'

'Aye well, Sewell. Just as lang as we find a buyer quickly. Divven't want to spend all day lugging this tackle aboot.'

'What is it with ye, Gerry? Ye've been doon for ages.' Moving one of the boxes, Sewell edged slightly nearer to his friend. 'Ha'way, what's the matter with yus? Yer mam's getting better. Yus've all shifted, and she likes the new hoose. And once we get shot o' this stuff, why, there'll be nee stopping wor. In fact, mebbes we can gan straight from Whitley Bay and get wor Season Tickets.'

Gerry looked at Sewell as though he were far away. 'Aye, mebbes.'

Sewell brightened. 'Your Sean'll be getting oot soon an' all.'

'Sewell.'

'And ye nivver kna, Bridie might show up.'

'Listen to us.'

'Ah kna we haven't got all we need yet, but we're well and truly on wor way.'

'Sewell man, ah've got summink to tell ye.'

There was a roar of laughter from a crowd a few seats behind Gerry and Sewell. The sweetly acrid smell of cannabis wafted down the carriage. 'Soon we can gan back on the good things of life too,' smiled Sewell, breathing in the smoke fondly. Rusty sneezed and licked his lips reproachfully at the smoke. Folding his hands over his stomach and putting his feet up on a stack of boxes, Sewell ruminated, 'Ah cannet believe we've gone withoot for so long. Does yer heed in at times mind. First thing we'll dee after we've got wor Season Tickets is buy a load of tac and get some cans. We'll get mortal, man. Pure radgie.' Sewell's eyes glazed over. Miming smoking a joint while simultaneously drinking from a can, he tapped Gerry on the shoulder. 'A bit tac, man. A bit drink.' But still there was no response. Sewell sighed and, bending down, busied himself with Rusty for a while. When he uprighted himself he was smiling again, and there was a faraway look in his eyes. 'Mebbes ye're reet, mebbes we should wait until after the first match. Aye, that's it. After wor first match with the tickets we'll gan hyem and get totally peeved. Completely wrecked. Smashed. Mortal. Pissed and stoned as farts.'

'For godsake man, there is nee Season Tickets. There nivver will be!' Gerry's voice rang out like a bell.

'Eh?' stammered Sewell. 'We'll get a one each next season. They're making the groond bigger. There's nee need for a bond. The pot ponies . . .'

'Me auld man, he took it.' The words wrenched themselves painfully from his mouth. 'He foond the tin and took the money. We've got next to nowt, Sewell. It was just after the Sun'lun' match. All we've got left is what we've managed to get since. The proceeds of aboot five o' these.' Helplessly, Gerry kicked a box. 'It's not enough, man.'

Silence seemed to seize the carriage. The blood drained from Sewell's face. Rusty's tail hid itself between his legs. The metro train stopped at Whitley Bay and all the passengers got off. Only Gerry and Sewell stayed put as though paralysed.

'H . . . h . . . how?' stammered Sewell at last.

'He found it in Bridie's wardrobe.'

'Why didn't ye tell us sooner?'

'Ah couldn't.'

Sewell's face crumpled. 'There's summink else ah need to tell ye an' all,' began Gerry.

The train stopped again. Gerry stood up mechanically and, pressing the button, stepped out through the electric door. 'Tynemooth,' he read from one of the signs. 'We'd better get oot here. Ye hold the door.'

'What aboot the boxes?' Sewell said.

Gerry shrugged. 'Why bother noo?'

'Gan and get them,' ordered Sewell abruptly. 'Ah'll hold it up.' Sewell jammed the electronic doors with a foot. Sighing, Gerry went back on the metro train, scurrying box after box on to the platform.

'Ah'm sick o' carrying this lot,' Gerry said, after the train had finally departed. 'Not that it matters.'

'We'll take some o'them, and leave the rest hidden to come back for,' decided Sewell, stacking the boxes beside a gritting box.

'Aye, at least neeone'll twoc them,' muttered Gerry.

'Why not?'

'Who'd be stupid enough to dee that?'

Toiling under their burden, eventually they reached the beach. The sea was spread out before them, blue and vast as the sky. People were paddling in the water, their faces screwed up as though they were being tortured, as though they had forgotten that the North Sea is always cold. All around, children were shouting, and sandcastles were being constructed. Rusty ran delightedly across the sand. 'Ah just cannet, cannet, CANNET believe it!' Sewell repeated like a mantra. Gerry was silent, his eyes fixed on the sand as though searching for treasure. 'Believe it ... believe it ... ah just CANNET believe it!' exclaimed Sewell endlessly, shaking his head. 'Ye nivver told us all this time.'

'How ye.' Gerry beckoned a bather half-heartedly. 'Want a souvenir?' Taking one of the pot ponies, he held it out. 'For yer lass like.'

'What is it?' asked a bodybuilder whose shoulders measured a full yard across.

'A pony.'

'Looks more like a camel.'

Sewell and Gerry climbed up from the beach and, passing the old priory ruins, the road dipped again. In silence they began to walk along the pier, a concrete arm which extends into the sea for half a mile or so, terminating in a lighthouse, perfectly mirrored by its double across the bay in South Shields. At their backs the kittiwakes seethed on the cliffs, vying for space in the precipitous cavities, calling out their own name to each other in a cacophonous symphony. Sewell picked up Rusty, Gerry struggled with the boxes, and they climbed down a metal ladder to the old railway track, which runs on a ledge just above the water. A flock of turnstones ran before them. 'Gerry man, are ye sure there's an amusements at the end o' this?' asked Sewell.

Gerry did not answer.

They passed the anglers, strung out over about fifty yards in twos and threes, leaning against the railing. 'So he took haad of it,' one of them was saying as they walked by. 'Grabbed it, y'kna, and smashed it against the wall. Didn't even blink. It was a real monster, man. So he hoyed it back in . . .'

At the end of the pier, they ducked beneath the railings and edged round until they were right at the tip. The lighthouse towered above them. Below them boiled the open sea. Rusty curled up, squeezing himself against the cold concrete of the pier. The boxes teetered on the edge. Gerry and Sewell's toes curled above the drop. A hooter sounded. They looked out to see the ferry coming in. 'From Norway,' said Gerry flatly. The hooter sounded again. The ferry loomed nearer, passing no more than a hundred yards from them. It was a huge vessel. The passengers were lined on the decks waving. Instinctively Sewell waved back. 'Ah wish we could gan to Norway,' he said wistfully.

The ferry entered the Tyne and carefully negotiated the midden rocks, where, in November 1864, five ships were lost in five days of blizzards, thirty-four crew and passengers perishing within sight of the shore. 'Norway?' mused Sewell. 'North Tyneside's aboot the limit of wor roamin'.'

'Sewell man,' Gerry began wretchedly. 'Ah've got the money with us, how much we've made since me auld man stole it. So if ye want to spend it, ah'll understand.' Gerry took out a note and some coins, and forming a bowl by joining his two hands together he offered them to his friend. 'It's not much. But it's yours. Ah feel terrible aboot it, but what could ah dee? Me auld man's a bastard, and that's all there is to it. So take it and be done. Most of it's from them ponies any road.'

Sewell looked at Gerry. Then he looked back out to sea. Then he looked at Gerry again. 'Haddaway, man,' he breathed softly, trying to force the money back into Gerry's pocket. 'Divven't give up. We'll think of summink. Mebbes even if we cannet afford two, we can get one and share it. Ye one week, me the next. Aye, that's what we'll dee.' Sewell beamed excitedly. 'Or me first half, ye second. It doesn't matter. Just divven't give up. We can dee it.' Some of the coins spilt on to the ground. Sewell bent down and picked them up. As he was forcing them back in Gerry's hands, he knocked one of the boxes. They watched the whole stack teeter, and then fall one after another into the sea. With a cry, Sewell tried to stop them, but his arms flailed emptily. As he teetered on the brink himself, Gerry leant over and pulled him back.

With an air of finality, Gerry put the money back into his pockets. 'There's something else ah've got to tell ye. Ah divven't want to tell ye this, but ah've got to. Ah've tried to put it off. But noo. Well . . .'

'Aye?' asked Sewell, kneeling down to stroke Rusty and hide his confusion.

'Ah've thought of other ways oot of it like, but there is none. Ah even tried to dee it once mesel' without ye knowing.'

Sewell buried his face into Rusty's warm flank, and kissed his dog. Gerry leant down and ran the curled tail through his hand.

'This is why ah've brought ye here. So ah can tell ye. It's like this, man Sewell. We've got to get rid of the dog.'

A herring gull swept down at them, yelling angrily, trying to jockey them away from its favourite perch. Landing in the water, it rode the waves, screeching at the intruders huddled at the edge of the pier, pecking suspiciously at the cardboard boxes which were slowly rolling out to sea.

'It's awer dangerous, man,' Gerry continued. 'Firstly that Matthew kid's lookin' for us . . .'

'Ah can have him easy,' interrupted Sewell.

'He's a radgie, man. A pure psycho.' Gerry paused for a moment as though he couldn't bring himself to continue. At last he spoke. 'It's not just that though. We've been on the telly.'

'Eh?'

'*CrimeStoppers*.'

Slowly Sewell drew his face from the dog and looked up. His hands still clung anxiously to the dog's pelt.

'Ah didn't see it like. Wor Clare told us aboot it,' Gerry explained. 'It wasn't a clear picture. She says ye cannet tell it's us. But Rusty . . . well, he's as clear as day. It's that bit where we passed each other at the door in Marksies. Then later on in that bookshop. It's all their technology, man. They've caught up with wor.'

'But it was ages agan.'

'It takes them that long to get the tape an' that.'

'Mebbes we can lie low.'

'They've issued a statement, man, asking people to keep a look out for two youths and a dog. One youth five foot. The other six foot dressed in a bench coat. The dog, white with rusty spots, with a tail that curls over on its back. It was on last night, Sewell. It'll be repeated at lunchtime today. Which is any moment now. We'd have to be world champion limbo dancers to lie low under all that.'

Rusty nuzzled at Sewell's hands which had fallen lifeless. The dog licked at them, pawing at his master's bench coat. 'Well, there's nothing for it then,' Sewell resolved, beginning to unbutton his coat. 'Ah'll get rid of me bench coat.'

Gerry stared at him, and shook his head sadly. 'Na. That's not enough.'

'We've nee choice, have we?' asked Sewell slowly. 'It's got to be me dog. Even a dumbo like me can see that.'

Sewell closed his eyes momentarily. Then, stiffly, he got up from where he had been kneeling. Rusty stood up too. 'Doon,' ordered Sewell. The dog searched his face and tried to get up again. 'Doon,' repeated Sewell, his voice breaking. Rusty flattened his ears and lay down with his head resting on his paws. His eyes implored Sewell. 'Divven't,' pleaded Sewell as Rusty barked invitingly. 'Divven't,' he echoed weakly. The gull flew up out of the sea and wheeled round shrieking after the boxes which were being carried away on the flow of a raw sewage line. Rusty was shivering. 'It's nee good,' choked Sewell, his face red, his eyes puffy. 'Ye dee it, man Gerry, ah cannet, ye dee it. Ah just cannet.' And turning his back, Sewell handed over the length of twine.

'Divven't worry, man,' murmured Gerry, taking the lead. 'He won't suffer.'

Sewell paused. 'Ah love that dog, me,' he said through clenched teeth. When he began to walk away, Rusty made to follow him. 'Stay,' croaked Sewell. Rusty cocked his head to one side and emitted a single, heartfelt whine. A battle raged within Sewell and then, nearly falling into the sea, he stumbled away, ducking under the railings and back along the pier. His head was down. He looked neither to the left nor to the right.

'Sewell man!' called out Gerry. 'Ye should be the one to dee this. It's only right,' he said and, holding out the twine, its end looped into a noose, he approached the dog. The dog came forward to greet him. Then stopped uncertainly. 'Ah'm sorry it's got to end like this,' Gerry apologised softly. Below them a seventh wave crashed against the pier end, sending up slivers of foam as though the mirror of the sea had just been shattered. A fishing boat entered the harbour, followed by its loud constellation of seagulls. Its wake foamed up to the pier. Gerry looked down at the sea. The pot pony boxes were bobbing further and further away. Then he looked at the dog. The dog looked up into Gerry's face. The nails of his paws began scraping nervously against the concrete. 'Sorry,' Gerry repeated. 'We cannet have people seeing ye. That tail's a real giveaway, man, the way it curls back on ye. Dead cute. But a giveaway, man. Ye've been a good dog, but, well, y'kna . . .' And still talking in soft, coaxing tones he slipped the noose around Rusty's neck. Passively the dog stood there. He didn't try to struggle. When Gerry began pulling him, he looked baffled, and belatedly tried to slip the lead. But he was held secure. Surrendering himself, he stared up piteously. 'So long,' said Gerry. 'Been good to kna ye.' And taking the dog right to the tip of the pier, Gerry tied the other end of his lead to a hook that was fixed to the brickwork. 'There,' he explained finally. 'Someone'll come alang here and love ye for a pet. Mebbes one of them fishermen, or a courtin' couple.' Rusty looked deeply into Gerry's eyes. 'What?' asked Gerry. 'Ye didn't think ah was gonna hurt ye? Ye're nee pot pony, y'kna.' Shaking his head, he turned away from the dog.

In the distance Gerry could see the hunched figure of Sewell. One of the anglers began to reel in his line. Gerry watched the struggle between angler and fish as he passed by. The line was reeled in empty. 'Felt like a real monster an' all,' the unsuccessful angler was explaining to his companion. 'Ah once hoyed back a one that was three-foot long, man. A real monster . . .' Gerry walked on. When he looked up Sewell had disappeared at the other end of the pier.

Having reached the shore, Gerry turned back up the hill alongside the ruins of the priory. There was no sign of Sewell. Closing his eyes, he felt the unaccustomed warmth of the sun on his face. Children were rolling down the steep banks of the priory, on grass cut immaculately short and sprinkled with daisies. Delighted voices filled the air. An ice-cream van was serving a queue which snaked twenty yards down a path. An early bee meandered by. Reaching the top, Gerry wandered to the esplanade with its panoramic view of the enclosed yellow sands of King Edward's Bay and the sea beyond. From here the arms of the piers looked like two fingers from the same hand, beckoning. Elderly trippers walked along the esplanade, their plastic macs folded neatly over forearms. Lovers promenaded by. Mothers threw out despairing hands for tottering toddlers. On the benches people were feasting on fish and chips. The world was enjoying its Easter holiday.

Gerry drifted with the holiday crowds. Popping in and out of shops and amusement arcades, he searched for the familiar bench coat. In the distance a clock struck one. The news would have been on the television. Now he was a fugitive. He shrugged nonchalantly.

Gerry wandered past the bus shelter on the main street. It was a stone structure with a wooden board running along its walls for people to sit on. At the back was a window, through which the sun shone sharply. Through this dazzle of sunlight, Gerry could make out a figure slumped below the window, with its head on its chin, draped in a big, thick coat despite the unusually pleasant early spring day. Gerry smiled, and stopped. Meditatively, he looked beyond the shelter, up at the old priory whose ruins stand above Tynemouth, gripping desperately to the edge of the headland, trying to fend off the gravity which sends more of its ancient stones crashing into the sea every year. Then he turned back to the shelter, and went in. The figure did not move. Gerry held up his hand to try and shield his eyes from the glare of the sun. 'Ah'm sorry, man,' he said. 'But what else could we dee?' Stealthily he sat, and remained motionless for a while. At that moment some people walked past the window, blocking the sun, and with a shock, Gerry saw the figure clearly. For a while he did not move. Then, putting his shaking hands in his pockets, he brought out a dow end and lit it. The smoke curled up and drifted towards the window. Gerry got up and sat down beside the figure. There was stirring in the depths of the coat. He could see now that it was not like Sewell's. First, hands became visible as the figure unfolded its arms and straightened them out before itself with a stretch. The ears showed next, burrowing from the depths of the coat like rabbits from a hole. Hair followed, and then the face: forehead, cheeks, eyes and finally the mouth. 'What ye deein' here, Bridie?'

The girl looked at him dopily as though she had just woken from a deep sleep. She examined his face and his feet, blinking and rubbing her eyes. Then, gathering her strength together with a shudder, she got up. Her long, fine, gingery-blonde hair was plastered over her skull in tangled strands; her heavily freckled face was pale. Open-mouthed, Gerry stared up at his sister for a while. 'Ha'way, man Bridie,' he urged eventually when she looked as though she might drift away. 'It's me, Gerry.'

Gerry noticed that Bridget's fingers shook as she pulled the big coat round her. She stood there for a while, looking out at the opening to the shelter, which was shrouded in shadow. She looked drawn and exhausted. Fixing her concentration on something that seemed impossibly far away, she screwed up her eyes in thought and then sat back down.

'Areet, Gerry,' she said quietly.

Gerry took out his packet of cigarettes. Reaching over, he gave her the only full-length cigarette that was left. She took it, a questioning expression briefly flaring over her face before being replaced by a sleepy passivity. She smoked without taking the cigarette out of her mouth, keeping it wedged between her lips so that it tilted up and then down as she inhaled and exhaled. She concentrated on it as though it were taking up all her faculties.

'One o' nana's?' she asked at last. Gerry nodded, leaving her to smoke on in silence. The ash curled from the cigarette like an uncut fingernail and then fell off of its own accord, sprinkling itself over Bridget's coat.

'Where've ye been all this time?' began Gerry at last, his voice small, unsure.

'Here,' replied Bridget with a shrug.

'Why?' asked Gerry.

'Ye know why, man Gerry.'

''Cos of . . . him?' said Gerry, struggling over the word as though it were a stone he had to swallow.

There was another long silence. A wheelchair was pushed past the opening of the shelter, its wheels squeaking, its occupant eating an ice-cream. 'Ah just couldn't stand it,' Bridget confessed.

Gerry trapped a stone beneath the toe of his shoe and scraped it slowly across the concrete floor of the bus shelter. 'We've moved again. This time he won't be able to find wor. It's a canny hoose. Ye should see it. It's . . .'

Bridget interrupted him softly. 'Ye always say that he won't find us, but he always does.'

'Ye'd love it, man Bridie,' Gerry persisted as though he hadn't heard her. He spoke quickly and excitedly. 'It's dead near the Metro Centre. Ye'd just be able to stumble oot the door and there it is. The school bus gans by dead near an' all. Ah've checked for ye. Ye'd be able to catch it in the morning just like ye used to. Ye could start in the sixth form. Ye've got yer own room an' all, unless Clare and the babby come back again. And . . .'

'Ah'm not coming back.'

'And the river's geet close so ye can come fishing with wor again,' Gerry's eyes were shining. 'Remember the time ye did with me and Sewell and we caught summink? Ah divven't kna what it was exactly but we caught it all the same. Sewell can catch owt. Ha'way, Bridie, if ye moved back we could dee all these things. And . . . And . . . Ah've got so much ah want to tell ye. And . . . Look. Ah'll tell ye what. Ah'll just give ye the address so ye can pop in if ye're ever near.'

'Na,' Bridget told him, still softly, but this time much more firmly. 'Ah've told ye. Ah'm not coming hyem.'

'But . . .'

'Na.'

Far, far above a jet climbed up the sky, leaving its lonely trail of white in the vast blue of the northern spring. But neither

Gerry nor Bridget could see it. 'How've ye been?' Gerry asked. 'How've ye been living?'

'Sleeping on floors mainly, y'kna, of friends. Lived with a bloke for a few weeks, he's got a flat looking oot awer the sea. Ah've been living all awer here. Whitley Bay, Cullercoats, North Shields. Ah even got the ferry once and spent a few days in South Shields.'

'Is it areet?'

'Sometimes ye get caught oot and have to spend a night ootside. But ye just take a pill, that gets ye through it all reet. Ye divven't notice the cold then, man.' Gerry tried to return his sister's smile but he couldn't. 'Ah've been taking everything, man Gerry,' she said, her eyes glinting coldly like coal chippings in a winter sun. 'Tac, E, wobbly eggs, speed, poppers, even smack, man. Owt ah can get me hands on.' Bridget paused and sniffed loudly at the membrane of snot which had strung itself down her nostril. She wiped her nose with the sleeve of her coat, then finding Gerry's gaze on her she looked away. 'What aboot ye, Gerry?' she asked after a while. 'Ye and Sewell still playin' the radgie gadgies? Gannin' mental on tac an' that?'

Gerry shuffled his feet uncomfortably. 'Na. We've stopped that for a bit, y'kna.'

'Why?'

'Just for a laugh really. Ah even went to school.'

Bridget shuffled closer to Gerry. He recoiled slightly from the shocking stench of her coat. 'Ye carryin' owt noo?'

'Ah've told ye, man Bridie.'

'Nowt much, y'kna. A bit tac?' There was an edge to her voice. Her face seemed to become sharper. Her hair looked thin and frail, dead like a clump of October grass on the wasteland where the travellers like to camp. 'Ha'way, man Gerry. Ah kna ye've got summink. Share it with wor, man. Ah'm desperate.'

Flinching, Gerry moved away, inching down the wooden seat. His hand strayed to his pocket. He could feel the contours of the money. He counted the coins through the material of his jogging trousers.

'Ye must have summink!' A crazed look flashed in Bridget's normally gentle eyes. 'Or some money. Give wor a couple of quid, man Gerry. Ha'way, man. Help us oot. Ha'way! Ah'm begging ye. Ye've got to help. Ye've got to . . .'

Gerry stared at his sister, horror on his face. Then abruptly she slumped back from him weakly. 'How's everybody?' she asked gently.

'Areet,' replied Gerry. 'The babby mings a bit mind.'

'Ye did an' all, man,' smiled Bridget.

'Mam hasn't been in hospital for a while. Why, not for the usual thing anyway.'

'Fell doon the stairs again, did she?'

Gerry looked down. 'Aye,' he replied.

Bridget shook her head sadly. There was a pause. 'So how's Sewell deein'? Still wearing that old coat o' his?' she said at last.

'Cannet get him oot of it. Fancies this lass but.'

'Oh aye?'

'Gemma. Ye kna her. Sewell's mental aboot her. She's a canny lass like, but she's been gannin' oot with this gadgie for months, man. He's a proper chaver. Plays ice hockey and that.'

'Sewell's hard enough to look after himsel', man.'

'Aye,' agreed Gerry. 'But there's this Matthew kid after him an' all.'

'Not the dog boy?'

'Aye.'

'He's a psycho.'

'Ah kna.'

'Sewell's hard, mind. Can ye remember the time he took on them three West Enders?'

Gerry nodded nostalgically. 'Oh aye. When we were selling the tac. Headbutted one of the cunts. Kicked the other two in the balls. All but killed them. Ah'm not saying that Sewell's not hard. Ah mean Sewell's canny hard himsel' like, but he's not, well y'kna, mean. He's not a killer. This ice hockey player and his mates would break his back withoot even stopping for a tab.'

'Sean still inside?'

'Me and Sewell are gannin' doon to see him, just as soon as we've got a bit o' business oot the way.'

'What aboot me nana?'

Gerry smiled sadly. 'She misses ye, man. There's neeone for nana but wor Bridie.'

'Haddaway.' Bridget threw her head back and laughed, for a moment the girl she used to be when she went to school and did her homework and never stole a thing.

'Thinks ye're the best, man,' Gerry continued, his voice imploring. 'She thinks ye're away at college or summink.'

'Na. She's clever that one. She knows how things are. She knows all aboot . . . things, y'kna.'

'Bridie man, me dad'll nivver find us. Come hyem, hinny,' said Gerry openly begging now. 'Ha'way. Nana misses ye. We all dee.'

Bridget shook her head and smiled sadly. 'It's not hyem any more. It's been taken away from wor. This is me life noo. This.' Bridget gestured at the bus shelter with a weary flourish. Closing his eyes, Gerry saw his father again through the distortions of the flashing light and siren of the ambulance that had taken his mother to hospital, and amid this searing strobe he saw the bleeding heart of Bridget's First Holy Communion Christ, and the broken glass on the floor.

'Ah'll kill him,' he resolved flatly.

'Who?' asked Bridget.

'Me dad. Ah'll kill him.'

'Divven't be stupid, man Gerry.'

'Ah divven't care what they dee to me. They can bang us up for the rest of me life and ah won't mind, because ah want to kill him.' Gerry's voice rose angrily. 'Ah want to kill him, me!'

Bridget sighed. 'What good will that dee?' She reached over and put a hand on her little brother's cheek. 'Divven't cry, man.'

Brother and sister looked at each other for a long time. Gerry put up his hand to meet Bridget's which was still resting on his cheek. 'Come back, Bridie. Ah'll look after ye. Ah've been looking after yer things.'

'Gerry?' Bridget took her hand away and shuffled back along the bench. 'Ye've got to promise me summink.'

'What?'

'Divven't tell anyone that ye saw me. Areet? D'ye promise?'

'Bridie man . . .'

'Promise, Gerry. Divven't tell a soul. If ye do, then me dad'll find oot where ah am.'

'He won't . . .'

'And then he'll come for us. Ah know he'll come for us. Ah couldn't stand that. Divven't dee that to us.'

Gerry stared at the ground. Flicking up a Beck's Bier bottle top he kicked it. It hit the wall opposite him. Bridget sighed. 'Ye'll tell them, won't ye? Ye cannet help yersel'.'

'Ah want ye back,' replied Gerry.

There was a long pause. An elderly couple looked into the shelter and took a step in as though meaning to sit down. But they seemed to change their minds as soon as they saw Bridget and Gerry. Bridget's arms began disappearing back into the folds of her coat.

Gerry took out his cigarette packet and shook it. There were two dow ends left. Selecting the bigger one, he lit it and handed it over to his sister. Then he lit the smaller one, nothing more than half an inch of tobacco, and he flinched as its acrid smoke stung his eyes. 'Mam's got all these pills an' that. Been telt not to smoke. Should have seen her, man Bridie! Created hell, couldn't dee withoot the tabs for one hour to the next but nana wouldn't let her or anyone else oot the hoose to buy any. Climbed the walls, man. But aye, she's gettin' better. Coughs sometimes. At neet mostly. And in the morning. Sometimes during the day. But she's areet noo.'

'Good,' nodded Bridie. 'Canny good.'

Gerry threw a glance at his sister. 'That Drama teacher was asking after ye. Told me to tell ye to get yoursel' back.' Gerry narrowed his eyes. 'Bridie man, ah've been thinking. Ah suppose ye could gan back to school without even moving back hyem with us. Ye could get a flat or summink by the school and live there.' He paused and looked at his sister. Slowly she was slipping back into her coat. Her hands had already disappeared. Now her chin and then her mouth sank under, and her nose was lying on the surface of the coat's collar as though exhausted with the struggle. He leant back and stared. Her eyes were heavy-lidded, half closed. She looked like somebody who was drowning but had lost all fear of the water. He had not noticed how thin she was at first. Now she seemed no more than a few bones rummaging in a coat. 'Did ye say ye were hungry?' he asked desperately. There was no reply. 'Ah tell ye what, ah'll gan and get fish an' chips. Fish an' chips, man Bridie. Plenty of salt and vinegar. Ah won't be a minute. Just ye wait there.'

The money jingled in his pocket as he ran down the street to the fish and chip shop. He put down a hand to settle it. He wanted to get there as soon as possible, he couldn't bear to think of that appalling thinness. He closed his eyes and ran with all his might. When he reached the chip shop there was a long queue. 'Ha'way,' he cajoled, pushing his way through the bodies. 'Ha'way,' he urged.

'Ee, who does he think he is?' complained the queue. 'What's yer game, lad? Calm doon, son. Where's the fire?'

'Me nana's disabled,' explained Gerry wildly.

'What d'ye want, pet?' asked the woman who was serving, her forearms showing chunkily red against the white T-shirt and blue stripes of her apron.

The question threw Gerry for a moment. He seemed unable to concentrate. At last his thoughts settled down. 'Fish an' chips,' he said. 'Fish an' chips once. For me nana,' he told the queue which was regarding him with some menace. 'She's disabled.'

'Open or wrapped?'

'Open.'

'Salt and vinegar?'

Nodding, Gerry took the note and coins from his pocket and slapped them down on the counter. Without counting he pushed over a pile of coins, scooping the rest back into his pocket. 'Here! Ye've got change,' she shouted after him. He didn't look back. The people in the queue shook their heads. A man in a tweed hat took the change and placed it elegantly in the charity box standing on the counter. 'Some people,' he frowned.

Cradling the paper of fish and chips in both hands, Gerry left the shop and hastened down the street. The smell of the food was warm and delicious. His mouth watered. He felt his stomach rumbling. He crossed the road and wove between a couple of parked cars. Idly he noticed that one of them wasn't locked. It was a blue Ford Escort, parked with its driving seat beside the pavement. There was no steering wheel lock either, just a deodorising plastic Gromit sitting on the dashboard. In the back there was a baby seat. Hurrying on, he cast one last glance back at the car. His shoes had holes in them and a stone jagged against the sole of his foot. But he didn't dare slow down. He had to get to the shelter. He had to get the food to Bridget while it was still hot. He had to get to Bridget.

When he had reached the bus shelter, Bridget wasn't there. He looked round the back. He looked up and down the street. He ran over to the esplanade and looked over King Edward's Bay. But she wasn't there. She was gone.

The fish and chips were beginning to cool in his hands. He could feel the sogginess spreading through the paper as the fat congealed. A family walked by where he stood leaning against the railings. They were all wearing Newcastle United tops. The black-and-white stripes flashing in the sunlight dazzled him momentarily. Holding the fish and chips he walked towards the priory.

Benedictine monks had built this priory nearly a thousand

years ago when the mouth of the Tyne was a quiet wilderness and both the Shields were silent, unpeopled places. Chosen for its remoteness, its position had been on the very edge of the world. Aside from a few arches and the crumbling walls of a refectory and a library, all that is left is the lilt of the kittiwakes screeching on the cliffs below, which is the purest dialect of Geordie it is possible to hear spoken, and the sea which pulses endlessly against the ribs of the headland. Finding a secluded spot, Gerry sat down, his back resting against a block of crumbling masonry, the short cropped grass comfortable beneath him. He laid the fish and chips down too. A tiny squall of wind tugged gently at the paper before passing on to run its fingers through the early daisies.

'How did ye know ah'd be here?' Sewell asked, when he stood up from behind his resting place ten yards in front.

Gerry smiled.

'Ah was coming to look for ye,' said Sewell, a huge smile annexing his whole face as far as his eyes.

'Look, Sewell, mebbes ah was wrong, mebbes ye could have kept Rusty hidden. Mebbes we should gan back and get him from the end of that pier . . .'

'Nee point,' Sewell told him solemnly.

'What d'ye mean?'

'Ah've been there, he's not there any more. Someone's taken him.'

Gerry dug his fingernails into the grass, piercing the soil below. 'Sewell man, what can ah dee eh? Ah feel terrible. But ah just divven't kna what to dee. Ah make mistakes. Ah'm nee fuckin' good me.'

Sewell looked over at the fish and chips. 'Nice one, Gerry man,' he enthused, rubbing his hands together.

'They're cold,' Gerry said, plucking despondently at the grass.

'Ah'm sure he won't mind. Would ye mind?' Sewell called out in a loud voice. 'Would ye eh? Coast's clear, Rusty! Fish an' chips!'

Charging out from behind the ruins, Rusty ran at Gerry, and licked the full length of his face from chin to hair roots. Then he fell to on the fish and chips.

'It's his favourite. Divven't worry, man.' Sewell climbed on to a stone and, tottering self-importantly, tapped his chest with his forefinger. 'Ah worked it all oot as ah walked doon that pier. We cannet leave him. It'd break his heart, man. But divven't worry. This is what we'll dee. We'll smuggle him back to Gatesheed in me bench coat. Use it like a carry-cot y'kna. That way ah'll have killed two birds with one stone. Rusty and the bench coat like. Then ah'll give him to Gemma to look after until it's all blown awer. Ah had to gan and get him. Ah couldn't leave him on the end of that pier, man.'

'Would she dee it like?'

'Who?'

'Gemma?'

'Why aye!'

'Ye seem pretty certain, man.'

Sewell blushed. 'Ah'm seein' her, man.'

They looked down at the dog bolting the food, and then back up at each other. Gerry groaned. 'Ye cannet be serious, man.'

'Why cannet ah?'

'Because the lass is engaged to be married to an ice hockey player, that's why ye cannet.'

'Well, ah am.'

A cloud strayed over the Easter sun and the temperature fell suddenly, reminding a blackbird perched on a pile of stones just how early in the year it still was. 'Sewell man,' said Gerry in a quiet voice. 'The only question noo is who's going to get ye first? Matthew, the radge dog merchant, or Gemma's lad. He plays ice hockey, y'kna.'

'So?'

'So?'

'Aye, so?'

'Ever seen it on the telly, man? They'll come for ye, all

together, his whole team, when ye're least expecting it and kill ye.'

'Ha'way,' said Sewell. 'Let's get busy.'

'What d'yus mean?'

'We've still got eighty-two pot ponies to shift.'

'Why divven't we just forget aboot the pot ponies, Sewell?'

'Na.'

'What's the use? We're not gonnae . . .'

'We will. Together. We'll work it oot. Starting with the ponies.'

The laughter began with a titter from Sewell. Despite himself, Gerry took on the chuckle and turned it into a building, body-shaking ha-ha-ha. For a while they were both insensible with hilarity. Then, rolling the fish and chip papers up tightly, Sewell threw them to Gerry who kicked them at Rusty. 'And another great save!' shouted Gerry. Sewell tossed the ball to Gerry who headed it into Rusty's mouth. 'And they still cannet get past this keeper!' yelled Gerry delightedly. 'And it looks like neeone is gonnae win the pot pony challenge cup.' The final whistle blew with still no score, and the two friends dropped to the ground, rolling round with Rusty. Then, passing under the standing arch, they re-entered the streets of today.

Falling serious, Sewell took off his bench coat, wrapped it round Rusty and in one movement swept the dog up into his arms. 'Neeone'll kna there's a dog in here,' he said, gesturing at the package in his arms with a stab of his nose. 'Mebbes they'll think it's a babby.'

Gerry and Sewell both doubled up with laughter again. 'Ha'way, man, divven't drop the babby.'

Riding this fresh tide of hilarity, Sewell swayed off the pavement, just catching his balance in time. 'Divven't twist aboot in there,' he whispered to Rusty. Gerry was walking a few steps ahead, his forehead lined with thought. Sewell watched him for a while. 'That's it,' said Sewell at last. 'Get back to yer auld self. Think. Work things oot for wor. Ye'll come up with an idea. Ye'll see. We'll have them Season Tickets yet.'

'Well, ah suppose we better gan and reclaim wor merchandise from the station.'

Sewell smiled. 'That's it. Ha'way, it's a canny step away.'

Gerry turned abruptly. 'What we need for them boxes is transportation.' He walked up a line of parked cars, stopping beside the blue Ford Escort. Gerry opened the door, and felt for the immobiliser. With one or two expert ripping movements and a deft joining of wires the car hummed into life. 'Taxi for two, bonny lads?' said Gerry.

Sewell got in the passenger seat. 'Now we're buzzin'!' smiled Sewell.

'Ye can gan free, but the hoond costs,' said Gerry as Sewell lifted Rusty on to the baby seat in the back.

'Ye cannet charge a babby!' laughed Sewell, carefully arranging the little seatbelt round the bench coat.

With a roar, the car sped off down the street. Reaching the metro station, Sewell got out to collect the boxes. He came back a moment later, scarlet with rage. 'The bastards,' he growled. 'Ye cannet trust anyone these days, man.'

'What is it?'

'Someone's only gone and twoced the pot ponies!'

Shaking his head, Sewell got back into the car. Gerry drove on to the coast road back to Gateshead.

'Ah cannet believe it,' said Sewell. 'Ah just cannet believe how anyone would pull such a low trick.' Slipping into the outside lane, Gerry changed into top gear. Sewell continued to chunter: 'What we gonnae dee noo? Mebbes yus were right before. Mebbes it is all over. Mebbes we should just give up, and gan back to tac and tabs an' that. What d'ye think? Eh? What d'ye think, man Gerry?'

'Shh. Ah'm concentrating. There has to be summink ah can think of.'

'Ah mean what can anyone dee with eighty-two pot ponies? Ee, why!' The car wove through a band of thicker traffic.

'Nice driving,' said Sewell. Glancing up at the driver's mirror, he looked at Rusty sitting obediently in the baby seat. 'Could have brought Keegan alang an' all,' he mused.

'Eh?' said Gerry, turning to Sewell.

'Watch the road, man!' shouted Sewell.

'What was that ye just said?'

'Ah said we could have brought the babby.'

'The babby?'

'Aye, your niece. Keegan. For frigg's sake, watch the road!'

Suddenly the brakes screeched, and the car careered out of control. With arms juddering on the wheel, Gerry guided it on to the hard shoulder, where it skidded thirty yards before shuddering to a halt. The smell of burning rubber filled the air. Gerry leapt out. 'What is it, what is it?' Sewell demanded. By the time Sewell and Rusty had emerged, Gerry was already over the dual carriageway barrier and into the wide open fields of Wallsend.

'Ah've worked it oot! Ah've frigging well worked it oot!' Gerry called back over his shoulder.

'What aboot the car?' Sewell shouted.

Gerry was laughing wildly. 'Got to leave it. Cannet run any risks. Not noo it's all worked oot.'

'Eh?'

'Ha'way, Sewell. Them Season Tickets are as good as ours.'

Sewell stared over the fields with the tethered ponies, and saw, in the distance, the tall shipbuilding cranes standing sadly above the Tyne. Then, with a joyful shriek, he began to sprint.

9

The baby struggled to her feet and, steadying herself by holding the side of the armchair, stood upright. Emboldened, she launched herself over the carpet, but without the stabiliser of the armchair, came crashing down to the ground. She lay there dazed for a minute, hit the carpet angrily with the palm of her hand and then crawled back to the armchair where she once again began to haul herself to her feet. Outside the rain lashed against the window, testing the door of the house like an opportunist burglar.

It was dawn on a rainy Mayday morning. 'Hallo, pet,' Mrs Macarten crooned, coming from the kitchen into the living room and sitting down on the settee. 'Show yer nana how ye can walk.'

Gurgling happily, the baby let go of the armchair. Mrs Macarten held out her arms. 'Ha'way, pet,' she whispered with an infinite gentleness. 'Ha'way.' Concentrating on these two familiar arms, the baby took two steps, then three; stumbling on her fourth she managed to rectify herself for her fifth; her sixth was accomplished faultlessly, and it was only on her seventh that inexplicably she found her legs taken away from beneath her. 'Divven't ye cry,' soothed Mrs Macarten, taking the baby into her arms. 'Nana's here, pet.' She cradled the baby in her spindly arms, and her tired mouth widened to a smile. 'Nana'll always be here for ye.' The baby threw out a hand to feel her grandmother's face. She touched the lined forehead, smoothed the two gaunt cheekbones, and traced a fat finger over the drawn mouth. 'Shall ah sing to ye?' Mrs Macarten whispered, kissing her granddaughter. 'Shall ah sing to me little Keegan?' The baby laughed, staring up with huge eyes. 'Ah'll sing ye a song me own nana sang to us when ah was a bairn like ye.' Rocking the baby gently in her arms, she began to sing. Starting quietly, almost in a whisper, her voice was broken by the frequent and hungry breaths; but steadily the song filled the chill room with a warmth like that of a small fire. Mesmerised, the baby listened.

> Ah can-net get to my love if ah would dee
> The waters of Tyne run between him and me
> And here ah must stand with a tear in my e'e
> Oh sighing so softly my sweetheart to see . . .

> Oh where is . . .

Seized by coughing, Mrs Macarten managed to lay the baby gently on the floor before rolling into a ball beside her. When the worst of the coughing had abated she was able to look around and to hear again. The postman stopped to push letters through the door. Feebly she turned to see them fluttering down on to the floor. The junk mail, bills and giro seemed to fall loudly, piling up on top of each other noisily like metal sheets. Then there was silence.

The house seemed so quiet. She could not remember such quiet in any of the houses she had ever lived in. It was like being under water, as though she and the baby were lying not on a carpet but on the thick mud-bed of the Tyne. Holding her arms out in a swimming movement, she tried to raise herself, but she could not. Besides, it was so quiet lying there. How she loved this new-found silence, the peace which was pooling all round her. The words of the song she had been singing floated around her like inquisitive fish, and her mouth mumbled after their shapes. She lay there until the baby, puzzled by this solitude, crawled over to the resting adult, doggy-paddling her way with arms and legs scrabbling. Mrs Macarten felt the flail of a little hand and she reached out for the child, pressing her to her chest like a lifebuoy.

Slowly she felt herself rising back up to the surface. With a huge, desperate, screaming gulp, she found oxygen again. Breaking free of the silence, she heard the worn bellows of her breathing. She looked about her. The settee and the two armchairs seemed to bob at eye level. Moving over, still holding the baby, she threw out a hand to try and grasp them. 'Ee, hinny,' she whispered to her granddaughter. 'Ah thought ah wasn't gonnae come back that time.'

Gerry came downstairs to find his mother sitting on the floor with the sleeping baby. She was pale, her cheeks as white as paper litter that has been blanched and soddened by the full four seasons. Her mouth seemed stretched wide across her face and her eyes poked deeper into their sockets. He reeled slightly at the sight, trying not to look at the deep bags which were pouched under her eyes. 'Areet, Mam,' he greeted her, yawning.

She stared up at him blankly for a while, before seeming to recognise him. 'Areet, Gerry. What ye deein' up at this time?' Walking to the window, Gerry looked out. His face crumpled with disappointment. He drummed his fingers agitatedly on the sill. 'What's the matter, hinny?' asked his mother.

'It's rainin'.'

'It's always rainin', man.'

'Ah kna, but ah didn't want it to the day,' Gerry said disappearing into the kitchen. 'Is there owt to eat, Mam?'

Smiling sadly to herself, his mother hauled herself and the baby up to the settee. 'Ah'll gan oot later and get some things. When ah've cashed me giro.'

'There's nivver owt in,' complained Gerry.

'Gis a chance, man. It's the crack o' dawn. Last time ye were up this early ye were nee bigger than this one.' She rubbed the baby's back with a gentle hand. 'There's some soup, isn't there? Y'kna, that poodered stuff.'

There was the sound of a spoon hitting a bowl, of paper tearing and of a tap running. Gerry came back into the living room carrying a bowl of soup. 'Ah used the hot water tap,' he told her, switching the telly on as he sat down on an armchair. Gerry ate rapidly, his spoon knocking urgently against the bowl. His foot tapped insistently. His glance roved constantly from the cartoon on the television screen to the front door. He got up to flick through the channels, but returned to the cartoon. Then sank back in the armchair. 'Great telly that but,' said his mother.

'Aye,' said Gerry. 'Divven't let anyone in to take it this time.'

'They come roond. Ah cannet stop them gettin' in. We owe on the catalogues.'

'Just divven't answer the door, man Mam. Or look through the curtain first.'

'Is that soup areet?' Mrs Macarten asked.

'Canny,' replied Gerry. 'Mediterranean Tomato flavour.' Energetically, he stood up, and took the bowl through to the kitchen. Coming back, he lifted the corner of the curtain hanging over the window, and peeked up and down the street. With a sigh, he sat back on the arm of the armchair.

'Ha'way, hinny,' began his mother. 'What is it the day?'

'Why?' asked Gerry.

'Ye're like a cat on hot bricks.'

'Aye well, it's a big day, man Mam.'

'Why?'

'Put it this way, if everything gans to plan the day, then me and Sewell will have done it. Pulled off a miracle.'

Mrs Macarten laughed gently, the baby cooed. 'Ee, what's he like? Yer uncle Gerry and his best mate Sewell. They're always up to summink. What is it this time?'

Gerry smiled widely. 'Ye'll find oot soon enough.' Then, he frowned. 'But only if he gets a move on.'

They sat for a while in silence. Through the corner of his eye Gerry became aware that his mother was watching him rather than the television.

'If ah . . .' she tried to say. 'If owt happens to wor. If ah have to gan to the hospital again, but this time for a really long time, would ye ... would ye be areet, pet?'

Gerry shifted uncomfortably, slipping from the arm into the chair. 'But ye're not gannin' anywhere,' he said.

'Ah kna, but if ah were. Would ye be areet?'

Gerry pretended to be absorbed by the television.

'This one'd be areet,' smiled his mother, taking up the baby who flopped contentedly in her arms. 'She's knackt hersel' oot. Ee, Gerry, ye should have seen her. She walked straight across the room.'

'Did she?'

'Why aye, man. Straight across. She's gonnae be a reet Bobby Dazzler this one. Ye were still shufflin' on yer arse at her age.' There was a short pause as his mother concentrated on the baby. Gerry stiffened as he felt her eyes fasten back on him. 'Ee, where do the years gan? Ah remember ye this size. And Bridget an' all, God love her. Before her wor Sean. And first of all of yus, Clare. Ah wasn't much older than ye are now when ah had Clare.' Smiling, for a moment she turned into a beyond that only she could see. Then she turned back to Gerry. Her voice was urgent. 'Listen, pet. If owt does happen, or if ah dee have to gan back to hospital or somewhere for a long time, ah ...' Suddenly Gerry sprang up and went to the window. He returned impatiently to the armchair. 'Gerry, ah need to kna that ye'll be areet without wor for a time.'

Gerry looked his mother in the face. 'Ye're areet. Ye're better now. That trouble ye had ... it's gone. Ye're not gannin' anywhere.'

'Aye,' his mother echoed, smiling a sad smile. 'Ah'm not gannin' anywhere.'

The silence was shattered by a knock at the door. Before Gerry had time to open it, a banging could be heard on the ceiling above. Muffled, Clare's voice penetrated the floor-boards. 'If that's him tell him ah'm oot!'

'Met a lad doon the Bigg Market last neet,' Mrs Macarten explained with a wink. 'Got off with him y'kna, but doesn't want owt to dee with him. Didn't ye hear her come in last night? Pissed oot of her heed. She woke the babby up.'

Striding over to the window, Gerry shook his head.

Upstairs, bed-springs could be heard complaining as Clare sank heavily back into the mattress. 'Aye, mortal she was,' repeated Mrs Macarten, smacking Keegan lightly on her bottom. 'Yer mammy was pissed oot of her heed, hinny Keegan lass,' she crooned to the baby, who cooed and dribbled appreciatively.

There was some more knocking. Carefully Gerry lifted the curtain at the window. His face broke into a wide smile. 'It's areet,' he said.

'Areet all, Mrs Macarten, Gerry,' said Sewell as he entered the house, rain still dripping from his coat.

'Ee lad, ah cannet believe it. Ye up at this time an' all! What's gannin' on the day?' she said, greeting the newcomer with a smile. 'Well, come in, Sewell lad, divven't be standin' at the door all day. Sit doon.'

Sewell looked significantly at Gerry and sat down in the other armchair. 'Just for a minute but.'

'And take that coat off, bonny lad,' Mrs Macarten added. 'It's soaking.'

'It's areet, Mrs Macarten.'

'How's that dog of yours, Sewell lad?'

'Canny, Mrs Macarten. He's being looked after by a . . . by a mate. *CrimeStoppers*, y'kna,' finished Sewell, stumbling over his words under the unbalancing push of Gerry's frown.

'Ah wondered why he wasn't with ye. Ah had that Matthew lad roond the other day.'

Gerry looked up quickly. 'Ye didn't let him in, Mam?' His mother looked away. Gerry sighed loudly.

Mrs Macarten looked back over to Sewell. 'Well, take yer coat off anyway. Is it not all wet?'

'Na. Well, it'll dry but.'

'He's not stoppin' for long. We're late already,' Gerry said.

'Raining,' she said, sitting up with a pull of great effort and craning her neck to see through the window. 'Just like a winter's day. Ee and it's May. It's the first of May. Isn't it supposed to be a nice day, May Day? A good time for courtin'. Eh, lads! What d'yus say aboot that?' Growing suddenly breathless she struggled for her words. 'Ah courted yer father in May, man Gerry. Behind the Spartan Redheugh, with all its lovely flowers.' She tried to say more, but couldn't. With a soft sigh, she slumped back in the settee. Sweat glistened moistly at the roots of her hair. 'Mebbes it rained that day an' all but.'

Gerry shook his head at Sewell. 'Where've ye been, man? We said crack o'dawn.'

'Ha'way, it's time to tell us what it's all aboot. Tell wor, man. Tell wor! Ah haven't been able to sleep a wink for weeks.' Walking over to the baby, Sewell began laughing excitedly.

'Ha'way. Nee time to lose,' said Gerry, nodding at the kitchen.

'Keegan,' said Sewell, tickling the baby under the chin.

'Aye, Keegan,' replied Gerry mysteriously, his eyes shining. 'Ye're on the reet track there, bonny lad.' Striding over to the television set, he turned the sound up. 'Top secret,' he intoned mysteriously.

Sewell bustled after Gerry into the kitchen. 'But we've already tried using the babby,' he said.

'There is more than one Keegan in this world, man,' explained Gerry.

Sewell stopped. 'You mean?'

'Aye. The man himsel'.'

'Kev . . .'

'Keegan.'

'But he isn't at Newcastle now, Gerry man.'

Gerry shook his head and, smiling knowingly, took out a piece of paper from his pocket. He handed it to Sewell.

'Carlisle. 3.00 p.m. Fulham,' Sewell read stutteringly. 'Eh, what's all this aboot?'

'What this is aboot, Sewell, is that today we are going to Carlisle to pick up wor Season Tickets.'

'Now ye've done it.'

'Done what?'

'Lost me.'

Gerry sighed. 'Areet, we'll start from square one. Who's the manager of Fulham?' Sewell snorted impatiently, and rolled his eyes with irritation. 'What is it, Sewell man?'

Trembling with agitation, Sewell flushed. 'Weeks back ye telt wor we had it all worked oot. Did ye then gan on to tell us how? Na. Ye left us in the middle o' Wallsend to find me way all the way back to Gatesheed. Ah've been asking everyday for weeks. Last neet ah came roond here to find oot what it was all aboot once and for all. And ye telt wor to come back in the morning. All neet ah'm tossing and turning. Sweating and wondering. Me heart gannin' radgie. But still ah have to get up at the crack o' dawn. And noo . . . and noo . . . and noo yus start quizzing us on third-division football teams!'

'Who's the brains?'

'Ah divven't . . .'

'Who's the friggin' brains?'

'Ye, but . . .'

'All will come clear if ye jus know some patience. Yus're too impatient ye. Like a big fat bull in a friggin' pot pony shop. If ye'd only waited to hear wor oot, then ah would have telt ye that Keegan is noo the manager of Fulham. Then ah would have telt ye why we are gannin' awer to Carlisle the day. Which explains the godforsaken hour. Then ah would have finished by saying that by five o'clock this afternoon we will be the prood owners of a pair o' Season Tickets.'

'Eh? How?' expostulated Sewell, hurrying after his friend.

Gerry smiled and led him over to the pantry that ran down a few stone steps almost forming a little cellar. 'Walls have ears,' Gerry explained as they crept into the pantry, leaving the door ajar so that they could see a little. Gerry cleared his throat and stared at Sewell like a master tactician waiting to begin his brief. 'We get the train at the Metro Centre and stay on for as long as we can. We'll probably not get all the way to Carlisle withoot tickets but wherever we get hoyed oot we'll hitch the rest.'

'Aye, aye, aye,' Sewell stammered. 'Ah kna that bit. It's the other bit ah divven't get.'

'We could have taken a car, but ah decided against the risk. We cannet let anything jeopardise me plan. We're getting off nice and early. Cannet leave owt to chance, man Sewell.'

'WILL YE JUST TELL WOR WHAT ALL THIS IS FRIGGIN' WELL ABOOT!'

Gerry smiled knowingly. 'Turn the piece of paper over, and read it.' Lighting a match, Gerry held it over the piece of paper which his friend still held. A halo of light fell over a page of tightly written letters. 'Dear Bev,' began Sewell.

'Kev, man!' Gerry burst out. 'Dear Kev.'

'Dear Kev, how ye deein'? Shocking that ye had to leave the toon, but we hope that ye're deein' areet at Fulham . . .' Gerry shook the match out as it reached his fingers. Gloom returned to the pantry. Quickly he lit another, its flare sending their shadows over the empty shelves and cavities of the pantry.

'Dear Kev,' Sewell began.

'We've done that bit, man,' snapped Gerry.

'Sorry,' mumbled Sewell, searching for his place with a finger. 'Aye, here it is. How ye deein'? You were our mess . . . mess . . . mess . . .' Sewell paused, and shrugged uncomprehendingly.

Gerry shook his head. 'Sewell man, are ye serious or what?'

Sewell took a step back in defence. 'Course ah'm serious.'

'Ye sure?'

'Aye ah'm sure.'

'Because we divven't stand a chance if ye start acting the arsehole.'

'Eh?'

'You were our messiah. That's what it says. Our messiah.'

'Aye. They called him that. The messiah. Special K an' all.'

'Gis that.' Gerry snatched the piece of paper just as the

match went out. 'Ye give us a light and ah'll read it.' Another match flared.

'These are nee good. Pass us them,' Sewell said, indicating the pile of *Gateshead Herald* free newspapers revealed momentarily at the back of the pantry. Tutting, Gerry leant down to pick one up, and handed it over. Sewell tore off a page and, twisting it into a reefer, put it in his mouth. 'Smoke tac, man!' he said, lighting it.

'What the fuck is it with ye the day?' demanded Gerry.

'Cannet help it. Ah'm just excited,' mumbled Sewell.

'Aye, well. Bring that friggin' light awer here.' Sewell held the light near the paper. 'Watch me face, man. Ye nearly singed me eyebrows off. Reet. Dear Kev, blah-blah-blah. Ha'way. Here we are. We are glad to welcome ye back to the North even just for a day. We have both been toon supporters since the day we were born which was within spitting distance of the Tyne, and my baby niece is called Keegan.' Pausing to see the effect of his words on his friend, Gerry added: 'Personal details, y'kna, makes all the difference.' Clearing his throat he prepared for the finale. 'The tragedy is, we cannet get in to see wor team, so please give wor a Season Ticket each for the toon. From Gerry and Sewell. PS, Me big mate, Sewell, has just lost everything in a tragic fire.'

The newspaper burnt low. Dextrously, Sewell twisted his wrist so that the bottom of the torch burnt too. Then, using its last flame, he lit another twist of paper. The red embers of the used torch spiralled to the ground. Gerry stared at him expectantly. 'Well, what d'yus think?'

'Could ye read it again?'

'Eh?'

'Ah'm sorry, man Gerry. Ah didn't get that last bit. The plan bit like.'

'Oh for godsake! Kevin Keegan's gonnae give wor a ticket. That's the plan, reet? Kevin friggin' Keegan is gonnae hand wor a pair o' tickets. That's it.'

Silence greeted the end of his declamation. Sewell busied himself lighting another torch. 'What's that bit aboot the fire?'

Gerry sighed. 'We needed an angle, man. There's thoosands of wor oot there, wanting a Season Ticket. We have to stand oot from the crowd. We cannet have yus blind again. So ah came up with that.'

'Fire?'

'That's what we'll say.'

'Na.'

'It doesn't have to be a fire.'

'And where's me auld man gonnae gan?'

'It doesn't have to be a fire. Could be anything bad. Y'kna, catastrophic. Owt in the nature of a personal disaster.'

'It'd kill him to have to move.'

'Sewell, are ye listening or what?'

'If ah'm gonnae burn doon any hoose, then it's yours. Yous lot are always moving aboot anyway.'

'What are ye rabbiting on aboot?'

'Ah couldn't dee it to him. Me auld man's always lived in that hoose.'

Gerry grabbed hold of his friend by the bench coat, and stared into his eyes. 'Neeone's gonnae burn doon nee hoose. We're just pretending, ye soft get!'

'Really?' Sewell asked at last.

Gerry's eyes shone brightly in the light of the flaring torch. 'It's just wor angle. We'll come up with summink else if the fire upsets ye. We could say ye had a life-threatening illness. Or that ye've lost yer whole family.'

'That's true but. Almost anyway.'

'Look, Sewell. What we're dealing with here is hype. It doesn't have to be true. We just want to dee a bit strum on the auld heart strings.'

'Why does it always have to be me?'

'Areet, areet, it'll be me. It'll be me what's got the rare liver disorder. Now. This is the note we're gonnae hand him at half-time; then we'll see him as he's getting into the coach after the match. It took ages writing it. Had to twoc a pen an' all last neet. All the betting shops were closed. Worth it though for the Season Ticket.'

Sewell began to shake. 'Ah cannet believe it. We're gonnae get them then?'

'Aye.'

'We're really gonnae get them?'

'Aye. It's all worked oot. Ah've been thinking aboot it for ages. All this time we've been barking up the wrang tree. All this time, we've missed the obvious. The human element but. Ye kna what he's like, man. Auld Kev Keegan. Heart o' gold, man. He does loads of things like this. Cannet help but help people. Ah've seen him dee it on the telly, which is why ah thought ah'd put the bit aboot the fire.'

'Special K!' Sewell suddenly shouted.

'Messiah!' yelled Gerry.

The light phiffed into extinction. Gerry and Sewell started dancing in the pantry. Jigging and shouting hysterically. 'If ye love Kev Keegan clap yer hands! If ye love Kev Keegan clap yer hands! If ye love Kev Keegan, love Kev Keegan, love Kev Keegan clap yer hands!' The pantry rang with clapping and whoops of joy.

'A simple plan,' said Gerry. 'But ah think ye'll find it'll deliver! A return to first principles, like.'

'Ah always knew yus'd dee it.'

'Got there in the end, didn't we?'

'Except . . .'

'Except what?'

'Why Gerry man, what if he gives wor tickets for Fulham?'

'Y'kna summink, Sewell? Ye're always pissing on the bonfire ye.'

'Eh? Ah thought it didn't have to be a fire.'

Gerry sighed, then spoke gently: 'Divven't worry aboot nowt, Sewell man. It's all worked oot. Ah promise.'

In the sudden thoughtful silence that followed, Gerry's

mother could be heard singing. The words of the song drifted from the sitting room, only just managing to reach them, pressing through the gap of the pantry door and flapping inside weakly like a dying butterfly. Gerry and Sewell did not move a muscle, allowing the song to brush their faces and tangle in their hair, the whites of their eyes the only sign of each other in the darkness.

> Oh where is the boatman my bonny hinny?
> Oh where is the boatman, please bring him to me
> To ferry me awer the Tyne to my hinny
> And ah will remember the boatman and thee . . .

'Canny singer, yer mam like,' said Sewell.

Gerry was embarrassed. 'Ah can remember when she sang that song to me.'

'Must have been good that,' mused Sewell. 'Having a mam.'

Breathing unevenly, Mrs Macarten's voice seemed to struggle over the words, pausing every now and again as though actually defeated by a physicality as real as a river. She had to pause and rest before the last verse. Rallying her strength, she sang as loudly as she could.

> Oh bring me a boatman, ah'll give any money
> And ye for yer trouble rewarded will be
> To ferry me awer the Tyne to my hinny
> Or scull him across that rough river to me.

Silence thickened the darkness of the pantry.

'What's that?' cried Sewell, suddenly flinching.

'What?' asked Gerry.

'That! A rat or summink!' Sewell pointed at the foot of the door which had been opened by something about ankle-height. 'Bloody hell, ye've got rats!'

'It's the babby,' explained Gerry, bending down.

'Oh,' smiled Sewell. 'She's come to see wor,' and walking

up the steps he bent down and picked up the baby. 'She needs changing again,' he remarked mildly.

'Bloody hell!' said Gerry, trying to dodge the stench as though the infant were wielding a baseball bat at his head. But despite his efforts it hit him right between the eyes. 'Where's nana?' he cooed unconvincingly as he backed out of the pantry, up the steps and resurfaced into the kitchen.

'Nana,' echoed Sewell. 'Tell Uncle Sewell where nana is.'

'She wants yer bench coat,' laughed Gerry, pointing at the baby's hands which were both firmly gripping Sewell's coat.

His mother was bent double when they walked back into the living room. Seeing them she righted herself quickly and looked up with a smile. 'They told us in the hospital that ah had to dee these exercises from time to time.'

'Are ye areet?' asked Sewell.

'Why aye,' she said brightly. 'Champion.' The baby started crying. Gerry's mother reached out for her. 'Hand us me grandbairn,' she said. 'Ha'way, pet.' Gerry and Sewell watched her. A moment later there was a knock at the door. 'Ee its like Central Station here,' she remarked before dissolving her words into a mash of baby talk and cooing sounds.

Gerry went to the window, and peeped through an inch of raised curtain. 'Oh,' he said, and opened the door.

Sewell's face lit up like a firework when he saw Gemma come in. 'Areet, Mrs Macarten,' she said.

'Areet, bonny lass,' replied Gerry's mother.

'Areet, Gerry?' Gemma asked.

'Areet, Gemma,' Gerry replied.

Gemma was holding a plastic bag. 'Ah've just brought this for ye,' she said, handing it over to Sewell. Sewell blushed. 'It's mostly for Sewell 'cos ah kna he'll eat the most being so fat,' she laughed. 'But it's for ye an' all, Gerry.'

'What is it?' asked Gerry.

'It's wor bait, man,' said Sewell proudly, his fingers already exploring the contents of the bag.

'A few sarnies and a couple o' cans. Some cake an' all,' said

192

Gemma. 'Ah went to the petrol station shop. It's the only place open at this time.'

'Isn't she the best, man?' boasted Sewell happily. 'Isn't she the best?'

'Na,' giggled Gemma, blushing with pleasure. 'Ah'm just feeding me man. Ah kna yous are gannin' on a mission the day.'

'Do ye?' asked Gerry.

'Aye.'

'Oh.' Gerry's voice dropped and he narrowed his eyes at Sewell.

Unable to control himself, Sewell moved across the room to slide an arm round Gemma's waist. 'Ah cannet keep owt from me lass.' Then, holding up the bag of food, he added, 'There's even a few hairs from Rusty in it!'

'Belter,' said Gerry in a chilly tone. 'Purely belter.'

Sewell put the bait in the largest pocket of his bench coat. 'We've done it, pet,' he said, nodding furiously. 'We've friggin' well done it! Gerry's just telt wor all aboot it.' Moving both hands over the contours of Gemma's body, Sewell began kissing her, his mouth widening with each passing second. With thrusts and jerks and committed little moans, she responded. Breaking off the kiss loudly, Sewell bent down to her neck. There was a squelching, sucking sound. When he had finished there was an angry red welt on her neck.

'Is it showin'?' Gemma asked excitedly.

'Aye,' said Sewell proudly. Winding their arms round each other again their lips sought each other's.

'Ha'way,' coughed Gerry. 'We'd better be gannin' before yous two swallow each other.'

'Ah'll stay with yer mam a bit,' said Gemma.

From under the shelter of the door frame Gemma and Mrs Macarten waved Gerry and Sewell off. Gemma was holding the baby. She bounced it and waved its little hands. It was raining. The air was chilly. The last thing Gerry heard as they crossed the waste ground was his mother coughing.

'So ye think he'll help wor?' Sewell asked.

'Ah kna so.'

The train followed the course of the younger Tyne as it sparkled over its stones and under its stone bridges, pouring through the little Northumbrian towns. The carriage was crowded. Gerry and Sewell dodged the conductor, hiding in the toilet, getting off and then back on again at each station. 'We've done it,' whispered Gerry with a concealed smile as the train began to climb up to the wild terrain which is the upland border area of Northumbria and its cousin Cumbria. 'Part one nearly complete,' said Gerry. 'Next stage: get the letter to Kev. Ah was thinking, Sewell, ye any good at putting on a one o' them speech impediments?'

After Greenhead junction the conductor managed to corner Gerry and Sewell in the compartment before the driver's cab. He was sweating when he reached them. 'Ah've got yous at last,' he said, then added in a flat, triumphant voice, 'Tickets please!'

Gerry and Sewell made a great show of searching for their tickets. They emptied empty pockets and felt for non-existent wallets. They sighed. They emptied empty pockets again and re-felt for non-existent wallets. Every crevice and cranny of the bench coat was searched with a jabbing forefinger, and double-checked with an index finger. 'Cannet find them,' admitted Gerry at last. Then, before the conductor had time to speak, he launched into Sewell. 'Ah gave them to ye, man.'

Genuinely offended, Sewell returned, 'Na ye didn't.'

Desperately trying to make Sewell realise that they had rehearsed this, Gerry's voice soared up and down in tone. 'Ah did, man. Remember?'

'Na. Ah divven't remember.'

'Think aboot it. Ye had them.'

'Ah didn't, man Gerry. Ah nivver had them. Ah've nivver had a ticket.'

Gerry coughed loudly, nodding manically at his friend. 'He

cannet help it,' he explained to the conductor. 'He's an orphan. Aye, yus've got all confused, poor daftie, haven't ye?'

Sewell was adamant. 'But y'kna very well that we nivver got tickets.'

'When you're finished!' snapped the conductor, who had been watching this conversation without emotion. 'Where did ye buy yer tickets, lads?' he asked wearily.

'We got on at Haltwhistle,' said Gerry, relieved to be able to remember the name of the last station.

The conductor laughed joylessly. 'Yous have been on this service since we left the Metro Centre, haven't yous? Ah saw ye both.'

Suddenly the train came to a screeching halt and the conductor was thrown against the door. Sewell and Gerry piled against him. Cursing, he yelped in pain. 'That's me bad shoulder,' he told them. Turning round he banged on the driver's door. 'What's up, George?' he shouted.

'Coos on the line,' came back a thick voice.

The conductor opened a little panel in the wall above him. There were the two familiar metallic beeps and then the electric doors to the train shuddered open. He jumped down. A line of cows was spread over the line in the distance. When he came back he was fuming.

'What we gonnae dee, George?' he shouted.

'Wait for them to shift,' George replied phlegmatically.

The conductor seethed. He jumped off again. This time Sewell and Gerry followed him up the track. 'Cush!' he shouted, running towards the cows with his arms spread wide. One of the cows, actually lying over the line, looked up and regarded him coldly, its jaws chewing disdainfully.

'Cush! Cush!' shouted Gerry and Sewell, charging at the cow.

Still it wouldn't move. The conductor scratched his head and diving into the thick undergrowth of the railway cutting, came back holding a stick. 'Cush, you bastard,' he menaced.

Gerry and Sewell looked at each other. 'Are we near Carlisle?' asked Gerry.

The conductor shrugged his shoulders. 'Aye. It's just awer there.'

Gerry looked at Sewell. Sewell looked at Gerry.

'Run for it!' cried Gerry, hauling Sewell behind him. They scampered up the steep railway cutting. 'We're here, we're here!' Gerry laughed.

'Will wor see Carlisle's groond when we reach the top?' puffed Sewell heavily.

'What we'll see is wor Season Ticket!' shouted Gerry. They began to cheer. The cheering grew louder, crescendoing as they reached the top. Then there was silence.

'Where is it?' said Sewell. 'Where's the groond? Where's wor Season Ticket? Where's friggin' Carlisle?'

A harsh, bleak landscape of moor and coarse, tussocky grass tumbled from their feet, stretching unendingly in all directions. The more they looked, the vaster it seemed. Far away, the Solway estuary showed as a glimmer of silver where a distant sun shone on its treacherous muds. The Northern Pennines of England, the Southern Uplands of Scotland and the mountains of the Lake District ringed the other horizons. Below them, they heard the train moving off.

'Ah cannet see Carlisle,' said Sewell. 'Ah cannet see owt at all, me.' Feverishly, Gerry climbed the fence and sprinted over a field to where the land rose to a summit. 'Na,' announced Sewell, when he caught his breath. 'Ah still cannet see owt.' A strong wind blew into their faces. The train whistled as it disappeared round a fold of land. 'What we gonnae dee?' asked Sewell.

'It's aboot eleven o'clock,' replied Gerry.

'How d'ye kna?'

'Ah'm speculatin'.'

'Eh?'

'Ah divven't kna for certain, it just seems aboot that time.

We caught the ten o'clock morning train. Kick-off's three o'clock. That gives wor four hoors.'

'To dee what?'

'To get to Carlisle. Ha'way, Sewell. If we cannet walk there, then we'll find a road, and hitch. Ah mean, it's got to be oot there somewhere.'

They set off overland, scaling crumbling dry-stone walls, and scrambling under barbed-wire fences, sending sheep scattering. They forded becks swollen by spring rains and negotiated the assault courses of sudden, tight-knit conifer plantations. Gerry moved quickly, Sewell struggled after him, chest heaving.

'Oh, bloody hell!' moaned Sewell as his feet sank past their ankles in a concealed bog. 'That's it. Ah'm not gannin' any further.' Pulling himself free, he made for a nearby cluster of birch trees and, leaning his back against a trunk, slid to the ground.

'We're not there yet,' said Gerry.

'Ah'm not taking another step until ah've rested.' With two almighty heaves, Sewell pulled off his shoes and peeled off the socks. 'That's better,' he breathed, rubbing his wriggling toes.

'Ye're right. Mebbes we should rest,' conceded Gerry, sitting down beside him. 'Aye. Rest here, and then get off even quicker. Ah think ah've spotted a road. Ha'way then, let's have wor bait.' Sewell looked away guiltily. 'Ha'way,' urged Gerry. 'Ah'm starved.' Sewell continued to evade his friend's eye. 'Sewell man!' exclaimed Gerry. 'Ah'm talking to ye.'

Solemnly Sewell reached into his bench coat and brought out the plastic bag Gemma had given them. It was empty except for a few crumbs and two finished cans. 'Y'kna when ah went to the bog on the train and ah was ages . . .' he mumbled.

Gerry stared at his friend in disbelief. When he spoke it was softly. 'Ye fat, greedy get.'

'Ah'm sorry.'

Gerry's voice began to build angrily. 'Sorry. Ye said sorry

did ye? And ah suppose ye think that makes it areet. Sorry. Sorry?'

'Well, there's nee need to shoot, man. Ah am truly sorry.'

'Are ye?'

Sewell sighed magnanimously. 'Ha'way. Ah'll gan and find a shop.' Gerry laughed bitterly. Sewell got up decisively. 'Ah'll gan and get ye some crisps and mebbes a pasty or summink.'

Gerry threw his arms out wide. 'Sewell, man. Where's the shop?'

Sewell swivelled his head slowly in all directions.

Suddenly Gerry's frustration gave and he snapped like a Dobermann pinscher, his fingers leaping at Sewell's throat. 'We're in the middle o' bloody neewhere! There is nee shop. Nee pasties. Nee pies. Nee nowt,' he shouted. 'And it's not as though this is the first time ye've let me doon.'

Sewell knitted his eyebrows together ponderously. 'What d'ye mean?'

Gerry's voice quietened again, each word coiled, ready to spring. 'Not only have yus eaten wor bait, but ye've given away secrets an' all.'

'Eh?'

'The trip was supposed to be secret. Element of surprise an' all that, man. But ye told Gemma. All that time with ye pretending to be excited. Gannin' on aboot sweating it oot all neet. Tossing and turning 'cos ye didn't kna me master plan. Why aye, ye were sweating it oot, but not because of wor Season Ticket.'

'Surprise?'

'Top bloody secret.'

Sewell watched Gerry nervously. 'Why?'

'Because if they knew then everyone would dee it.'

Sewell opened his mouth wide in disbelief. 'What? Everyone would find themselves in the middle o' neewhere like this, with their feet soaked to the skin?'

Gerry exhaled exasperatedly. 'Well, not in this exact spot, man y'kna, obviously. But they'd want to try the same thing.

They'd gan to ask Keegan an' all. Mebbes even get there before wor. Think o' summink better than a fire.'

Sewell bowed his head in thought. 'Gemma and wor Season Ticket, man Gerry,' he began at last. 'Divven't get wor wrang, ah love her, me, but she's got nowt to dee with the Season Ticket. What ah mean is, she wants us to get it as much as ah dee.'

Gerry shook his head knowingly. 'It's not Gemma ah'm worried aboot.'

'Who is it then?' Sewell's face contorted with incomprehension.

'That lad she used to see. The ice hockey player.'

'She's finished with him.'

'Well, that makes things just perfect,' said Gerry sarcastically.

'We think so,' responded Sewell complacently.

'Now he'll really want to ruin wor plans. He'll dee owt to get back at ye, Sewell, and that means stopping us from getting wor Season Ticket.'

Sewell spat decisively on the ground. 'Gerry man,' he said. 'How's he gonnae ever find oot?'

Gerry paused a little before replying. 'Because she'll tell him.'

There was a silence. 'Na,' said Sewell certainly. 'She doesn't see him any more.'

'Grow up.'

'Eh?'

'Ah said grow up, man Sewell. She's probably still screwing him.'

Sewell looked at his friend with tortured eyes. He opened his mouth to speak but either forgot what he wanted to say or decided against it. He shook his head sadly a few times and then absorbed himself in vigorously rubbing his feet.

Above their heads the wind streamed through the canopy of the birches, thickening now with May. The trees were stunted, bonsaied by the cruel knife of the prevailing wind which runs unobstructed over this open moorland. Behind them a curlew raised itself up, calling desolately: Where I am going – where are you going – when will we know the place we are going? it's voice seemed to endlessly ask.

'We're lost,' said Gerry in a small voice.

'Oh, ha'way, Gerry,' encouraged Sewell. 'Ah wouldn't say that, man.'

Gerry snorted exasperatedly. 'What would ye say like?'

'What aboot that road?'

Getting up, Gerry trudged on purposefully, Sewell hopping after him as he put his shoes back on. The landscape never seemed to vary. Once they dropped a few hundred feet down a precipitous gill, but when they came up on the other side it was as if they had climbed back up the side they had just descended. The land on both sides of the small valley was identical: a never-ending roll of wind-bitten grasses and gnarled knots of mountain ash and alder. The wind freshened, slapping their cheeks like hands. A flock of lapwings blew by above them. 'Ah cannet take another step,' Sewell said, falling to the ground.

Gerry whirled his arms in exasperation. 'Oh, aye. What ye gannae dee like? Wait for the friggin' Angel to fly here with a pan o' bacon an' egg?'

Sewell hauled himself to his feet. They walked on, but they were getting slower and slower. 'Gerry? Ah wish ye hadn't said that.'

'Said what?' replied Gerry fifty yards later.

Panting heavily, Sewell paused on top of a fence at which Gerry had been waiting for him. 'Bacon an' egg,' he explained.

'Eh?'

'Ah wish ye hadn't said bacon an' egg. Back there ye said bacon an' egg. Ee! What ah wouldn't give to be sitting doon to a panful of bacon an' egg.'

Gerry narrowed his eyes and smirked. 'Burger,' he said. 'Double cheeseburger with chips.'

Sewell moaned.

'Pepperoni pizza.'

'Oh divven't!' Sewell begged breathlessly.

'Double pepperoni! Toast dripping with butter. Fish and chips. Pie and chips. A lovely juicy kebab from the Bigg Market. A sausage roll, piping hot, still in the bag from the bakery and the steam drifting off it like a dog's shite.'

'Chinky and chips,' simpered Sewell, revelling malevolently in his own hunger. 'Fish and chips. Pie and chips. Sausage and chips.'

'Sunday dinner from the pub.'

'Ham and pease pudding stotties. Beef curry. Lamb curry.'

'Chicken and mushroom pie . . .'

'And chips. With gravy.'

'Two lots of chips. All with salt and vinegar and tomato sauce. Pot noodles. Microwave chips. Pizzas. Every single kind of pizzas . . .'

'Nee more!' howled Sewell, arcing in the air like a whale coming up for breath and crashing to his knees. 'Ah cannet stand it me. Nee more food!'

When they were resting for the fifth or sixth time, it began to rain. 'Ha'way,' urged Gerry. 'Let's get as far as we can before it starts to piss doon.'

Stumbling to their feet, they staggered out of the deep gill where they had been resting. At the top they found their way blocked by trees. An immense line of trees. Dark evergreens, closely planted. 'Friggin' hell!' whispered Sewell, hardly able to speak for terror. 'Friggin', flamin', hell!'

Gerry followed the point of his friend's shaking finger. 'What?'

'That!' shrieked Sewell, just as a flock of goats came hurtling towards them. It was one of the ancient herds that roam the Anglo-Scottish border forests. The remnant of those brought here by Danes, more than a thousand years ago.

Scrabbling wildly on hands and knees, the youths hurled themselves behind a boulder.

'What the hell was that?' Gerry asked, when the drumming

sound of hooves had passed. Sewell could not answer. 'Frigg this for a game of soldiers.' In silence they listened wide-eyed as the herd disappeared into the gill.

'Ha'way,' said Sewell, getting up from the boulder and blundering under the eaves of the forest. 'At least there'll be some shelter in here.'

It was dark, and silent. Gerry and Sewell were jumpy as conifer followed conifer. Ridges of oaks sometimes rode up the land above them, and in one deep hollow, which they reached after about twenty minutes' walking, there were beeches, growing more widely apart. They began to relax again, but when they were enclosed by conifers once more, the air seemed to have thickened. A snapped twig, an unseen bird's song, a spoken word, all rang out loudly here. Disconsolately, they tried to return to the beeches, but could not find them. Rain was beginning to fall on the needles above them when they stumbled upon an open ride in the forest, and then an area of mountain ashes. Sheltering, they slumped down with their backs against a trunk, their bodies gradually assuming a supine position. 'What's that?' asked Sewell nervously after a while.

'What's what?'

'That. Sounds like someone whispering.' They both listened intensely.

'Mebbes it's the auld man of the forest,' said Gerry mysteriously. 'Ye kna. The spirit what was trying to warn wor off from coming into these friggin' woods in the first place.'

'Piss off,' replied Sewell uncertainly.

Gerry sighed. 'Look, Sewell. Them animals are nowt. Weird ah admit. But nowt really. Just animals. Sheep or summink.'

'Thems weren't nee sheep.'

There was a long silence. 'What time is it?' Sewell said when they had been lying under the rowans for a long time. Gerry ignored him. 'What time is it?' Sewell reiterated, rolling over to face Gerry, placing his head on his arm.

'One twig past the friggin' leaf,' replied Gerry.

'Keep yer hair on,' retorted Sewell.

'Well aye! Divven't ye gan and ask such stupid questions. Ye kna very well that ah haven't got a watch, man Sewell man.'

'But ye always seem to kna the time.'

'Well, ah divven't here. Ah kna nowt here.'

Gerry took out a box of matches. 'Ha'way, Sewell, gis that last tab what me mam borrowed wor.'

Sewell looked away.

'Ye've smoked it yersel', haven't ye?'

'Aye,' said Sewell miserably. 'Y'kna when ah said ah was having that monster shite?'

'Ye mean when yus were eating wor bait?'

'Ah finished it off with that tab an' all.'

Closing their eyes, they began to doze. Lulled by the peace of the place and their exhaustion, a shallow snooze deepened into slumber. When Sewell eventually woke, he found Gerry standing staring at an owl on the branch above them. 'Shh,' said Gerry, finger across his lips. They watched it for a while. 'Y'kna owls? In other civilisations, they're a symbol of death.'

'Piss off!' moaned Sewell.

Frightened by the raised voice, the owl flew off, its sweeping wings fanning Gerry's face. 'Noo, ye've done it,' he said.

'Done what?'

'Brought the curse doon on yer heed.'

'Grow up!' Sewell said. Then he stood up purposefully. 'Ha'way, let's get gannin'.' Gerry did not reply. 'Ha'way, cannet sit aboot here all day. We've got to get to Carlisle to see Kev Keegan.'

Gerry licked his lips. 'Ha ha,' he laughed. 'Hahahahahaha!'

'Why are ye laughing, man?'

'HAHAHAHAHA!'

Gerry faced Sewell. 'Look, we're lost, reet? Lost.' Then, slowing his words down as though he were talking to a baby, he said, 'Lo-st, we div-ven't kna where we are or where we a-re gan-nin'. We have been wand-er-ing for hours. Soon it will be gett-ing da-rk.'

The ash grove seemed to reverberate with Gerry's words, which continued to hum angrily long after he had spoken them, gathering under the thickly leafed boughs like swarming insects. Sewell started to swat the air about his face. Gerry twitched, and then scratched. They began to slap their wrists and ankles as though performing the preliminaries to a ritual dance. Leaping up, they hopped from foot to foot. 'Midges,' moaned Gerry. 'Everywhere!'

There was no escape, and the midges, having descended upon them suddenly, now tormented them beyond belief. Every inch of exposed flesh was thick with the tiny insects. Their nostrils, ears and mouths filled up quickly so that they could smell and taste the whining insects. Like a maddened animal, Sewell took off through the trees. Gerry followed him at a sprint.

Leaping a fallen tree trunk, they vaulted a ditch and ran down a bank. Bluebells carpeted the thick fabric of the grass forming that picture of England found in so many homes, but they did not notice the flowers. They reached a river. It was about ten or fifteen yards wide and, where it pooled under high ledges of rock, fed by the quick upland current, it seemed deep and slow. The water was dark with peat. Gerry and Sewell stopped on a small headland of grass and bluebells overhanging the pool at the height of two or three people. The small comfort that had come from speed was swept away by a fresh onslaught of midges. 'Ah cannet stand it,' whined Sewell, sliding his jaw from side to side in an increasingly condyle movement. 'Ah just cannet stand it.' Suddenly he opened up his bench coat and stepped out of it. Kicking off his trainers, he pulled down his tracksuit bottoms and lifted his sweatshirt over his outstretched arms. Fidgeting desperately, he stood still for a moment in only his underpants. Then, driven into fresh frenzy by another onslaught from the midges, he tottered to the edge and, with a deep gulp and a bellow of bovine panic, jumped. There was an almighty splash. It resonated profoundly against the rocks. The dark water was flecked with a few flats of foam created by Sewell's impact. Apart from that there was no sign of any disturbance on its tranquil smoothness. A few moments passed.

'Ha'way,' Gerry said, imploring the water. 'Ha'way, ye fat get. Surface, cannet ye?'

But still there was no sign. Shaking his head at the midges, Gerry crouched down and scrutinised the river below. It was as though Sewell had never existed. As though the river had completely digested him, or ushered him into another world deep within the rocks. Gerry shuddered. Then, just as he was about to jump in himself, fully clothed, an immense air bubble rose and exploded on to the surface of the water. Slowly, Sewell's head became visible a few feet under the surface. The rest of him followed as his ample body breached the water like a luxuriating water mammal. 'Belter!' exclaimed Sewell, floating on his back. 'It's purely belter!'

'Ah, me lads!' Gerry began singing as he stood naked on the bank. 'Ye should have seen us gannin'.' His words were shrieks as he arced through the air. He felt the slap of water on every pore of his skin and then he sank beneath the dark water. Still sinking, he looked about at the strange, black chamber which had taken him so utterly. For one terrifying moment he thought that he would never leave this dark silence, that he would never want to; for one terrifying moment he thought that at least he would never hear again the siren of that ambulance, nor be dazzled by the rip of the flashing lights; for one terrifying but seductive moment he considered the peace of this airless element. 'It's freezin'!' he yelled as he bobbed up to the surface.

From the water the woods looked different. The rocks towered above them, but protectively, like the inside of battlements. The bluebells raged like a blue fire. The trees, deciduous by the water, bearded with lichen and moss, seemed impossibly old. And all the time a delicate but insistent current tugged at the edges of everything. 'Cushdy,' repeated Sewell, surfacing and diving. 'Cushdy. Like swimming in a pint of Guinness.'

'Aye, that's been in a freezer!'

The skin of the water wrinkled a little where the raindrops landed. 'Are ye warm?' Gerry asked as he swam frantically from one bank to the other. Sewell came over to him. Laughing and shouting, swimming and diving, they ducked each other under the water. They swam a little upstream, reaching the place where the river poured itself over a lip of rock into the pool. There they lay in the massaging current as though it were a jacuzzi. 'Ha'way, man,' began Gerry when they had stopped playing. 'Canny spot to bring a lass.' He narrowed his eyes. 'Listen, ah've got it all worked oot. Gan for a swim with her first.'

'Aye,' laughed Sewell.

'Make sure she doesn't bring a cossie, eh?'

'Oh, aye.' Sewell's wicked laugh matched Gerry's.

'If she cannet swim too well ask her if she needs lessons.'

'. . . if she needs lessons.'

'Get a few handfuls in under the water.'

'. . . a few handfuls.'

'Then afterwards rub her doon.'

'. . . rub her doon.'

'Smooth away any, y'kna, goose bumps.'

'. . . goose bumps.'

'Then if she's cold take her under a tree and warm her up.'

'. . . under a tree.'

'Tell ye what, Sewell, ah could get another lass and ye could dee it with Gemma.'

No appreciative echo this time.

'Ah said that ye could dee it with Gemma,' reiterated Gerry. Still no reply.

'Sewell man, ah'm talking to ye.'

'Na.'

'Na?'

'Gemma's a lady.'

'So?'

'So ah wouldn't just dee them things.'

'Wouldn't ye like?'

'Na, ah'd ask her first.'

Gerry suddenly began to shiver. They started a water fight, splashing each other with mill-wheel arms, but Gerry fell back in the water, shivering. 'Ye see, Gerry,' said Sewell, streaming into deeper water, and rolling on to his back. 'Being thin isn't all it's cracked up to be.'

'What ye gannin' on aboot?'

'Well, say if there was a geet, freak wave noo, and we were smashed against them rocks, and both broke a leg, then ye would die before me.'

'Oh aye?'

'Aye, ah'd last longer. Ye'd soon peg oot. Look at yersel' noo. Ye're shivering like a half-droowned rabbit.' Grabbing hold of the bank by the roots of its grass and flowers, Gerry hauled himself up. Shuddering with the cold, he smoothed off the droplets from his body. 'Ye see me? Ah'm still warm,' said Sewell as inch by inch he strained himself up the bank behind Gerry. Reaching the top, he stood there with his hands on his hips. The water coursed down his legs. There were fewer midges now. 'Ah wish ah hadn't gone in with me undies on though,' he added wistfully. When they were dressed, Gerry began walking further into the forest. 'Now ah kna how a babby feels like in a wet nappy,' remarked Sewell miserably, following at a waddle.

'Ha'way, ah thought ah saw summink,' Gerry told him without turning.

They stopped where the conifers stood like a drawn curtain, barring the greater light of the mountain ash trees, reducing the undergrowth to an orange carpet of needles and a few tangled bramble bushes. 'It's in here somewhere,' explained Gerry. 'Ah saw it before we went swimming.'

'What is it?' asked Sewell.

They trudged on for another few yards, pushing through a sudden elder thicket.

'That,' said Gerry pointing.

There before them, standing in a clearing of dark green bracken, were the ruins of a cottage. Only three walls still stood but in the far corner there was a doorless opening leading into a small chamber where the walls and roof were still intact. Breasting the bracken they approached the building. When he poked his head through the crumbling cavity Gerry saw a fireplace fanning up to a chimney. A window held its glass, which was begrimed with dust and cobwebs. There was even a table standing, attended by two chairs. He went in.

Sewell sighed and began plodding away.

'See sense, man Sewell. It's getting late . . .'

'Ah thought ye didn't have a watch,' Sewell interrupted.

'We've been lost for ages. It must be late. The match'll be over by noo.' Gerry took a step towards Sewell and looked him in the eye. 'Face facts, man. We've missed Kevin Keegan. We've missed wor chance.'

The owl hooted from somewhere in the distance. The sun was sinking below the treeline; the light in the clearing was fading. The gradual slide into darkness which is a British late-spring night, had begun. The trees and bushes were melting themselves into shadows. It had stopped raining.

'Ah'm hungry,' moaned Sewell softly. 'Hungry.'

'Me too.'

'What are we gonnae eat?'

'Why ye asking me?'

'Hungry,' repeated Sewell, his voice rumbling like a stomach.

'Ah kna,' Gerry told him. 'Ye've already told me.'

'Na. Ah mean hungry. So hungry that ah would eat anything! D'ye hear me? AH COULD EAT A SCABBY HORSE, ME!'

Wriggling free of Sewell's feverish grip, Gerry took a step

away. 'We need summink to eat. But there is nowt. So, if Mohammed cannet come to the moontain . . .'

'Just tell wor where to get food!' exclaimed Sewell desperately.

Spitting casually, Gerry pointed down to the river. 'Ah've nivver known a better fisherman than ye, Sewell.'

Sewell's mouth widened with bewilderment. 'But ah've nee tackle or bait or owt.'

'As ah said, if Mohammed . . .'

Sewell crashed into the bracken. 'We'll need slugs,' he shouted, stooping to the base of the plants. 'And ah can use the drawstring bit o' me bench coat.'

'Ah'll have a fire gannin',' said Gerry. 'And Sewell,' he added. 'Take them undies off, man. Ah cannet stand to see ye walk in them. Makes ye look like a crab. Ha'way, ah won't look.'

The underpants were taken off and left in a soggy pile on a crumbling wall of the cottage. Gerry approached them with a stick and speared them up. 'Ah'll even dry them for ye.' He watched his friend as he slipped into the shadows, whistling. Gathering some wood, Gerry piled it on what was left of the cottage's hearth. He stacked the thinnest bits into a pyramid in the fireplace and placed some dry lichen delicately under the structure and then lit it in three separate places. Stooping, he blew gently. The lichen glowed, its powder popping into flame. The pyramid glowed and then fell in on itself. After a while he added the larger pieces. 'An arsonist is the man for a fire,' he said, cackling to himself. 'And that's one job ah've got the references for.'

The darkness came, relieved only by a moon which winked out from behind a gathering cloud cover. The owl began hooting again from somewhere behind the cottage, deeper in the conifer forest. It fell silent for a moment only to recommence, but this time from much closer. Gerry rubbed his hands together. It was getting colder. The fire licked at the wood, spitting angrily at the pockets of gas it found, its light sending a glow over the hearth and shadows on to the walls. The air was icy at the open door. He threw more wood on the fire and huddled closer. Hugging himself, he rubbed his hands restlessly. At last, he got up and stumbled through the doorless door, out into the main shell of the cottage and then into the forest. The cold hit him like a hammer. Thick sleet was beginning to fall. 'SeweLLLL,' he shouted. 'Are ye areet, SeweLLLL?' There was no reply.

Longingly, Gerry looked back at the warm glow of the fire, but tearing himself from it, he set off towards the river. 'SeweLLLL?' The sleet fell harder and harder, its thick, wet flakes a lighter presence in the gathering darkness. Gerry slipped and his feet gave way beneath him. He crashed on to a soft bed of pine needles. Pulling himself up, he hurried on. 'SeweLLLL!' The sleet grew drier and fell harder. At last he thought he could hear the whisper of the river's current. Something over his shoulder took fright and bolted. His heart lurched. 'SeweLLLL!' Gerry slowed down, but his momentum took him skidding over the light sprinkling of snow. 'The river,' he whispered to himself urgently. 'Divven't fall into the river, ye prize chump!' He couldn't see much, but the river was louder than ever. Cautiously he felt out in front of him with a toe. The grass gave way to air. He was right on the edge of the bank. He swore under his breath and slowly retraced half a dozen steps.

'BOO!' somebody shouted, jumping out from behind a tree. Gerry crashed to the floor under the impact of a rugby tackle. He and his assailant slid dangerously near the edge of the bank. 'Doon ye gan, boy,' the tackler laughed. The snow stung Gerry's face. His fingers dug desperately into the cold earth, trying to brake their slide. They came to a halt with their legs already kicking out over the river.

'Sewell ye prick!' seethed Gerry, smoothing the snow off his clothes and chin. 'Ye could have had us in. Ah'll get ye for that.'

'Ha'way,' said Sewell. 'Ah've caught wor tea.' Gerry looked at his friend. He could only see his outline, but he seemed to be holding out something. 'Can ye believe it's snowing?' Sewell said. 'Makes wor feel all Christmassy.'

'Oh, aye,' mumbled Gerry.

'Cheer up, man,' said Sewell. 'And divven't mumble.'

They walked back to the cottage in silence, concentrating on keeping the hardening snow-storm from contact with their faces.

The fire was still glowing. Gerry added a thick bundle of wood and sat down. The fish were both about the length of a hand, and the width of a fat finger. 'What are they?' Gerry asked.

'Divven't kna,' admitted Sewell.

'How d'ye catch them?'

Sewell shrugged enigmatically. Digging in a pocket, he brought out an ancient Swiss Army penknife with which he began to gut the fish. In the silence, the wood crackled warmingly. 'Me dad taught us.'

Gerry looked at the fire and then returned to his friend's fingers. 'Did he?'

'When ah was a bairn like.'

'He was always deein' things with ye when ye were a bairn.'

'Aye.'

Although the fish were small they seemed like a feast to Gerry and Sewell, who ate every single scrap and licked each finger thoroughly. Sewell had brought water from the river in the two empty cans left in the bait bag. 'Guinness,' laughed Gerry.

The light from the fire filled the small room, but on the walls Gerry's and Sewell's shadows were driven into a frenzy by the freezing wind. The patch around the opening was covered in snow. Without a word Sewell took off his bench coat and hung it over the empty door frame. With the help of some stones taken from the fallen fourth wall in the main part of the cottage, they were able to secure the coat into a kind of door. The room immediately became warmer. 'We can make tea oot o' them,' Sewell said, pointing at a clump of bracken growing in the wall. 'Ah've seen Ginga dee it.'

'Mebbes later,' said Gerry.

Sewell suddenly jumped up, and went over to his coat. 'Aha, ah'd forgotten aboot the secret pocket!' he exclaimed triumphantly, bringing out two bars of chocolate.

Like two little boys, they cheered immediately. 'Thank God yer so thick, man,' said Gerry.

They savoured the chocolate, eating it piece by piece, feeling the warmth spread within them.

'We'll sleep here the neet,' decided Gerry. 'In the morning we'll gan back to Gatesheed.'

'Aye,' agreed Sewell.

Gerry sighed with satisfaction. 'That's if we ever get oot alive.'

'Eh?' demanded Sewell.

'Why, this hoose it's bound to be haunted. In fact, shh, listen . . .'

Sewell got up, his chair falling behind him, its clatter echoing eerily. 'Pack it in noo, man, or ah'm gannin'.'

'What aboot the spirits o' them radgie sheep? What aboot the mad shepherd, and his ruined cottage?'

Sewell took a step to the improvised door. 'And ah'll take me bench coat with us an' all, mind,' he threatened.

'Ha'way, Sewell, ah was only having yus on.'

Slowly Sewell walked back, and picked up the chair. 'Ye just open yer mooth once more about them what-ever-they-weres, and ah'm friggin' off.'

'Keep your hair on,' replied Gerry seriously, adding, 'As the mad axeman said to the gadgie what foond himsel' alone in the deep, dark wood. They were weird, but. Them sheep.'

In one movement Sewell had dashed over to Gerry and, throwing his arms round his neck, levered him back on to two legs of his chair. 'Promise?' demanded Sewell.

Gerry held out for a few moments, struggling in Sewell's grip. 'Promise,' he conceded eventually. Sewell sat back down. 'Ye should see yer face, mind,' began Gerry after a while. Sewell bristled angrily. 'Your cheeks and chin an' that are purely white but your ears are geet red. Like a turnip between two beetroots.'

Sewell nodded nonchalantly. 'Oh aye,' he remarked. 'Ah used to gan like that when ah was a bairn.'

'Really?' asked Gerry.

'Aye,' responded Sewell seriously. 'When ah was a tot. If ever ah had a shock or owt like that, all the blood drained to me ears.'

Lapsing back into silence, they stared into the fire. 'Listen,' Gerry said. 'Ah mean just listen.' Sewell listened. 'What can ye hear?' Sewell shrugged. 'Nee cars, nee shouting, nee police helicopter,' Gerry continued. 'Nee nothing.'

'What would they think if they could see us noo?' mused Sewell.

For a long time they sat there on the two chairs by their fire, and the grey, unquiet streets of Gateshead seemed very far away. 'Me mam's not very well,' said Gerry at last, his voice following the rhythm of the fire as its flames rose and fell.

'Ah kna,' replied Sewell.

'She'll be areet y'kna, it's just that she's not too well.'

The fire burnt well, freeing the different shapes of Gerry and Sewell into dancers on the crumbling wall. One big, one small; both nimble.

'Did yer auld man really learn ye how to fish like that?'

Sewell shifted position and looked deeply into the fire. 'Ah've nivver known me auld man. Ah live with me granda. Ah call me granda dad.'

Rarely taking their eyes from the ordinary mystery of the fire, Gerry and Sewell began a conversation which was to last deep into the night. They talked slowly, allowing long pauses between replies and comments. Sometimes they would take so long to answer each other that they had forgotten what they were talking about. It did not matter.

'My auld man nivver did owt like yours,' said Gerry. 'Yer granda ah mean. Teachin' ye things an' that.'

Sewell screwed up his nose in thought. 'He was great when ah was a bairn, with me not having a mam an' dad y'kna. Took me to matches, learnt wor how to fish, with or withoot a rod. He was from the sticks, oot the back y'kna. From oot Chopwell way. A lang time since. After the mine closed, he nivver had another job. We always seemed to have enough but. Had an allotment. Did a bit poaching. But when they tore them doon, the allotments, summink just died in him. Ah kna everybody says he's doo-lalley-tap. Ginga's the only mate who's stuck to him. And one or two others from the allotments. Ah kna he's mental. Gettin' worse an' all.' Sewell paused, consulting the fire by way of preparation. The firelight lined his face, wrinkling him, ageing him, painting his future portrait. 'Ah have to take him to the netty y'kna. Wipe his arse for him when he's finished. The only thing he can dee is make a cup o' tea. Not much that mebbes, but ah've always thought that if he can dee that then things aren't too bad. A cup o' tea. That's a normal thing, isn't it? Everybody in England makes a cup o' tea. Mebbes even the Queen. So as long as me auld man could make a cup o' tea ah didn't worry too much. But the other day ah walked into the kitchen. He didn't see me. He was making a cup o' tea. He put the bag in the cup and then went to the tap. He used water from the tap. It wasn't even hot. Just a bit warm. That's how he makes his tea noo. With water from the tap. Na. He's gone. He's mental. He's purely radge. But ah still . . . well ah still love him y'kna.'

'What aboot yer mam and dad?' Gerry's voice was hushed as all around them the vast silence urged and encouraged their secrets.

'Nivver met them. Either of them. Ah've seen a picture of him, nivver even seen a picture of her like. He's inside. On a canny lang stretch.'

214

'D'ye not, y'kna, want to visit him?'

Sewell thought long and hard. A vole scurried over the ground, disappearing into the wall. The scuttling of its claws was audible for a while and then fell away. 'Mebbes. But they've gone from wor, man Gerry. Just gone.'

A squall of wind pressed itself against the bench coat. A fox could be heard barking.

'Sewell?' began Gerry, taking his turn when the fox had also grown silent. 'Sometimes ah wish me dad was dead.'

'Bridget,' whispered Sewell.

Gerry got up and resecured part of the coat which had been blown loose. He sat back down, perching lightly on the edge of his chair. 'How d'ye kna aboot that like?'

'Everybody does, man.'

'How?'

'Oh, y'kna.'

'Ha'way! How does everybody kna aboot me dad and wor Bridie?'

'He gets wrecked, doesn't he? Stands on the road and shouts for her. Doon the club an' that. Always gannin' on aboot it. Defending himsel'. Says it's not true. Ah'm sorry, Gerry. Ah thought ye knew.'

Leaning over to the pile of wood, Gerry took the biggest log. He placed it gently on the fire. It burnt slowly, taking a while to produce heat, but when it did it radiated so much warmth that even the back of the room felt its effect. 'Sewell?' Gerry began. 'D'ye ever wonder?'

'What aboot?'

'D'ye ever wonder aboot the way we gan on?'

Sewell thought about the question, inspecting each fingernail minutely before answering. 'What d'ye mean?'

'Twocing and robbing an' that. Everything, y'kna.' Gerry rubbed his hands in front of the fire, warming them on both sides. He put his feet over the flames and wriggled his toes. 'D'ye ever wonder why things are the way they are, and not different?'

'Different?'

'Different. Ah mean it's not as if every bugger's oot robbin' the day they hoy off their nappies.' Gerry stared at his friend, thought about spitting in the fire and then stopped. 'Sometimes ah wonder if there's anyone up there. Y'kna. Looking over wor or summink.'

Sewell half shrugged. 'There's the Angel.'

Gerry nodded. 'That's what ah mean. Is there summink that stands above wor like the Angel stands above Gateshead?'

Sewell leant forward and brought his face to rest on two upturned palms. 'Ah hope there is.'

'Summink to look after wor,' said Gerry, dreamily repeating his own words. 'If there is then ah hope it's like the Angel and not the pollis helicopter. Summink to, y'kna, help, not chase.'

'Mebbes a summink like Kevin Keegan. Making everything better like. Or . . .' Sewell stopped abruptly. 'Like a dad. A good dad. One that loves ye an' that. One that really wants ye.'

'Aye,' smiled Gerry sadly. 'Mebbes like a good dad.'

The wind changed direction for a moment and came moaning down the chimney. They listened. The wind died down, searching for itself deeper in the forest. Slowly Gerry turned to Sewell and looked in his friend's eyes. 'They call us scum,' he said. 'All of them dee. And even when they divven't say it to yer face, ye kna they're thinking it all the same. Scum, they're thinking, ye're all just scum. Caird. The swots in top sets. The doctor. The pollis. Them at the Job Centre. They all think we're scum.' He paused and sat rigidly upright. 'Sewell man, mebbes we cannet change it. Mebbes things cannet be different. But there is summink we can dee. We can nivver give up on wor Season Ticket.'

Sewell turned his head to look over at Gerry. 'Ah nivver did.'

Gerry smiled. 'Cannet ye see? We're nowt withoot a one.' Gerry relaxed, idly stoking the fire with a twig. When he looked back to his friend, the firelight caught a steely, decided, irrevocable set in his face. 'It was a crap idea. Gannin' to

Carlisle. And the rest. All of this stuff we've done up to now, well it's all been bairn's stuff. Bits here, bits there. We'll nivver raise the money this way.' Gerry fell silent for a while. Then, in a voice that seemed nothing more than a whisper said, 'It's got to be a big job, Sewell. Get the money in one fell swoop. There's nowt else for it.'

'A job?' asked Sewell after a long time.

Gerry nodded. 'A job. Big time. Dee it all in one fell swoop. Willing to risk it?'

'Why aye.'

Outside the snow had stopped falling, and there was such a profound silence that the endless ranks of conifers could be heard creaking slightly, puzzled by their unseasonal burden. The clouds had blown away and the moon shone uninterrupt-edly over the immense forest which incorporates Wark, Spadeadam and grows into the mighty dark green of Kielder. Free from the light pollution of the cities, the stars looked down, their curiosity blazing in the sky. Did they see the two figures nodding fitfully by the wood fire in a ruined cottage, counting their dreams drowsily like sums that will not add up?

10

Sewell and Gerry were walking quickly through the streets of Gateshead. At their heels lowped Rusty. 'Where we gannin'?' Sewell asked again, sweating in his bench coat under the June sun. Increasing his pace, Gerry did not answer. 'Gerry man, where we gannin'?' Without turning to his friend, Gerry whistled the opening lines of The Blaydon Races. 'Canny,' purred Sewell, rubbing his hands together in appreciation. 'Canny.'

They trotted across Bensham. Bensham has a large Orthodox Jewish community. The Jews make Bensham a unique, exotic, almost dreamlike place. They are a community that grows along with the others of Gateshead like a tall, mysterious, separate evergreen tree on a heath of scrub. Go through Bensham on a Friday and vanishing round corners you will glimpse the coat-tails of a world that elsewhere has been savagely disappeared from Europe. Sewell and Gerry hastened past Jewish shops and the synagogue, a teacher-training college and a Talmudic institute. The dark-clothed Jews stared after them for a brief moment before looking away again, as though returning to concerns so many centuries, continents, worlds away.

Gerry and Sewell began to run. They ran through the little parks where small children were scaling multicoloured slides assisted by the secure hands of their grandads, ex-miners made tender at last; they ran past pubs heaving with happy people, past Job Centres seething with disgruntled ones; they ran past betting shops whose horses never come in, and past the pigeon crees whose flocks always return. They sped the entire length of Gateshead. 'When?' asked Sewell, puffing to keep up. 'When? When? When?'

'The day,' Gerry told him simply. 'The day.'

When they slackened their pace for a moment, Gerry turned to his friend quizzically, and pointing at the dog said, 'Ah thought Gemma was lookin' after the hoond.'

'She is,' panted Sewell. 'But he keeps on getting oot.'

'We cannet have him with us for what we want to dee.'

'Ah kna, ah kna. Ah'll take him back.'

'He'll get ye, y'kna. The dog boy.'

In the distance a church clock struck four. The rich smell of melting tarmac greeted them as they entered the Teams. Gerry caught sight of three figures gathered by a cut between derelict houses. 'Let's gan this way,' he said to Sewell. But behind him Sewell and Rusty had already crossed the road. Cursing, Gerry turned to join them all by the cut. The three figures stopped what they were doing and turned to face the two newcomers.

'Areet,' said Jimmy.

'Areet,' said Sewell.

'Areet,' said Gerry.

'Areet,' said Mally.

'Areet,' said Sewell.

'Areet,' said Gerry.

'Areet,' said Darren.

'Areet,' said Sewell.

'Areet,' said Gerry.

'Aye,' they all replied.

The greetings were followed by a silence. Picking up a bottle of Lambrella Pear Perry, Jimmy offered it to Sewell and Gerry. Gerry shook his head; reluctantly Sewell mirrored him. 'What is it with yous two nooadays? Yus nivver dee owt for a laugh.' Jimmy held the bottle to Rusty. 'What aboot the hoond, stopped his fun an' all?' Sewell shook his head. Jimmy shrugged his shoulders, tilted his head back, and took two huge, Adam's-apple-bobbing gulps from the bottle. Then he passed it to Darren. 'Are ye seein' Gemma?' Jimmy asked Sewell, his baby face contorting into an impish leer.

'Why?' asked Sewell sharply.

'Nee need to bite,' replied Jimmy. 'Ah was only askin'. It's your life, Sewell.'

'What d'ye mean by that like?'

Jimmy raised his eyes knowledgeably. 'Ye might be hard, man Sewell, but ye're nee match for Gemma's auld lad and his mates. Not all o' them.'

'So?'

'Put it this way. He knows aboot ye and Gemma.'

Just at that moment there was a shout from one of the boarded-up houses. A second later, the metal hoarding blocking the first-floor window was sent clattering to the ground. Dust puffed up from where it landed in a rubbish-strewn yard. The dust cloud shimmered on the hot air. A voice thundered out. 'Divven't ye move. Ah'm comin' doon!'

Jimmy laughed. 'Ah forgot to tell ye, Sewell. The dog boy's after ye an' all.'

There was a splintering of wood. A foot appeared through a hole in the boards over the door of the derelict house. A scrawny, mongrel-like figure emerged into the growing heat. 'Shit,' whispered Gerry.

'Psycho bollocks wants a word with ye,' giggled Jimmy, moving off down the road. Darren and Mally followed him. 'He's oot of it, man,' they laughed, gambolling with each other like hyenas. 'Divven't hang aboot.'

'Ha'way,' said Gerry, taking three or four steps in the same direction. 'He's radgie, off his heed.' Putting his hand down, Sewell gently massaged Rusty's ears. 'Sewell man, divven't look for trouble!' Gerry implored, urgency causing his voice to rise an octave.

Matthew slowly approached the neck of the cut in which Sewell stood waiting, motionless. Wearing only a pair of shorts, Matthew's meagre body was yellow in the sunlight. His arms seemed very long on his scrawny frame, hanging in a cordage of sinew and bone. Even from where Gerry stood, he could see the length of his fingernails. Matthew continued towards Sewell, advancing carefully now that he was so near, as though he was stalking him. Every so often he leant his head on one side and seemed to sniff exploratively. 'Mat-theeewww!' howled Jimmy and his friends, having stopped a safe hundred yards away. But Matthew did not seem to notice them. His attention was fastened completely on Sewell. Uncertainly, Gerry took a step back to the cut, but went no further. 'For godsake,' he whispered urgently. 'Run, man.'

When he was within spitting range of Sewell, Matthew stopped. Sewell tried to clear his throat. His mouth had run dry. A low growl was emanating from Matthew and he curled his lip. The whine turned to words. 'Ye took my dog.' Sewell narrowed his eyes, his hand fell stiffly from Rusty's ears, and, searching for a resting place, began to fiddle awkwardly with a bench coat pocket. 'He's mine, and ye twoced him.' Matthew took another step forward so that now they were almost within touching distance. Sewell took his hand away from the pocket, and raised both forearms so that his elbows tensed into right angles. 'Mine.' Sewell blinked slightly under the impact of the growled word.

Down the road the hyenas, sensing the coming climax to the conflict, fell silent. Helplessly, Gerry scuffed at the road with the toe of his training shoe. From where he stood he could see the unpredictable stringiness of Matthew edging ever closer to the solid mass of Sewell, and to one side, lying in an uneasy, unhappy ball with his nose hidden under his tail, Rusty. 'Watch oot for a weapon!' he called.

It all happened very quickly. Matthew's eyes grew suddenly and staggeringly large, the skin on his face began to twitch. Then he launched himself. Sewell stood up against the flailing bone of elbows, wrist and knee, until, wincing under the sharp jab of serrated fingernails slashing at his face, he staggered, dropping his arms for a split second. In that moment, Matthew was able to leap at his throat. Sewell bellowed as the teeth sank into his soft flesh. Wildly he hit out, a fist sending Matthew sprawling over the ground. Landing on all fours, Matthew immediately scuttled out of range. He remained on his hands and knees for a while, whimpering, then slowly approached Sewell again. In a flurry of elbows and feet, Matthew hurled himself at Sewell's shins. Sewell kicked out, but he could not stop the momentum. Bending down, he grabbed Matthew's arms. He was just about to punch when he became aware of Rusty. Ears and tail cringingly low, the dog howled imploringly, nudging at Sewell's grip. Then Sewell looked down at Matthew. With a shudder, he loosened his grip. Matthew had begun to howl with the dog. A fly buzzed heavily by, and Rusty fell quiet, rolling playfully on his back, but still Matthew howled. 'Ah didn't take him,' Sewell said. 'He followed me.'

Matthew rolled over to the dog. Rusty fussed at him with his nose. The boy's tears fell quickly, lying on the ground before being absorbed in the dust. Sewell rubbed his hands smartly against each other and then walked off. Rusty came after him. 'Stay,' said Sewell sternly. Rusty turned back, and began to lick Matthew's motionless face and hands. Sewell turned to look back when he heard Rusty bark. Matthew had the dog cradled lovingly, desperately in his arms.

Gerry fell in with Sewell when he walked past him. Together they moved through the gawping group of the other three, who, open-mouthed, parted for them. 'Ha'way,' said Gerry softly, gently stopping his friend by placing the palm of his hand on his chest after they had walked on ten more yards. 'What aboot the hoond?' Sewell shook his head and carried on walking. 'What do ye mean?' persevered Gerry, drawing next to him again. 'Ye cannet leave Rusty, man. Ye just cannet. Ye love him, ye daft get.' But still Sewell did not reply and, shaking his head, Gerry followed him. 'Sewell man!' he exclaimed, this time laying a heavier hand on his friend's sleeve, forcing him to halt.

Sewell lifted the corner of his mouth slightly in a way that could have been a half smile or a half grimace. 'When?' he asked quietly. 'When's it gannae be? Wor job. Wor one fell swoop.'

Gerry nodded his head robustly and, darting his eyes about, spat decisively. 'Today. Now. We're on our way.'

Together they walked on in silence. They had not gone far when they heard shouting. They stopped. Gemma ran over to them, she was out of breath. A little boy with piercing blue eyes and ginger curls was holding her hand. He stared up at Sewell and Gerry, fascinated. 'Ah'm sorry,' Gemma began. 'Rusty's got oot again.'

'Ah kna,' replied Sewell.

'Ah couldn't stop him. Ah'd just taken this one to the toilet, he's one o' Audrey's friend's bairns.' With a nod Gemma indicated the little boy while her hand ruffled the child's hair, her fingers twiddling the curls. 'We'd only left the window open a crack like. When we came back doonstairs, Rusty was through it and gone. Quick as lightning. Wasn't he, pet?'

The child nodded seriously, his brilliant, sky eyes widening with every moment. 'Gorra tab, gadgie mista?' he asked Sewell, who shook his head distractedly. 'Ah love yer dog. The way his tail's geet curly.'

'Aye,' said Sewell at last.

Gemma wiped dust from Sewell's bench coat. 'What ye been doin', pet?' she asked. Then she turned to Gerry. 'Ee, Gerry. Ah've seen yer dad.' Gerry froze, his shoulders rising rigidly. 'He was looking for yer mam.'

Sewell's rapidly expelled air was like a gasp. Without smiling he accepted a cigarette from Gemma and then a light. Not pausing to inhale he handed the burning cigarette to Gerry. Gerry took it with no sign of recognition, and held it stiffly between two fingers. He did not seem to notice when the little boy took it from him. 'Ha'way then,' he said suddenly to Sewell, his voice toneless. 'Time for wor to get gannin'. Time to gan to work.' And without waiting for a reply, he walked off.

'Look after yerself, man,' said Gemma urgently to Sewell,

her voice softening. 'Ee, ah didn't see that cut!' she gasped, caressing Sewell's neck.

'We're gannin' on a mission,' Sewell explained, staring after Gerry. 'Divven't worry aboot the scratch. Divven't worry aboot the dog neither. He'll come back when he wants to.'

Gemma threw her hands to her mouth. 'Ah nearly forgot. Me ex knas all aboot wor an' all.' Swatting her concern aside, Sewell kissed her quickly. A sudden coughing from the little boy jolted them. 'Gis that!' Gemma exclaimed, snatching the cigarette from the child's lips. 'Fingers crossed for the job,' she called to Sewell, who was shambling after Gerry. 'And watch oot, man!'

Sewell caught up with Gerry and began to whistle The Blaydon Races. 'Forget aboot yer auld man, man,' he urged. Gerry made no reply.

They wandered over the waste ground, sat on the bridge for a while without talking and then, skirting the Soccer Superpitz, they walked behind the Spartan Redheugh factory. After the heat of the day it was pleasantly cool there, the sun gentled to various shapes of tree shade that dappled the path. The rose bushes in bloom, frothing the path into an avenue of whites and pinks. Sitting on the bonnet of a wrecked car they went over the plan again. Poppies flourished through the empty, buckled windscreen of the wreck. 'Divven't take the coins,' Gerry said. 'Just the notes. Afterwards we won't gan back into Gateshead, but we'll hide in them auld buildings on the Quayside then slip away when the pollis have gone.'

Sewell nodded his head slowly.

'We gan in, me first, a minute later ye follow. We wear wor Newcastle hats so the gadgie cannet get a view of wor. When ah shout, we pull the hats doon awer wor faces. Divven't worry, Sewell, ye'll be able to see through the holes ah made for ye. But remember, in all of this there's summink ye have to dee.' Gerry waited for Sewell to speak, but he did not. 'What is it that ye have tae dee, Sewell?'

224

Sewell did not hesitate this time. 'As soon as we get in the shop, ah put the closed sign up on the door.'

Gerry snapped a poppy at the stem and waved it in the air like a wand. 'Whatever ye dee, divven't forget that. Nee closed sign, nee Season Ticket. Understand?'

Nodding, Sewell repeated the words. 'Nee closed sign. Nee Season Ticket.' Then he fell into thought. For a while they both listened to a blackbird singing from the roses. 'Gerry,' tried Sewell. 'There's nowt ye can dee. Yer auld man ah mean. At least when we have the Season Tickets ye'll have summink to be proud of.'

Gerry sprang up from the wrecked car. 'Ha'way.'

A shift finished in one of the factories beside the Spartan Redheugh building, and a thin stream of workers dribbled out, a few cars, a few bikes, mostly walkers with their knapsacks over their stooping shoulders. 'They get paid nowt these y'kna,' said Gerry. 'Wor Sean once had an interview as a security guard in the Team Valley.' Sewell laughed. 'Straight up,' Gerry continued. 'A hundred poond for a sixty-five-hour week. Why! Where's the point in that?'

'Ye wouldn't get a Season Ticket with that,' said Sewell.

'Ye wouldn't get nowt with that,' agreed Gerry darkly. 'They give ye time off to gan and sign on. Dodgy business. Not worth it. Ah'm telling ye, man, this is the only way.'

Reaching the Tyne, they followed its course towards the swing bridge. The tide was in, swelling to the walls of both banks. Pausing for a moment under the metro train bridge they listened to a train clattering above. Undisturbed, the cormorants continued to hold their wings out to dry, a patient, prehistoric presence persisting in the heart of the city, perched inviolably on the concrete islands of the bridge's raised foundations. 'Ye've really worked it oot this time,' smiled Sewell. 'We'll take a few hundred nee bother.'

'Nee rough stuff,' replied Gerry. 'Unless he doesn't open that till.'

'Gerry man,' Sewell whispered. 'Them tickets are as good as ours.'

Walking over the swing bridge from Gateshead, Sewell and Gerry entered the Newcastle Quayside, a chaos of ancient and new buildings built around a maze of dark alleys and passageways. The clock of the eighteenth-century church of All Saints was striking six. 'Quarter of an hour,' said Gerry, leading Sewell to the very rim of the quay. They sat facing each other on two huge capstans which, like oversized mushrooms, still buttoned the wharf despite the fact that no ship had stopped this high up for years, apart from The Boat night-club which was moored opposite them on the Gateshead side. 'We'll gan there to celebrate the neet,' said Gerry, pointing to The Boat with a smile.

'Grab a granny!' laughed Sewell.

'Why aye! Ye divven't look at the mantelpiece when ye're stoking the fire.'

'What's a mantelpiece?'

'Divven't kna. It's just a saying.'

The gulls gathered over the tidal in-flow. Soon the tide would be at its height. 'Have ye got yer hat?' Gerry asked. Sewell dipped into his bench coat pocket and brought out his black football hat. A jogger jogged past. Gerry hunched himself up and looked away. 'Divven't look conspicuous,' he hissed to Sewell.

'What does that mean like?'

Gerry swore. 'That jogger saw ye, didn't he?' Sewell nodded. 'Ah told ye not to look conspicuous.'

'And ah would have done but ah didn't kna what ye meant.'

Gerry stared at the jogger who was receding down the river. 'Ah'm getting edgy. Mebbes he didn't see ye,' sighed Gerry. He twisted round so that he could see the church clock; time had slowed to a crawl. Every minute seemed to take an hour. 'Ten minutes,' said Gerry. 'Ten minutes until the Season Ticket.'

A woman dressed in a suit, laden down with shopping bags,

walked past them with a suspicious look. Gerry had already looked away, but Sewell had not. The woman put the bags down to get a key from her pocket and opened the door to one of the cars which was parked close by. When the car had gone, Gerry spat. He looked at Sewell who smiled back. 'Ah divven't kna aboot this, man Sewell.'

There was a long pause before Sewell replied. 'What d'ye mean, man?'

'Summink doesn't seem right. Ah divven't kna what exactly. People have seen us. Ah mean there's supposed to be more traffic.' He gestured at the empty road at their backs. 'Usually this place is heaving at this hour. Ah thought we could melt into the crowd, like.'

'Gerry,' Sewell began uncertainly. 'Is yer dad an' all that gettin' to yus?'

Gerry's voice registered a slight pause, then he spoke mechanically. 'There's supposed to be loads of people just walking aboot here. Ah thought we'd have the cover of a busy road and pavements. It's too quiet.' He paused a moment. 'Sewell, mebbes we shouldn't dee it the day.' Pulling out his black hat, Sewell's fingers played nervously with it. A tight, anxious interlude followed. 'But what can gan wrang?' said Gerry, relenting. 'Nowt. Ah kna for a fact that there's nee film in the shop's security camera. As long as ye remember what ye have to dee, it'll all gan canny.'

'Ah'll remember,' Sewell replied adamantly.

'Tell us then, man. Gan through it again.'

Sewell sighed. 'Ye gan in first and look roond the shop. Ah come in a minute later. As soon as ah'm in ah put the closed sign on the door. That's the most important bit.'

'What happens after ye've done the sign?'

'As soon as ah've done the sign, ye shout, and we pull wor slash masks doon. Then ah jump awer the counter and grab the man while ye come and get the cash.'

'What d'ye dee if he resists?'

'Threaten him.'

'And if he still doesn't give wor the money?'

'Ah bat him one.'

Gerry narrowed his eyes. 'And if he still resists then ye'll have to knock him oot. Only if he resists, mind. There shouldn't be a problem, ye're twice his size, man.' Sewell smiled. 'So what's the most important thing again?' Gerry quizzed.

Sewell closed his eyes like a child in school trying to remember the words of a poem learnt at home. 'The closed sign,' he recited.

Gerry twisted round to see the clock again. Five minutes to go. He waited for what seemed like an hour, then, panicking in case he had waited too long, he turned round again. It was still five minutes to go. 'Ah wish we had some tabs,' Sewell drooled. He began to laugh. A nervous giggle became a body-shaking fit.

'What's up, man?' asked Gerry. Sewell tried to answer but could not.

'Ah was thinkin'!' Sewell spluttered eventually.

'Well divven't,' Gerry said.

'Ah was thinkin'!' he repeated. Breathing deeply and frantically like an asthmatic during an attack, Sewell tried to compose himself. 'We'll gan into the shop and say . . . and say . . .'

'And say what?'

'All yer money, and a packet of Lambert and Butler!' Sewell burst out finally. 'Ha ha ha ha!'

'Ye fat get!' Gerry snapped. 'Ye'll dee nowt of the sort. D'ye hear me? Nowt. Just dee what we planned, eh? Just dee as we planned.' Chastened, Sewell stopped laughing. 'It's Premier League stuff noo, a job like this, but Christ, if you're not up to it mebbes we shouldn't . . .' His words petered out in a vague gesture. The sun was deliciously warm on his face. Making himself more comfortable, he shielded his eyes with a hand. 'Mebbes we should just sit here, and build up wor tan.' Gerry glanced downstream and then up again. He saw the huge, crumbling buildings of the Quayside behind him. On the Gateshead side, he could see the tall Dunston Rocket, and the Staithes that used to take coal from the Durham coalfield to the world. It was at this point, according to a local story, that the ferry had docked, bringing the body of St Cuthbert from the Holy Island of Lindisfarne to his resting place in Durham. Gerry seemed to be searching for something there, but with a sigh he turned back to the Quayside. 'Wor Season Ticket,' he breathed.

'It'll be great, man,' beamed Sewell. 'We'll gan to every match.'

'Sitting in wor own seats.'

'Drinking wor own tea.'

'And neebody to tell us what to dee.'

Behind them the hands of the clock clicked. It was a quarter past six. Gerry tried to speak, but his suddenly tight, dry voice yielded only a murmur. Sewell understood. They stood. Together they took one last look at the buildings by the river – the old Customs house, the old Baltic flour mill and the new Courts of Justice – and then they set off.

It seemed to take Gerry hours to cover the few hundred yards from the capstans to the shop, as though he was floating or slipping back on a treadmill. He saw mundane objects with a stunning clarity. A pavement stone was slightly raised, a pub window had a hairline fracture, a thread was fraying on the knee of his jogging trousers. But then everything speeded up, and suddenly there was the shop, looming towards them like a train. They pulled their black hats low over their foreheads. Both spat. The spit hung in the air like balloons, and hit the ground in two simultaneous explosions.

The first thing Gerry noticed inside the newsagent's was the heat. It hit him like a wall. The air was humid and cloying. The smell of milk turning in the heat was nauseating. Disorientated, he reeled. Finding his balance, he moved cautiously round a stack of greetings cards with his back to the counter.

The bell jingled. Gerry's heart raced sickeningly on seeing Sewell. Gulping the nausea down, he worked closer to the counter. Behind him, near the door, something clattered to the ground. The shopkeeper's soft voice hummed on the pulsing heat. 'What ye deein', bonny lad?' Gerry turned to see Sewell tugging and pulling at the signs and notes stuck to the door of the shop. 'What ye deein'?' the shopkeeper demanded. The metal grille on the inside of the door came off in Sewell's wild hands. 'Hey ye, what ye deein'?' roared the shopkeeper.

Instinctively, Gerry pulled the hat over his face. Heat immediately engulfed him. Blinded by sweat, he clawed at his eye-sockets. His temples throbbed. His darkness seemed to fill with sirens. He shook his head savagely, but the wailing grew to a crescendo, matched now by a strobing in his skull, so that he seemed to be sitting in the ambulance with his mother again. Suddenly, shockingly, the sirens stopped, and in the moments that followed Gerry was left with a vision and a hearing that were almost unbearably lucid. The shopkeeper was staring at him. Sewell was scrabbling at the door. 'All yer money!' Gerry heard himself cry, but although he was shouting, his voice did not seem loud. He could see the fleck of sweat on the shopkeeper's unshaven top lip. 'Give wor all yer fuckin' money!' Gerry shouted again. The tendons on his neck swelled, taut as cables, but still his voice seemed no more than a whisper. The shopkeeper was pale. Gerry saw his eyes dart between him and Sewell. Then Gerry looked back for Sewell again. In this one quick glance, he took in the whole of the shop so completely that he would never forget it, and even in later life, if he had been asked, would have been able to describe the interior and its contents in flawless detail. The racks of magazines and papers stretching from floor to ceiling on the right of the door; the flimsy central stand of greetings cards; the cubbyholes full of loaves; the large fridge of chilled pop cans and mineral water; the window, dirty, and throbbing with a fat bluebottle buzzing desolately over the other fly corpses on the sill. Sewell was on his hands and knees, scrabbling desperately under the magazine rack by the door. 'Hand it over!' Gerry screamed, finding his voice at last.

'It's been cashed up,' the shopkeeper said, speaking suddenly, nodding furiously. 'Cashed up and gone.'

'Look,' stammered Gerry. 'Just give us yer money.'

'But there isn't any . . .'

Helplessly, Gerry turned round. 'SEWELL!' Not responding, Sewell was still worrying the area round the door. Choking back vomit, Gerry screamed wordlessly over to his friend.

'Ah cannet find the closed sign for the door,' Sewell hissed miserably.

'Pull yer mask on, and friggin' get here!'

When Gerry looked back to the counter, the shopkeeper was halfway to the door that led through the back of the shop. With a strength born of desperation, he leapt up on to the counter and sprang from it. He landed on the fleeing man's shoulders. The shopkeeper flailed at Gerry, but his grip was too tight. Suddenly Sewell was towering above them both on the counter. Shrieking, he jumped. In the impact Gerry was knocked from the shopkeeper's back. Picking himself up, the shopkeeper struggled to the back door, and reaching it, began fiddling frenziedly with the locks. He had managed to slide open one bolt when Sewell's foot flew up and kicked his grip aside. For a moment the shopkeeper continued to scrabble against the door before Sewell dragged him jerkily back to the counter, where he dropped him.

'Where's yer sign?' Sewell demanded, squatting down to lift up the shopkeeper's head to within an inch of his own.

The man's lips scrabbled for words. 'Haven't got one,' he managed to spit out eventually.

Sewell knotted his eyes dangerously. 'What d'ye mean, you haven't got a one?'

The shopkeeper looked up wildly at the masked face lowering above him. 'Ah've got a wife and two bairns,' he yelped at a high pitch, urinating into his trousers.

By now Gerry was rifling through the cash register. A fountain of coins spurted out as he ripped open the drawer. Sewell raised a fist. 'How can a shop not have a closed sign?'

The man started sobbing. 'Ah don't know.'

'Shut up!' roared Sewell.

'A bag,' Gerry groaned, his breath rapid. 'We didn't bring a friggin' bag.' Ripping off his sweatshirt he laid it on the ground and poured the money on to it. Then, folding it up into a bundle, he scooped the sweatshirt to his breast.

'He didn't have a closed sign,' Sewell said simply.

'Forget aboot the sign!' croaked Gerry, the pent-up force of his words making Sewell wince. Desperately Gerry scrabbled up some of the coins and the notes which had evaded the sweatshirt, and stuffed them in his pockets.

Sewell took the man's face between a thumb and a forefinger. 'Ye should have had a sign,' he told him, almost tenderly.

'Take the money, just divven't hurt us,' the man said with a weird calmness. 'Ah've a couple of bairns at home like you. Divven't hurt us.'

Dashing around the shop, Gerry was wildly dusting their fingerprints from anything that came into view. 'Reet,' he ordered Sewell.

'Ye had nee sign!' Sewell rumbled. The man gargled at the back of his throat as Sewell grabbed him by the upper arms to raise him. 'Nee sign,' said Sewell, bewildered. The man seemed to smile, then gripping Sewell's wrists, began gulping at the air. Sewell tried to shake him off, but the shopkeeper's grip would not loosen.

'What's the matter?' demanded Gerry. The man was turning purple. Gooselike rasps tore from the back of his throat.

'Divven't stare at us,' menaced Sewell shrilly, unnerved by the way the man kept his eyes fixed on him.

'Drop him!' shouted Gerry. 'Let him go. He's having a heart attack, man.'

Sewell shrieked. 'Ah cannet. He's got hold of wor.' Wildly,

Sewell swiped at the shopkeeper's hands, chopping at them with no heed for his own pain. Eventually the grip loosened, and the man rolled off.

'We've got to be missin'!' bellowed Gerry, shoulder-charging Sewell towards the back door.

'He shouldn't have hidden the sign.' Sewell didn't move.

With as much patience as he could muster, Gerry softened his voice, compressing his tone into a gentle, coaxing insistence. 'They'll catch ye here if ye divven't come noo.'

Sewell stared wretchedly at the door and then at the shopkeeper on the floor.

'Ye've got to come,' begged Gerry, opening the rest of the bolts on the back door. Seeing a pile of money he had missed, Gerry squatted down. 'Ha'way!' he howled.

With a final, baffled shake of his head, Sewell followed Gerry. They opened the door, crossed the yard and then, ripping off their hats, tore down the Quayside.

The friends wove their way deeper into the maze of tall, derelict buildings. Turning into a narrow passage, their steps echoed loudly, and then abruptly stopped. Gerry lifted two loose boards from a window and climbed inside. When Sewell had scrambled after him, Gerry carefully replaced the plank, shutting them in. The darkness was damp and heavy. Half crawling up a broken flight of stairs, they crept through dusty rooms, finding the deepest, safest corner, instinctively, like animals. They did not speak. Slowly their eyes grew used to the dimness, but it never grew light. It was like being under the surface of the murky river.

'We leave the money here,' explained Gerry, hugging the sweatshirt close. 'Find a loose floorboard, then when it's safe we'll come and get it.' Gerry's voice echoed under the tall ceiling. 'Ha'way, Sewell. Light a match and let's count it.' Sighing, Gerry cradled the sweatshirt on his lap, his fingers caressing it worriedly.

'Sorry,' said Sewell at last.

'What for?'

'But ye see he didn't have a one. Ah looked everywhere.'

Gerry looked up at the dark shapes of the half-rotten beams on the ceiling. In another distant room, lit by shafts of light which slanted in through gaps in the roof, he could see that the ceiling had fallen in. Once this had been a busy place, the offices of a thriving shipping line, and the dust of a thousand obsolete ledgers, the dust of a thousand thoughts, the dust of a million clerking hours rode the air like ghosts.

Sewell's voice was tiny. 'We're in trouble, aren't we?'

'He isn't deed,' sighed Gerry, the coins clinking dully as he placed the sweatshirt on the ground.

'How d'ye kna?'

'Well, people divven't always die of a heart attack.'

'Ye're just saying that.'

'Ah'm not, man.'

'How d'ye kna then?'

Gerry consulted the gloom, but he couldn't find anything to say.

The silence became brooding, like a thunderstorm brewing. 'It's all gone wrang,' said Sewell.

Without answering him, Gerry raised himself up to a crouching position and began feeling the floor in front of him. Finding a loose board he lifted it up and placed the sweatshirt beneath it. He crushed the sweatshirt between two hands and felt the money. 'We'll coont it later. Ah'll leave a mark so we kna where it is.' Gerry picked up a stray coin. As he scuffed it against the floorboard, his elbows pulsed frenetically in the darkness.

Sewell stirred but then fell back again into his corner like a wounded animal. 'Now we'll nivver get a Season Ticket.'

'Gis a hand, man,' Gerry said, taking the loose notes from his pockets and stuffing them into the sweatshirt. 'Did ye pick any up? Any notes or coins?'

'Ah keep on thinking aboot that auld gadgie in the shop,' said Sewell. 'D'ye really think he's gonnae be areet?'

Carefully Gerry replaced the floorboard. There was a long

silence. Although he was no longer out of breath from running, he could feel a pounding against his ribs. His fingers clasped his wrist and he felt the pulse there too, urgent, insistent, increasing. When Sewell spoke to him again, the voice seemed to be his own heart. 'Was it murder?'

For a long time they did not move at all. Gradually Sewell shrank into himself, tucking his arms into his body, raising his knees up to his chin, until he was a ball. Then he started to rock. Gently at first, the movement almost imperceptible to Gerry who sat only a few feet away; then quicker, more urgently, building up to a frantic climax. As he rocked, he moaned. Afterwards, when Sewell had grown still and his laboured breathing had eased to nothing, an even deeper silence seemed to fall on the darkened building. 'Nee sirens yet,' remarked Gerry dully. 'Nee flashing lights.'

Gerry dug at the wall against which he rested, gouging out an ever-growing hole, heaping the broken, flaking plaster at his feet. There was a sudden disturbance from a room above, a series of quick movements as of a struggle. Then pigeons could be heard cooing. Sewell turned to Gerry, the whites of his eyes showing. 'Why didn't he have a closed sign?' Standing up, Sewell looked down at Gerry decisively.

'Where the hell are ye gannin'?' Gerry hissed.

'It's deein' me heed in.'

'Talk sense, man.'

Sewell sank heavily to the ground. Time seemed to pass even more slowly. Every so often Sewell cleared his throat, and Gerry would sometimes try and cheer them up by whispering. 'He's not deed, man. He was just pretending,' or, 'When we've coonted the money, ah bet we've got enough.' But his words sounded thinner and thinner, and eventually he lapsed into silence. Whenever the pigeons scuffled above them, their hearts were sent racing. Gerry played tensely with the plaster he had picked from the wall, grinding it into ever-finer powder until it ran effortlessly through his fingers like grains of rice. Outside, a group of early-evening drinkers sauntered down one of the alleys. They were women. Their voices echoed shrilly. The beat of music from one of the pubs which line the Quayside flared up suddenly and then died. It sounded again, this time quieter, but gradually creeping up until it reached its former level. Its rhythm probed the darkness of their hiding place as though searching, making the walls pulse dully. Gerry stiffened. The lights and the siren played in his head for a dreadful, intense moment. Shuddering, he turned to Sewell in his confusion. 'Is that the pollis?' Sewell grunted a negative. They listened to the music blaring from the pubs and clubs, as song followed song, their fingers uneasily obeying the rhythm.

'Can we at least gan and see if he's areet,' said Sewell at last.

'Eh?' replied Gerry distractedly.

'Ah'm gonnae have to gan and see if he's areet.'

Gerry sprang over and physically restrained Sewell. 'Ye cannet. Ye . . . ye just cannet. Think aboot it, man Sewell man,' His voice cracked. 'If they catch ye it'll . . .'

'He might be deed,' Sewell interrupted simply.

'He isn't friggin' deed!' Gerry's sudden shout in the long hush of their hiding place was shocking. For a while they simply lay there. Gerry looked over at Sewell. In the general shape of his friend's body, the face showed as a lighter shadow in the gloom. The forehead, cheeks, nose, were all indentations on the darkness. 'Ah wish it was me auld man. Ah wish he'd have a heart attack.' A long silence was broken by the impact of Gerry's fist punching the palm of his hand. 'Ah've got to gan somewhere, Sewell,' he said softly. 'Ah'm gannin' for a while. Ah divven't kna exactly how long.'

Sewell nodded. 'Ah'll come with ye.'

'Na. Ye wait here and ah'll come back for ye. D'yus hear me? Ye wait here. Divven't gan neewhere.'

Just before Gerry climbed back out through the boarded-up window, Sewell stopped him. 'Gan canny,' he said.

Stealthily, Gerry ran along the Quayside, creeping from alley to alley. At a wild dash, he crossed the Tyne into

Gateshead on the swing bridge. He passed the Ovoline Lubricants factory, sliding on the oil which flows from its bowels along the road and pavement into the river. He ran under the great bridges, their arches towering dizzyingly above him. He hurled himself blindly on, reaching the Teams without pausing. A police helicopter roared through the sky, and he flung himself into the tall grass of an unkempt garden. When it had gone, he sprinted down the street, playing children calling after him. He scrambled along the Spartan Redheugh rose avenue and scuttled across the waste ground.

When he reached his road, he began to stumble, sliding as though he were on ice. Unable to stop himself, he blundered into the door. It fell open. He stumbled across the living room. The television had gone. The radio. The new table. Everything that the social worker had got for their new home had gone. All that was left was an armchair. He threw himself at it and, tunnelling his face into its soft cushion, sobbed like a child.

'Who's that?' a voice called from the kitchen.

'Dad,' he whispered into the cushion. 'Please, Dad. Please.'

'Just piss off, whoever y'are.'

'Dad,' he breathed. 'Dad.'

When Gerry looked up, his father was standing over him. 'Yus've heard then?' his father said. Gerry stared into his eyes, which were red-rimmed and bleary. 'Satisfied noo, are ye?' his father asked. 'Ye nivver wanted me and yer mam together.'

'Did ye dee this?' Gerry asked, gesturing the empty room.

'What if ah did?'

'Did ye?'

'What does it matter noo?'

Getting up from the armchair, Gerry stood up to his father. 'Did ye nick all wor stuff?'

'Ye divven't kna, do ye?' his father said, falling into the chair. He buried his head in his hands and began laughing.

'Shut up!' said Gerry.

'Oh, God,' replied his dad. 'It's priceless. Ye divven't kna.'

Gerry ground his teeth over his bottom lip, until the lip burst. He could feel the blood warm on his chin.

His father's laughter had changed to sobbing. 'She's deed man.'

Gerry clenched his teeth.

'Yer mam's deed. Oh me hinny, me darlin' lass, she's gone.'

'Shut up,' said Gerry simply.

'Ah loved her. Despite it all, ah loved that lass.'

'Shut up,' repeated Gerry softly.

'Me hinny lass. Me hinny!'

'Shut up.' It was no more than a whisper.

'She's with Jesus and wor Lady noo,' said Gerry's father, weeping piteously.

Gerry's first blow landed on his father's back, taking his breath away. 'Shut up!' Then, coming round to the front of the chair, he kicked his legs. He began pounding his arms, his shoulders. After a pause, Gerry struck his father full in the face. Then he began to beat him mercilessly, indiscriminately, without thought, like a thunderstorm breaking. 'Shut up,' Gerry begged repeatedly, each plea following a blow and each blow emphasised by his own grunts. 'Shut up! Shut up! Shut up! Ye made me mam's life a misery. Ye filthy, nee-good bastard! Ye drove Bridie away! Ye broke up wor family! Ye've nivver been owt to us! Ye've nivver been owt to me! Ye've nivver so much as made a cup o' tea for us! D'ye hear me? Ah've nivver even had a cup o' tea from ye. And ah'm yer son! Ah'm yer son! Ah'm yer son!'

When he got up, he looked at his father curled in a ball in the armchair. His father peered back, terrified. Their eyes fused. In Gerry's head, the sirens blazed and roared away, getting fainter and less insistent, until they were gone. 'Why?' he breathed. And kneeling down, he vomited, retching until there was nothing left. He took one last look at his father, then left.

Retracing his steps Gerry began trotting. His breathing was even and calm. Then, behind the Spartan Redheugh, he suddenly stopped. 'Na,' he said, shaking his head furiously. 'She cannet be. She cannet be.' He set off again, more quickly now as though something was pushing him on. Quicker and quicker he ran, his elbows and knees pumping desperately. Turning from the houses, he hurled himself down the bank of saplings and scattered rubbish, bumping and clutching at the shoulder-high trees. Towards the bottom of the slope, the trees had been uprooted. Unchecked, his speed now ran out of control. He plunged over a pile of rubble and, flying through the air, landed awkwardly. Losing his balance, he was thrown forward. The metal rang out as he hit it. His wild momentum stopped, he crumpled, doubling up over the railings. Below him, the Tyne was flowing, the tide going out now. He breathed in the dampness. For a while he stared at the river, his breath gradually easing, his heaving chest slowly settling. In the darkness of the mud, a redshank suddenly lit up and, flying past, called plaintively.

A fine, cooling rain had begun to fall. The police helicopter roared back into view overhead. Gerry climbed the railings and, hanging down, lowered himself. Letting go, he felt himself hit the mud. It cushioned the impact as he sank up to his knees. Pressing himself closely against the wall, he watched the helicopter probing the water as it passed by. When it had gone, he moved on, prowling along the mud-line of the Tyne, his feet slopping in and out of the sludge.

He found Sewell staggering down one of the dank lanes of the Quayside. His bench coat had been ripped, and hung from him in shreds. His tracksuit trousers were covered in blood. His face was so badly pulped as to be unrecognisible. He could not speak coherently. 'They got ye, didn't they, son?' said Gerry softly.

'Ah waited ages for ye,' stammered Sewell. 'But ye didn't come. Them lads got us. Them ice hockey players. Cornered wor doon a lane. Cannet remember the rest. The next thing ah knew ah was . . . wandering. Then . . . then ah saw ye.'

Gerry bowed his head for a moment. 'Ha'way,' he breathed at last, 'ye'll be areet.'

'Will ah?'

'Why aye.'

'Gerry?' stammered Sewell, the word like a tooth being spat out. 'Gerry?'

'What is it, man?'

'Ah'm so sorry aboot the sign. In the shop. The sign in the shop. Ah'm sorry.'

'Forget aboot it.'

For a moment Sewell brightened. 'Ah've been thinking. Working it all oot. That man's areet. He didn't die. It'll be areet, man. Divven't worry. And if anyone sees us and asks we'll just say we saw two gadgies running oot of the shop and up the road into toon. Na. We'll say . . . We'll say . . .' Sewell stopped for a moment. His face began to glow with a flush of inspiration. 'We'll say we saw two wifies running up the road.' With a wide smile he looked to Gerry. 'That way we'll really fox them. Won't we?'

'Oh aye,' said Gerry, looking away. 'We'll really fox them.'

'See? Sometimes ah can be the brains as well as ye.'

From somewhere deep inside of Sewell, a gurgling began. 'Get home, man Gerry. Hide.'

'Ye're badly, man Sewell. We've got to get ye to the hospital.'

Flailing his arms weakly, Sewell fell heavily to the ground. Gerry knelt down beside him, and cradled his head in his hands. 'Leave me . . . make . . . anony . . . anony . . . anonymous phone call . . .' said Sewell.

Gerry shook his head. 'Na,' he said. 'Ye're badly.'

'Gerry,' gasped Sewell. 'Ah'll be areet. Get yersel' hyem . . . at least get yersel' away . . . ring from the pub.'

'Na. If ah gan anywhere, then ye're coming with me. Ha'way. We've got to get yer to a hospital.'

With a huge grunt of effort, Gerry pulled Sewell up on to his knees. Legs buckling, he tottered under the weight as he levered his friend upright. For a moment they did not move. Sewell leant heavily against Gerry; Gerry propped him up, his own chest heaving with exertion. Then they began to move off down the alley. Shuffling, swaying drunkenly.

The Quayside was thick with drinkers now, droving themselves in loud, lowing herds of ten and twenty from pub to pub. As they emerged on to the main thoroughfare, they slipped into the throng. They passed a woman squatting by a car wheel, her knickers around her ankles, her buttocks two glaringly white moons shining in the empty solar system of the gutter, as the urine foamed over her high-heeled shoes and ran away from her down the hill.

They had managed to make it on to the swing bridge when they heard the first siren. It grew louder, augmenting itself into two and then three. 'Gerry!' said Sewell desperately. 'Run! . . . Leave me . . .'

'Hospital,' Gerry remarked in a distant voice. 'Ye need a hospital.'

'Gerry,' growled Sewell, his broken hands clashing painfully against Gerry's face to get his attention. 'Listen to wor . . . the pollises . . . run, man . . . run . . .'

They were halfway over the swing bridge. The police car could be seen flashing its way down the Newcastle Quayside, its progress impeded by the staggering revellers. The way to Gateshead was clear. 'Gan on, man . . . run!' Sewell pleaded. Gerry smiled.

Two police cars arrived at the Newcastle side, blocking that end of the bridge. Another two arrived on the Gateshead side. The doors opened and slammed resonantly. Six police, three from each side, started to walk towards Gerry and Sewell. 'Ah well,' Gerry whispered to himself, 'the bloody Angel must have flown away.'

The air was fresh with the recent drizzle. Gerry leant over the parapet and stared down. Underneath them the Tyne slipped by, widening itself over the tidal mud, endlessly flowing, endlessly repeating itself like a story. He sighed as he lowered Sewell gently to the ground. The police were approaching. Gerry opened his arms wide in surrender, standing over his friend. 'Aye, that's reet,' he whispered when Sewell stopped murmuring. 'Ye've got it all worked oot, haven't ye, bonny lad? We'll be oot soon. Mebbes not this season. But soon. Get wor time shortened for good behaviour. Mebbes. We didn't mean to hurt that auld gadgie. They'll believe wor, 'cos it's the truth. Mebbes. They'll let us oot after a couple of years. Then we'll get wor Season Ticket. Nothing'll stop wor then. As soon as we get oot we'll get wor Season Ticket, man Sewell. Have a one each. And we'll just be able to sit there, with neeone telling us what to dee. With a cup o' tea. Mebbes. Milk. And as much sugar as ye want.'

BY JONATHAN TULLOCH
ALSO AVAILABLE IN VINTAGE

☐	**The Lottery**	009942214X	£6.99
☐	**The Bonny Lad**	0099284561	£6.99

FREE POST AND PACKING
Overseas customers allow £2.00 per paperback

BY PHONE: 01624 677237

BY POST: Random House Books
C/o Bookpost, PO Box 29, Douglas
Isle of Man, IM99 1BQ

BY FAX: 01624 670923

BY EMAIL: bookshop@enterprise.net

Cheques (payable to Bookpost) and credit cards accepted

Prices and availability subject to change without notice.
Allow 28 days for delivery.
When placing your order, please mention if you do not wish to receive
any additional information.

www.randomhouse.co.uk/vintage